Ruin the Friendship

ELLE RIVERS

Such A Funny Way – Sabrina Carpenter
Goodbye – Sabrina Carpenter
Adventure of a Lifetime – Coldplay
Man I Need – Olivia Dean
Don't Worry I'll Make You Worry – Sabrina Carpenter
When Did You Get Hot? – Sabrina Carpenter
Untouchable – Taylor Swift
SOS – Rihanna
Midnight Sun – Zara Larsson
Beaches – beabadoobee
Fuck Up the Friendship – Leah Kate
more than friends – Isabel LaRosa
Riptide – Vance Joy
Fearless – Taylor Swift
Dog Days Are Over – Florence + The Machine

Cover Design by Rachel Spendlove

Developmental Editing by Mae Peredo, Wildwood Author Services

Copyediting by Kasey Kubica, Basic Behemoth Edits

Proofreading by Mae Peredo, Wildwood Author Services

 Formatted with Vellum

a note from elle

Ruin the Friendship contains mature and potentially triggering content that some people might find upsetting. Please be advised that the following content can be found on-page unless otherwise noted.

- emotional abuse (not committed by main characters)
- explicit, open-door sexual content
- anxiety and panic with water phobia

Please take care of yourself and your mental health while reading any novel.

chapter one

WHEN THE FIRST thing I remember is face-planting onto the floor of my bedroom, I know my day isn't going to go well.

Muttering curses under my breath, I crawl to my light and flip it on. The thing that tripped me is the box of invitations to my wedding that I didn't need. My future mother-in-law had ordered way too many, and they're now collecting dust with all the other wedding stuff near the doorway.

I try not to glare at the pile of things I don't know what to do with. This wedding has taken over every aspect of my life, including my house, and it makes me feel like I'm losing my mind.

"Two days," I tell myself. "Two days and it's over."

By then, the engagement ring on my finger will be adorned with a wedding band, and I will be Mrs. Rob Norton. Then we set off on our honeymoon and into our happily ever after.

The wedding stress has gotten to me, and I haven't seen my fiancé, Rob, in a week. Back when this was funny, I joked that he seemed to take the superstition of not seeing the bride before the wedding *very* seriously.

It's no longer amusing to me now.

I know he's cramming in work before the wedding, so I try to take it in stride. But a wedding is stressful, and trying to plan a massive event with Andrea Norton as a mother-in-law is like having every one of my pubes plucked out one by one.

It's a terrible analogy my best friend Nate came up with. I hate that it's accurate.

After Rob's bachelor party tonight, he's promised to be more present. That should help, or at the very least, pull me back from the brink of insanity.

After putting the invitations back into the pile of wedding stuff, I haul myself off the ground and go to my kitchen in search of caffeine and breakfast. I start the coffee first and then grab the overnight oats from the fridge before I open my phone.

Nate sent me multiple videos late in the night. For nine months out of the year, he follows a normal sleep schedule so he can get to his job as a high school gym teacher on time. But during the summer months, he slacks off, often staying up into the early hours of the morning. I have a feeling he just went to bed only a few hours ago.

I laugh as I watch all the things he curated for me while I eat, and by the time I'm heading to get dressed for work, I'm feeling better.

I purposefully don't look at the pile of crap in the corner of my room as I pull out slacks, a button-up shirt, and a sweater vest for the day. After my clothes are on, I go to the bathroom to pull up my hair into its usual bun, but one long, dark strand falls out of the bottom. With a huff, I redo it, making sure it's perfect.

When I'm done, I face the put-together woman in the mirror. I may not feel like her on the inside, but I can pretend to be her until it's true. Most days, it's easy. Lately, I've felt more and more out of sorts as my wedding marches closer.

Before I leave for work, I tidy up the best I can so I don't come home and feel the same misery. There's one magazine on the dining room table, left out on purpose. I want to put it away, but I haven't so I can think about what Rob asked me to.

It's a list of amenities and floor plans at his apartment complex. He gave it to me when we were talking about who would move in with whom. I always thought the plan was to move here. He disagreed.

My house isn't much. It's a tiny two bedroom in an older neighborhood, but it's mine. After my grandma passed away, Mom took her inheritance and helped me with the down payment. I've worked hard to make every payment. Considering how expensive other homes are, I'm lucky.

And I'm so reluctant to give it up.

But Rob's made it clear he doesn't want to move in. He says it's not in a good part of town, despite there being hardly any crime here. This isn't the fancy part of Nashville people move to, it's the older part where the charm of the original city is barely hanging on.

My time is running out. I need to make a decision, and with how most things go with Rob, I'll end up giving in. I just don't want to this time.

But it's time for me to go to work, so I can't consider it anymore. With a sigh, I flip the magazine over, promising myself I'll talk to Quinn—my other friend and Rob's sister—about it when she comes over tonight.

Rob will be at his bachelor party all night, so I know I'll have time to talk it out.

After locking the front door, I head to work. I say hi to Sally and the other employees I'm close with before sitting to start my work for the day as a receptionist. I can't say I love what I do, but my boss pays me more than enough and I love the people I work with. That's what matters.

Besides, the busywork has been helpful. It leaves brain space for me to plan and survive my wedding.

I'm able to focus up until lunchtime when my stomach pulls me out of my work. I look around the office, wondering if my boss, Levi, happened to order anything for everyone. When I don't see anyone crowding the break room, I know I'm on my own. I didn't bring anything and I hate trying to go out anywhere by myself. It feels sad to sit and eat alone.

It's then that I notice a text on my phone.

NATE

Burgers?

Another great thing about summer is that Nate is almost always free, which means I have a lunch buddy when I want one.

MAISIE

Yes. Perfect timing too.

NATE

You're always hungry right at noon. Meet you there in five?

MAISIE

I'm clocking out now.

Nate pulls up in his blue SUV right as I'm walking up.

"Well, well. Fancy seeing you here," he says as he gets out of his car. I immediately have to look up. Nate is tall, like over six feet, and I'm stunted right at five foot two. He has wavy black hair and green eyes. Everyone I meet calls him ridiculously hot. I still see the annoying kid I met when we were ten.

"This weirdo invited me out for lunch. I assume you're gonna do your best-friend duty and fight him off?"

"Let me at him and I will."

I can't help but laugh at the idea of Nate fighting anyone. He's tougher than his lithe frame shows, especially since I've seen him training the teens on his high school football team, but he's so nice that I can't imagine him angry.

He's obviously been out swimming because he's got his usual summer tan. I have a crippling fear of the water, but Nate blossoms in it.

"Is this where we admit I'm the weirdo in this scenario and I get to buy you lunch?" he asks as he opens the door.

He's letting me get away with insinuating he's weird *and* he's paying? He's buttering me up for something.

"Aren't you on summer break? You should save your money."

"I have my checks split out so I get paid year-round. I'm *smart*, berry."

The nickname always puts me in a good mood, but I'm still suspicious of him. "You still can't tell your left from your right."

"Why would I need to know that when I have a built-in mechanism for checking?" He holds his hands up in two Ls. "Look. I know what I'm doing!"

I want to remind him of the time we were trying to get out of Nashville after a hockey game ended and he took the wrong left and we wound up stuck in front of the arena for an hour, but I know we'll never get our food if I go down that path.

And I want my burger.

We order our food and Nate slaps his card down before I can argue. I let him this time, only because I know I'll be broke after my honeymoon is over.

"Will you get the table to the right of the condiments stand?" I ask.

"This is just a trap to see if I know which way that is." He narrows his eyes. "But I'll let it happen if it means you get the food."

I only shrug and watch as he goes to the table. He, of course, picks the correct one and smugly stares at me as I wait. He's lucky our numbers are called quickly, because I'm very tempted to make an unsightly gesture in his direction.

I don't know what it is about Nate, but sometimes it feels like we're still the kids that met in the school cafeteria all those years ago. No one else can make me joke around like he can. It's why I cherish him so much.

"Been practicing?" I ask as I bring the food over.

"I also mess up when I'm tired." He grabs his meal. "Which is always, considering the career I chose."

"And yet you still love it," I reply as I cross my arms.

"Love is a strong word. But I do like it."

He's lying. I see his smile when I go to the games he coaches. I never thought Nate would be good with teenagers, but he is.

"You know, there's still room for you to come over tonight," I say as I grab a fry. "I'm sure Quinn wouldn't mind."

"I still have a thing tonight," he replies. "I'll come over tomorrow, though."

It's so rare that he doesn't join in on plans that I've been trying to figure out what could have come up. The best idea I have is that it's a date. Nate usually doesn't mention those to me.

As open as we are, some topics have become taboo over the years. He never asks me about anything intimate with Rob, and I do the same. I've met a few of the women he's dated, but it's only ever once, and they're no longer in his life after a few weeks.

"Are you finally gonna tell me what it is?"

He shrugs. "I'm still in the planning stages. Do you know of any decent bars in Nashville?"

I frown. "You're going to a *bar*? Why?"

"I'm trying something new."

Neither of us care for the party scene in the city. Rob does, so the only bars I know of are the ones he goes to.

"Rob has one he goes to a lot, but you wouldn't be able to go to it tonight."

"Why not?"

"Tonight's his bachelor party." I say it slowly. The bachelor party has been a point of contention between Nate and Rob for weeks. I hoped that Rob would rivite Nate as some sort of olive branch for the stony relationship between them. After all, they'll have to see more of each other after we're married. But Rob insisted this was for his guy friends only.

I despise being in the middle of disagreements, but especially ones involving the two of them. Nate was the one who backed off once he saw how uncomfortable I was as I tried to mediate.

"Ah. That's tonight. How could I forget? I'll have to do it some other time then. What was the bar name?"

"Winners something. It's on . . ." I trail off when Nate immediately pulls out his phone and looks it up. "Are you planning something?"

"Nothing you need to worry about."

I hum. "If you can't do whatever you're planning tonight, then you could come over."

Now he pauses. "Sure, yeah. I'll be late, though."

The second he says it, I know exactly what he's planning. "Nate. You are *not* crashing Rob's bachelor party."

My best friend freezes and he looks up at me slowly. "That's . . . not what I'm doing."

"For some reason, I don't believe you."

"He won't even know I'm there."

"I seriously doubt that. Why are you even worried about this?" I shake my head. "It's just a bachelor party. He's drinking with some friends."

Nate is quiet for a long moment. His mouth tugs downward into a frown, which looks wrong on his face. I know my best friend is capable of a lot of deep thought, but we keep things between us light for a reason.

"Bachelor parties are when a lot of things can go wrong. I understand he only wants his close friends there, but isn't that a little suspicious?" The lower timbre of his voice urges me to think about it.

Rob and I have had a fair share of issues over the years. Nate knows about some of them, but not all. There have been times when Rob seems to forget I exist. Times when I caught him liking other women's pictures on Instagram. And worse, times when I wondered if I should stay with him.

But he's been on his best behavior since asking me to marry him. He gets distant sometimes, but I do the same.

Still, he was *adamant* about not inviting Nate.

"I can see why you would be worried."

"I don't wanna make myself known. I won't even talk to him. But if something happens there, something that you don't agree with, I want you to know before you marry him."

Nate has never once stepped in between Rob and me. There was a time back when I first started dating him where I was afraid that Nate was upset with me for some reason. But that faded, and he returned to being the best friend I always knew. He's been there through some of the fights too. He's clearly been unhappy with Rob, but stepped back when I said I would forgive him.

If he has concerns now, then I better listen to them.

"Fine, but please don't get caught."

"I won't."

"When you find nothing, come over. I'm gonna tell you I told you so a hundred times, but then we can have fun."

Nate nods. "I think I can live with that deal."

The conversation slowly slides into silence. I'm trying not to think too deeply into Nate's worry when I see a familiar face walking into the burger shop.

"Be subtle, but my boss is behind you."

Nate immediately turns around fully, staring Levi down as if he's the coolest person in the world.

So much for subtlety.

"Come on, don't you know how to not let people know you're looking at them?"

"Nope," he replied. Of course, Levi can tell someone is watching him and his gaze slides to our table immediately. "Oh, look. I can say hi."

"You're lucky he's a nice guy," I hiss as Levi walks over.

"Hey, Maisie. Out for lunch?" Levi smiles at me like he always does in the office. He's kind and professional in the same way he's always been, but I know a lot about him through his wife, who I hang out with every now and again. At first, I'd been nervous that striking up a friendship with his wife would change things in the office. So far, he was the same kind boss I'd grown used to.

"Yep. He invited me out." I point to Nate, who immediately holds his hand out.

"Nate Hansford. I've heard only good things."

"You must be Maisie's fiancé who I've not met."

I'm glad that I'm finished with my bite or else I would have choked on it. "No, no, he's not my fiancé." I rush to say it.

Levi's eyes go wide and his cheeks color. "Oh, brother then?"

That was a stretch. Nate and I don't look alike, and we both hated it when we were called brother and sister.

"No, just a friend. Nate's been around me for my whole life."

Levi does what most people do when they find out Nate is not my partner. He looks between us, his brow furrows, and then he shakes himself out of it before smiling. "Well, it's nice to meet you. Is the food good here? I've been meaning to try it."

"I only take Maisie to the best places," Nate says, his voice light as always.

Levi hums. "I like that. I do the same for my wife."

Nate and I tense at the mere comparison of being like Levi and Amy. Those two are obsessed with each other in a way I didn't know was possible.

"I'll let you two enjoy lunch," Levi says. "It was great to meet you."

I let out a long breath when he walks away. At least Levi didn't ask the barrage of questions we were used to. Those ranged from if Nate was gay or if we'd dated a long time ago and it didn't work out.

The real answer is that we're simply . . . friends. We met when we were kids and dating wasn't on either of our minds. Then we grew up, real life hit, and it never happened. Our friendship is worth so much to me that I would never risk anything.

Then I met Rob in college and that was that.

"He seems nice," Nate says. "Friendly. He's the one who suddenly got married, right?"

"Yep. And I go to his wife's book club."

"You've had this job for, what, years now? I've not heard a complaint."

"It pays the bills."

"You *like* it." He smirks in my direction.

"Yeah, yeah. I do. You'll never let me live it down that you found the job listing."

"And got you to apply. You were so sure you wouldn't get it."

I sigh and cross my arms. "Fine. You were right about this one. *Don't* get used to it."

"Face it, I'm right about most things."

"Except when you mean to go left."

His smile drops. "You're never gonna let that go, are you? I got us caught in front of the arena *one* time—"

"It took hours to get outta there."

"But we had fun! We listened to the *Mulan* soundtrack and belted out every lyric!"

"And then not to mention the time when you got Dr. Pepper and Coke, and gave me the wrong one because the employee told you it was on the left. I *hate* Dr. Pepper, Nate. You tried to poison me."

He rolls his eyes. "And then I got you cheese fries to make up for it. Without you asking."

"Don't gloat about your apology skills. You've already tested the limits today."

He leans in, and the smile is back. "And you know I'll keep testing them. It's kinda my thing."

chapter two

I HAVEN'T EVEN TAKEN my sweater vest off when there's a knock at the door. I frown and check the time, wondering if it's later than it should be.

It's not.

Quinn is on the other side, but I know for a fact that she isn't supposed to be here until five. Her bleach-blonde hair is curled today and she's wearing a bright pink sweat suit.

"Hey," she says and holds up a bag of unpopped popcorn. "I hope it's okay that I'm early."

I blink and try to adjust my plans in my head. "I can make it work. I don't have everything ready, though."

She sighs as she walks into the house. "I'm sorry, I had to come early. I have a few birthday plans that I have to make it to, so I can't stay that late. Mom's insisting, or else I would cancel."

Andrea is not the kind of woman who takes no for an answer, and both of us know it. She's been a part of every single moment of wedding planning, including picking the date. She said that if the entire family was coming into town for something, she also wanted it to be near another big event. Quinn is turning thirty in a little over a week, and her party is going to be as big as the wedding.

I'm not upset that Quinn's birthday is going to be a massive event. This is just how things are in this family. What I am upset about is the fact that her party is the day after I get back from my honeymoon. Technically, it'll all work out. But there's a feeling of discomfort that's grown as I get closer to my big day. I don't know what it is, but it's persistent.

It's not like I can call it off. I have to get this over with.

"It's fine. We'll have time for a movie."

"Good," she says with a sigh of relief. "I can't wait for girl time."

I close the door and make popcorn before walking back over to the couch. The original plan was to change and be in comfortable clothes when we did this, but I don't want to delay us since she has to leave early.

"So, what do you wanna watch?" she asks.

I'm terrible at keeping up with movies. Nate likes them far more than I do. Usually, he finds one he likes and I watch it out of duty. "There's a new rom-com out. I can't remember the name of it, but Nate sent it to me." I open my phone and go through our many messages. "Here. This one." I show her the poster.

Quinn loves a rom-com. Coincidentally, so does Nate.

If only he were here.

"Oh yeah," she says. "I think it's on Netflix. We can use my account."

She pulls it up and I try my best to focus on the movie. I've gotten my love story, so I'm not all that interested in other people's. But I can make an effort.

Today, however, I feel far more bitter than I want to. My own love feels like a jumbled mess. I can't tell if it's not seeing Rob or if it's Nate's words from earlier.

We're about halfway through the movie when Quinn pauses it. "Something's bothering you, isn't it?"

"Am I that obvious?"

She shrugs. "A little."

"I know you're enjoying the movie. We can continue it and then talk when it's done."

"I'm not worried about the movie, I'm worried about you." She says it like it's obvious. "What's going on? Is my brother being dumb again?"

I wince. Quinn's always quick to be on my side when Rob and I fight. It's not something I ever expected when I started dating her brother, but she assured me that she knows him best, and that includes the fact that he can be a selfish moron. At the time, I defended him, but now, I find it hard to.

I don't even want to think about what Nate's doing, nor do I want to bring Quinn into it when it's only a hunch. But I do have one other issue I need to talk about.

With a sigh, I stand and grab the magazine off the table and hand it to her. "He wants me to move in with him. Into *his* apartment complex."

"Oh." She takes the magazine and flips through. "Yeah, this place is . . . something."

"And expensive. He's offered to pay for most of it, even if we get a new unit, but I prefer for finances to be more even. And . . ." I gaze around my own home. "I like it here."

Quinn hums. "What does Nate think about this?"

"Nate? I haven't told him yet."

"Really?"

I shake my head. "We don't tend to talk about relationship problems unless it's pretty serious."

"I'd say where you move is pretty serious. And didn't Nate specifically choose his apartment because it's close to you? He'd want to know."

"You're not wrong," I admit. "I have a feeling he'll tell me Rob and I should have talked about this a while ago. Or Rob should let it go, considering I own this place and he rents."

"Rob doesn't let anything go," Quinn says.

"Then I should move in with him." My shoulders sink as I say it, and I know I don't like that answer. Usually, I'm better about bucking up and dealing with things, but where I live is the one thing I've fought back on. Rob has gotten nearly everything he wanted from me. We're getting married where he chose, on the date his mom wanted. And the honeymoon is for *him*, not me.

"No, I think you should be the first to *make* him let something go."

"Really?" I ask.

"Yes. It doesn't make sense for you to move when you own your place. I'm not saying the two of you will be here forever, but he can't bulldoze you over it. And you can't afford his apartment complex."

"Thank you." A breath of relief escapes me as I say it. "I needed to hear that. Do you think it'll be hard to convince him?"

She scrunches her nose. "I'd get used to the idea of living apart for the time being. You might have to outlast him on this one."

He isn't going to like that idea, and I can easily imagine the fight that'll start. Rob can get mean when we disagree. He always apologizes, but over the years, I've learned not to start anything.

But this is something I can't let go.

"You'll help with this, right?"

"Of course I will. He needs pressure from all sides."

"Definitely." I bump my shoulder against hers. "Thank you. I really needed this. Should we get back to the movie?"

She nods right when a text comes through her phone. After pulling it out, her smile fades. "Actually, can we finish this another time? Mom has something else for me to do."

I'm really starting to dislike Andrea. But Quinn doesn't need to know that.

"Absolutely."

She apologizes for our night being cut short and hugs me one more time before she has to leave. She's gone by the time that she was supposed to arrive, and my stomach is still in knots about my living situation.

At least I have backup. And Nate will be on my side once I tell him.

I finally decide to get out of my work clothes. I swap my slacks for pajama pants and my top for a button-up, part of a set. But I don't feel better. Things feel so off even though I've gotten reassurance that I'm right when it comes to where I move.

Out of habit, I pull up Nate's location. He should still be at the bar, and I wonder how long he'll watch Rob.

The stalking of my best friend is interrupted by a FaceTime call from my mom.

"Hi, guys," I say. "What's up?"

My mom and dad live in my childhood home about thirty minutes away. Mom works at the same school Nate does and Dad is a carpenter. Mom volunteers with her free time, but still schedules her shifts to be the same as Dad's. They would have just gotten home and finished dinner by the time they called me.

"Hi, honey," Mom says with a smile. "I hope I'm not interrupting your movie night."

"Quinn had to leave early. *Andrea.*"

Mom nods. "She's a . . . special woman, isn't she?"

I hear my dad huff and I know he's sitting next to her, ready to enter the conversation whenever he has an opinion. He always does this when Mom is on a video call, purely because he hates seeing himself on a camera. But I can picture him. His arms are crossed tightly and he's probably doing all he can to keep his face straight. He makes it a habit to be as stoic as he can be. There are some things that he lets loose on, though.

His hatred for Andrea is one of them.

"I feel the same as you, Dad. Hope you had a good day at work."

"It was decent." That's all he says. It's about all I'll get from him too. I know he loves me and I love him. He's just a man of few words.

"What's Nate up to?" Mom asks. "I'm sure he would help salvage your night if you asked."

"Nate's out. He had plans."

"Does he have another date?" She gets close to the camera. "You'll have to tell me how it goes. I've been *dying* for him to not be single anymore! He's far too handsome for that."

Once upon a time, they'd thought *I* was the one for Nate, but with me staying with Rob for a decade, Mom's been hoping Nate would find someone too.

"Not with a woman, unfortunately. It's a date with . . . himself."

I don't usually lie to my parents, but I know they'll have questions about why he feels the need to make sure Rob doesn't say or do anything stupid. They have the same worry as Nate does, that Rob will betray me and we'll break up.

It's been long enough to prove that wrong.

He'd agreed to no strippers. He said this was just a night with the guys where he would let loose and have fun. Things were *fine*. And the twisting in my stomach is just Nate's worry bleeding into me and the fear of fighting with Rob over where to live. That is *all*.

Mom hums, but Dad has another question for me. "Getting ready for the big day?"

My marriage to Rob is the next step in our lives. This was expected and natural. I'd always wanted to be married before I was thirty, after all.

"I am. It's gonna be . . . busy."

I can't say I'm excited to see all of Rob's massive family. My own is tiny, and the people that are coming from my side aren't enough to fill up the huge venue Andrea booked.

"It's your wedding, honey. You have to at least pretend to be excited."

"It'll be the best day of my life," I say with a fake smile. "Is that better?"

"No. But once you're on your honeymoon, I bet you'll feel

better. I can't believe you asked for a cruise of all things. You've come so far with your fear of water."

I struggle to keep my face straight at the mention of water. I'd managed to get both Mom and Dad to believe that I had conquered my fear. Or at least it didn't stop me. But the truth is, I'm going on a cruise *for Rob*. This is what he wants, not what I want. When I agreed to do this, I'd hoped he would hear me out on living in my house and not his apartment.

So far, I've not had any luck. He reminded me that his parents were paying for the entire wedding and reception. Usually, the bride's family pays for that, but Mom and Dad hadn't been able to afford the wedding Rob wanted. All they could do was pull together enough savings to give us the honeymoon.

I'm hoping that I'll manage to have fun, but deep down, I'm afraid that it'll be just as miserable as planning this wedding has been. It's very possible our happily ever after isn't going to start until the wedding and honeymoon are over.

"Yeah, I'm growing as a person. Rob does that to me."

"He's the only person besides Nate who's managed it." Mom laughs. I try not to let any emotion show at the lie. Nate *is* still the only person that can drag me out of my life and make me do something fun. Rob's tried, but it always ends in a fight.

Just thinking of Nate makes me flip over to his location again. I pause when I see that he's leaving the bar and heading to my house early. And judging by how fast his little icon is moving, he's *booking* it.

"Uh, guys?" I start. "I have to go. I think Nate's plans changed."

"Is he coming over?"

"Yes, I think so."

"Can't I just say hi? I've missed him ever since school let out. He's the best coworker ever."

"I think this is a best-friend-emergency moment." In fact, I know it is as I watch him take a shortcut to get to me.

"Fine, but you'll have to let me know if something's wrong. I'll help him in any way I can."

"I will." I don't want to tell her that I don't think anything is going to be wrong with *him*. I have a feeling this is going to be directed toward *me*.

Both of them say their goodbyes right as Nate's SUV barrels into my driveway. He's at my door before I even open it.

"We need to talk." He's out of breath as he looks at me with wide eyes. "And you'll wanna sit down for this."

IN THE SHAKY VIDEO, Rob laughs into the mic like he's having the time of his life. "It's hard to believe I'm getting married in two days."

"Hell yeah it is!" one of his friends, Scott, shouts.

"You all know I just wanted to get into Maisie's pants when I first met her. Hell, I still do. All the time. It definitely makes up for the . . ."

"Bitchiness?" Scott says. My jaw drops at the word as Rob considers it. He doesn't even correct his friend.

"Boringness?" a guy I haven't even met adds.

"Her general nature," is what Rob lands on. "But the important thing is, she's mine. And she'll stay mine. Forever."

"Until you hate her." Scott snickers.

"I've had plenty of moments where I've hated her. You all know that. But still, when she's looking at me, I feel like I've won. She's the best prize I could ask for. And that's why I'm marrying her."

The video cuts off with a curse from Nate.

For a long time, I can only stare at the play button, wondering if I can stomach that again. But I feel like I need to. What I've just witnessed doesn't feel real. This has to be a bad dream.

Of all the things that had gone through my mind when Nate sat me down, this wasn't one of them. I thought that he would have cheated. Or that he was acting like a complete fool and I needed to go get him.

But this? This *hurts*.

Rob and I may not talk as much as Nate and I do, but I had no idea he felt this way. I had no idea his friends talk about me in this way. They've been nice every time I've hung out with them.

I press play and watch it all over again. As it repeats, I realize I would have preferred him to have hired strippers. Maybe even flirt with a woman at the bar.

Because this has my stomach sinking into my ass. This hurts me deeply. He *hates* me at times. And we're supposed to get married.

The video ends and I go to play it a third time, but Nate pulls the phone away. "I think you need to breathe," he says. This isn't the first time he's seen me at my lowest. Hell, I've seen him at his lowest too. When everything with our families fell apart in high school, it was all we could do to remind each other to survive.

I had hoped it would be a long time before I showed Nate that kind of hurt again. Obviously, tonight is the night to bring it back.

I take a shaky breath and it does nothing.

"What else did you see?" I ask.

"They were talking like this for a bit. I didn't record that, mostly because I was in shock. I figured the speech would be bad, but not *that* bad. I'm sorry, berry. I knew once I had the video, I needed to show you."

"I know. It just . . ." I don't have words as I curl into a ball on the couch.

"Maisie, I—"

"I don't understand. If he hated me at times, why would he continue to date me? Why not just talk to me?"

Mom and Dad have fought. And I've seen it. I'm sure Mom

briefly felt like she hated Dad and vice versa. But they always talked it out. That has been my goal too.

I've always had an idea of what I want in love. It should be warm and inviting, like a cozy blanket on the softest couch. That's what Mom and Dad have.

Did I have that with Rob?

Could I ever, if he'd often thought he hated me and never brought it up?

"Can you send me that?" My voice shakes and I must be close to crying, but no tears escape my eyes. Probably because my body still feels like it's in free fall.

"Only if you promise not to rewatch it."

"I won't. I need it for something else."

"And what do you need it for?"

I have a feeling Nate doesn't want me to reach out to Rob, but I have to know if this is how he really feels. I need his side of the story. So I take Nate's phone before he can try to stop me. Once the message is sent, I throw it back at him.

"Maisie, what are you doing?" Nate asks as I get my own phone out.

"Nothing."

"You don't need to talk to him. Just take a minute—"

My message is already sent. I've forwarded the video too.

MAISIE

Is this how you really feel?

Rob doesn't respond immediately. He doesn't have his read receipts on, so I have no idea if he's even seen it.

And I frown. I remember that I asked him to turn those on months ago.

"Maisie, talk to me." Nate's voice is urgent, and I don't blame him for it. When I go silent is usually when something *big* has happened.

"What is there to even say?"

"How about what you're feeling?"

"I feel exactly like any woman would when she finds out her fiancé *hated* her at any point in their relationship." I run a hand over my face and find tears on my cheeks. "I mean, was it obvious to everyone? Am I just an idiot?"

"Not that he hated you. I always thought he talked a different way with his friends, but I didn't think it would be . . . *this*."

"Fuck," I mutter as I stand. "I can't—why would he say this right before our wedding? Couldn't he have told me this, I don't know, before he proposed?"

"He didn't think he would get caught, Maisie. This is probably why he didn't want me there."

It makes complete sense.

That's when my phone goes off.

ROB

How did you see this?

He's more worried about how I saw it than what he said.

Every cell in my body burns. I'm angry. I'm devastated. And the idea of putting on that stupid white dress hanging in my room makes me want to scream.

"What did he say?" Nate asks.

ROB

It's not as bad as it sounds. It's just some guy talk.

"Guy talk. He says it's guy talk."

My phone is out of my hands and Nate's reading the messages with a furrowed brow. "Come on, he's not even denying it."

I hear a *ding* and now Nate's glaring at my phone. He doesn't get angry often. I've only seen it happen twice. Once when someone rear-ended me and tried to blame me for it, and once when his mom tried to make his graduation about herself.

"What the *fuck*," he mutters as he reads it. I sit beside him and do the same.

ROB

Who sent you this? Was it Nate?

"Like I wouldn't let you know what he was saying," Nate says. I grab my phone just as another text message comes in.

ROB

Let me guess, Nate snuck in. He has it out for us, Maisie. He's probably spinning this to be something it isn't. Don't listen to him. I didn't mean it in any negative way.

I thought I was burning before, but something about this turns up the heat.

I answer before my rare bravery fades.

MAISIE

All Nate's done is showed me what you said.

ROB

That was never meant for you to hear.

MAISIE

So you truly felt that way about me at one point and you didn't want me to know?

ROB

It doesn't matter now.

MAISIE

I think it does.

He calls.

Nate tries to stop me. "Maisie, don't—"

I answer it and go to my bedroom, slamming the door shut. "What, Rob? What could you possibly say to make this better?" I hiss out. Usually, I go into arguments wanting to fix things, to get things back to normal.

This time, I'm tempted to burn it all down.

"Maisie, don't get all in your feelings about this. You're logical. You know how guys talk." He speaks loudly, and I know he's still at the bar. He hasn't even left to come and try to see me in person.

I don't feel logical. "Oh yeah? You think it's normal to let your friends call me a bitch behind my back?"

"That's just how Scott talks. You mean to tell me you think Nate never calls you that behind your back?"

"No, I don't. Actually, I *know* he doesn't."

"Of fucking course you do."

"Hey!" I hear Scott in the background. "Get off the phone with her! This is supposed to be a guy's night!"

"Hang on! She's talking about that fucking best friend again!" It's muffled, but I hear Rob call it out.

"The one that you hate?"

"Yeah. He's putting ideas in her head again."

"Tell her it's you or him!"

My blood runs cold as I hear it. Rob sighs and comes back to the phone.

"Come over. Get away from Nate. I'll explain it all."

"I'm not leaving Nate." I say it immediately. "You know I won't."

I don't know if I'm talking about tonight or in general.

Both are true.

There are many things I'll let go. There are many things I won't fight about.

Nate is neither of those things.

"Yeah, because he's your best bud. I fucking *know*, Maisie." I can practically hear his eye roll. "But things will be changing once you move in with me. No more nights with him when I'm not around. No more hanging out, not in my apartment, or I'll—"

I hang up.

I wasn't moving in with him in the first place. Nor would I ever give up my time alone with Nate. Rob always said he trusted me. Now he's changing his tune.

Was he always going to do this? Tell me I needed to not be around Nate?

Rob calls again. I send one text.

MAISIE

I choose Nate.

ROB

Seriously? You'd choose him over your fiancé? Because of some guy talk?

MAISIE

Did you forget all you said about me tonight when you thought I wouldn't hear?

ROB

You're the one making it a big deal.

MAISIE

Because it is.

You'll get your ring back in the mail.

Then I turn my phone off before I take it back.

My heart pounds as I stare at the black screen. Did I really just dump him?

Until five minutes ago, that wasn't an option. I thought I could work it out. Sure, we may have delayed the wedding. We may have had to do counseling, but it could work out.

And then he made me choose between him and Nate.

I squeeze my eyes shut as I slide the engagement ring off my finger. Everyone is going to be *pissed* at me. The wedding is in two days, and I just called it off.

"Maisie, open the door," Nate says from the other side. "Please. I need to know you're okay."

I'm not okay. I'm very much *not okay*. My hands shake as I slowly do what he asks. Nate stands on the other side. His eyes go wide as he takes me in.

"What happened?"

"I . . . dumped him."

"You *what*?" His eyes dart to my hand, which is now bare. "I . . ."

Silence envelops us both as a tear escapes me. I'm pulled into a hug before I know what's happening. It's been a very long time since Nate and I hugged. Actually, I can't remember the last time we touched at all. The scent of orange and cedar is foreign to me, and nothing about him should be foreign to me.

Still, I cling to him, gripping his dress shirt tightly. I realize that his height has its advantages here. He's everywhere, and it's hard to have any other thoughts when he seems to be able to make the world melt away. He's the one stable thing in my life right now. How could I ever not choose him?

It feels right, just like this hug feels right. I miss this. I *need* this.

And that's when he lets me go. I blink back into the moment, trying to figure out how to ask him to do all of that over again. My entire body feels cold in a way that has nothing to do with the temperature.

"It's gonna be okay, Maisie. I can get sorbet and we can talk about how awful he is."

Another tear escapes and I wipe it away. He's mentioned the one thing I also really want.

"Good idea," I say. "Do you know what kind to get?"

"Lemon." He laughs. "What kind of question is that? Do you have any in your freezer?" I shake my head. "Then we'll go get some and then start shit talking."

"You expect me to go out like this?"

He raises an eyebrow. "Do you want to be alone?"

I don't. Both of us know it.

But the way he knows me makes me want to cry all over again. Deep down, I know that between him and Rob, Nate is the one who would know both the dessert that I need and that I don't want to be alone.

And that thought is humbling.

chapter three

The day of my wedding, my parents knock on my door. I'm lying on my couch in a tear-stained hoodie with my hair in a two-day-old bun. I *never* let myself get like this, but the doom of my engagement is good enough reason to sit around and be miserable for a bit.

Everything is ruined. I might as well join the party.

Slowly, I roll myself off of the spot on the couch that I'm sure has an imprint of my ass by now and shuffle to the door.

"Hi, sweetie," Mom says. "How are you feeling?"

Dad is behind her, his thick mustache blocking his mouth. It's amazing how he can look the same as the day I announced my engagement as he does today, when there's definitively *not* a wedding happening.

Still, even his eyes widen at the sight of me.

That doesn't mean anything good.

"Awful," I say.

"I brought you some food." She holds up a tray. "And I wanted to see you. Is Nate here? I made enough for him too."

Nate has crashed on my couch the last two nights. He was here when I cried and watched the video over and over. Now, he's handling the logistics of ending the wedding.

I don't deserve this man.

"No, he's out."

"Darn."

"I'll give it to him later," I say as I take the tray. "Thank you."

"What did he think about all of this?" Dad asks.

I think back to Nate's carefully guarded nature. I know he's angry, but he doesn't let it show. Still, I see his tense shoulders and gritted teeth as I've cried.

"He's supportive, like always."

Dad hums and says nothing else. That's pretty typical for him.

"We are too," Mom says softly. "That video was no way a future husband should talk about a partner."

"Yeah, I know. I'm sorry about the money you guys spent on the honeymoon."

Wasted money was one of the things Rob had been furious about, according to Nate.

I feel terrible. And that feeling has only gotten worse. Normally, it would be enough for me to bend to Rob's will, but this time, I'm not. I feel terrible *and* I'm continuing. The guilt is eating me alive, but I'm turning away from it.

That's not something I do. But I will for Nate.

"We didn't lose anything, dear. That's what we wanted to talk to you about."

"You paid for the honeymoon, which isn't happening now."

Mom and Dad glance at each other and then at me. "It still can," she says. She pulls out a pamphlet for the cruise. I resist the urge to groan. That whole decision was made for Rob's benefit. Looking back on it now, I was setting myself up for misery from the get-go.

"Mom, I—"

"You've had a rough go of it. But you need something to pick you up. I know you have a . . . complicated past with swimming, but there are plenty of other things you can do to care for yourself."

Complicated past is an understatement. When I was five, I fell into a pool when Mom's back was turned and she didn't see me struggling. By the time the lifeguard pulled me out, the damage was done. I was told it was only a few seconds. To me, it felt like a lifetime.

My young brain latched onto that moment and told me that water is unsafe. I've always followed that belief, avoiding water and everything to do with it.

The honeymoon was an exception. For *Rob*.

But Mom seems so hopeful, and I know I can't let this money go to waste, even if there's no way I can go.

Taking the pamphlet, I try to think of a plan for how the cruise can get used so I can stay at home and rot.

Mom and Dad are none the wiser.

"Thank you," I say.

"Just update the names when you know who's going. You can take Quinn."

"She's got her birthday party to plan for." I shake my head. "No way."

She hasn't even had time to see me. Apparently, Andrea has been on a warpath with the canceled wedding. I know she's taking some of the brunt of it along with Nate. I owe her far too much.

There's a part of me that hates that I hide out when things get bad, but I know if I face any of this, I'll take it back. And I refuse to do that this time.

"Or you could take your other best friend who loves swimming," Mom adds.

I nod absentmindedly. Nate does love swimming, and he's free since school isn't in session.

A plan forms in my mind. One where Nate can get the best thank-you I can muster.

"I'll figure it out," I say with a smile. "Thank you guys again."

Mom hugs me and squeezes me tight. Dad gives me one of his trademark nods. Something in my chest loosens. At least they're not mad at me.

They would be two of the few.

～～～

"Maisie," a voice calls from the doorway. "Are you still in despair?"

"A little, but at least there's food!" I call from the kitchen where I'm watching the microwave. I knew when Nate was on his way back from the wedding venue, and I started it so it would be ready when he walked through the door.

"You're cooking?"

"Kind of. My parents brought something for us."

"*Yes*," he hisses with a smile before he looks me over. "It's nice to see you up and moving."

"Well, I owe you. The least I can do is have some food ready for you."

"Berry, you don't owe me a thing. What else are friends for?"

"Sure," I reply as I take his plate out of the microwave.

"Is that lasagna?"

"You know it."

"Your parents do love us. There's enough for both of us, right?"

"There is."

"I've gotta tell them thank you," he replies. "I'll set the table."

I can't help but smile. This is so easy with him. Why the hell would I ever give it up? This, right here, is why I'm dealing with all the guilt. And it's worth it.

By the time I bring both plates out, Nate has napkins and silverware ready to go.

"Want a Coke?" he asks. When I nod, he disappears only for a second and is back with our drinks.

"How was everything?" I ask coolly as I sit. My voice sounds almost normal, but I'm staring at the melted cheese on top of my lasagna, not him.

"Do you really wanna do this again? Last time didn't go so well."

I'd asked yesterday and nearly broke down in tears. "I'm doing better today."

"You *seem* like you are," he says.

My spine straightens. Of course he would pick up on the fact that I'm pretending.

"How mad is Andrea today?" I ask. There's no better way to prove I'm fine than to talk about the woman who's been a thorn in my side for months.

He blows out a breath. "As angry as always."

My face falls against my will. I already want to run and hide at the mention of Andrea being angry.

Tapping on the table, I think about the run I'll need to go on to process this. Who knew ending a wedding would fill me with such anxious energy?

"Maisie," Nate says softly. "They'll get over it."

"I know," I say. "Did you see Quinn?"

"For a moment."

"And?"

"Quinn's fine. Still not mad at you. She never would be."

"I know. I just . . . need the reminder."

Nate reaches over and goes to put a hand on my shoulder. I pause as I remember when I'd been in his arms two days before. A hand on the shoulder is nothing compared to a hug, but I'll take it. But before he touches me, he stops and pulls away.

My stomach sinks. I want the contact, but now that I think about it, Nate and I don't tend to touch very often. When we were younger, things weren't like that.

When did they change?

"Maisie, you're doing the right thing. You know that, right?"

"I do."

"Then don't worry about anything else. Just recover."

Immediately, I shake my head. "I wanna try to be normal. No more crying on the couch. No more looking like . . . this."

"You look fine."

"It's sweet that you'd lie for me, but I'm a mess. I can't go on like this."

"Take as much time as you need. You don't need to rush."

I do need to rush this, only so he doesn't feel like he has to stay because of me. But he doesn't know that yet.

"I want to move on. Move forward. I can't mull in this for too long. You know that."

Nate only sighs. The summer before college, we both lost someone. For Nate, it was his mom. For me, it was my grandma, the woman responsible for my fun summers and warm Christmases.

Both of us fell apart. I tried to be there for him and he tried to be there for me, but we were a mess of grief with no way to process it. Eventually, Dad sat both of us down after two weeks and told us we had to at least *try* to do the things we loved, even if we didn't want to. Otherwise, the depression would only get worse.

I can't feel that way again, and Nate knows it.

"Want me to join you for your run tomorrow?"

Usually I would say yes, but not this time.

"You might have plans."

"The whole point of my summer is to *not* have plans." He raises an eyebrow. "Unless you have something for me."

"I might."

"What are you getting at?" he asks slowly.

I pull out the pamphlet for the cruise and hand it to him. "I'm thinking this."

He looks it over, eyes going wide. "This is your honeymoon cruise."

"Yep. It's still booked. Someone"—I look up at him—"could go."

"And by someone, you mean me."

"Yes."

"With you?" He says it slowly and I immediately shake my head.

"No! *No.* I'm not going."

His brow furrows. "And why not? Is being on a boat in the middle of the ocean suddenly not appealing to you?"

I roll my eyes as I lean back in the chair. Nate knows about my fear of the water, and he looked at me like I'd grown a second head when I originally told him where I planned to go for the honeymoon.

"You don't need to gloat."

"I'm not trying to gloat. I just didn't see why you'd choose to be around water on purpose."

My reasons seem stupid now. I thought that meeting Rob in the middle would make him more open to living in my house, at least temporarily. Now I know nothing I could have done would've been enough. Not without distancing myself from Nate.

"The point is, my parents paid for it. Someone should enjoy it."

"They could go."

"They want *me* to. I may have told them I conquered my fear of the water."

"Oh, did you?" Nate asks. "And let me guess, you don't want to admit you totally lied."

"I'm not gonna defend my choices here. Please, consider it."

Nate finally looks at the pamphlet, flipping through it as his lips press together. "You know, there's a lot on here that has nothing to do with swimming."

I have a feeling that's on purpose. Mom may have believed me, but she also was there when I nearly drowned, so she would give me an out.

"And?"

"You could *try* to go."

I huff out a laugh. "Are you serious?"

"What? It's your honeymoon."

"It's just a trip now," I remind him. "And do you really think I'm willing to go on a boat after all of this? Besides, you handled all of that stuff for me while I was a potato on the couch. You deserve it."

He moves the pamphlet toward me again. "No, *you* do. When was the last time you took a break, Maisie?"

I didn't take breaks. And I certainly didn't take vacations. Fear of water aside, I always preferred my routine. Hell, I've been dreading this cruise even before I realized how much of an idiot Rob is.

Nate uses my silence to go in for the kill. "I'm not going if you aren't."

This is his usual methodology to get me to agree to whatever he wants me to do. He always offers to do it with me.

"That's a terrible idea."

"And why is that?"

"This is a honeymoon cruise with only one bed in a tiny cabin. We'd practically be on top of each other for a week."

He immediately goes pale, as if being that close is actually his nightmare. *Ouch.* I don't need to take it personally, but I feel his reaction right in my chest.

"I . . . can handle it," he says.

I'm tempted to cry again, but I refuse to. "Sounds like you can't."

"I *can.*" He leans forward, and his tone has an edge to it that I've not heard before. When he leaves and I wind up crying again, I'll be thinking about this moment.

Harping on it, actually.

But for now, I have to keep it together.

"Just go on the cruise. Meet a hot woman. Have a great time."

It was rare that Nate gave women a chance. This could be a good time for him to.

"If it's a honeymoon cruise, how am I supposed to meet anyone single?"

"The cruise itself isn't only for honeymoons. It's an adult cruise with the honeymoon package."

He bites his lip as he considers it. I can't stop staring at the movement, wondering what his answer will be. His eyes are locked on the pamphlet, and I know he's considering this.

"And what about you?" he asks. "You want me to leave right when you just made a huge life change?"

"I'll be fine. I can deal with this."

"You need me."

My skin prickles at the words because he's right. I've known for a very long time that I do need him. "I can survive for one week."

"It's one hell of a week to do it."

"There's no one else I wanna give this to. And if my parents know that I'm not going, you're the next best thing. You know they consider you to be a son."

He sighs. "I see your logic, but I don't like it."

"Life will be easier if you admit I'm right and spend your week looking over the ocean and traveling the Caribbean."

"It wouldn't be a terrible way to spend some time," he admits.

"Good. You're seeing my point. Now, continue to see it while I eat." I grab my fork. "I'm starving."

chapter four

I DON'T REGRET LETTING Nate go on the trip until the morning he's supposed to leave.

After sending him a bunch of texts and heart emojis telling him to have fun, I sigh and put away my phone. I'm trying to work myself up to telling Levi that I'm willing to forgo my PTO and come to work, but I dread it. As much as I want to get back into the usual swing of things, I can't take another pitying look.

I don't want to admit it, but Nate had a point when he told me that I needed him. Usually when I had time off, he was the first person I called. Today, he'll be flying to Orlando and staying in a hotel. Tomorrow, he'll set off and be in the ocean.

Slowly, I lace up my running shoes, preparing to go out. The plan is to go on a run and call Levi when I get back to offer to return to work tomorrow. Then, I'll use the rest of my day to go through all the wedding stuff in my house.

But the plan is . . . not fun.

This feels terrible. It always does. After Grandma died, it felt like I was stabbing myself over and over again every single time I had to do something. And then one day, it got easier. And then it became second nature.

But this sucks, and I wish that I had told Nate to stay and help me. A run would be so much easier if he was running beside me, complaining the whole way.

As I finish up my second shoe, there's a knock at the door. I groan, hoping it's not a salesman or someone with well wishes after I ended my engagement.

But the second I open it, my jaw drops when I see a tall figure with wavy black hair.

"Nate, what the hell are you doing here? Shouldn't you be heading to the airport?"

To be fair, Nate does look like he's on his way. He's got on a wide sun hat with sunglasses that make him look like he's en route to the docks. He's traded his usual button-up shirt for the bright Hawaiian one I got him as a joke. On top of that, he's wearing sweatpants.

"I *am* heading to the airport. I just had to stop for one thing."

I narrow my eyes, racking my brain to figure out what he could have left here. "And what's that? Your sense of style?"

"Very funny. I thought you'd love that I'm wearing your shirt."

"It's sweet, but you look like you closed your eyes and hoped for the best when you got dressed this morning."

He rolls his eyes. "Here I was, coming to you to get the one thing I need, and you're making fun of me."

I cross my arms. "What do you need, Nate?"

"You." He says it so casually that, for a second, I don't think I've heard him right.

But he's leaning on my doorway, eyebrow raised as he waits for my response.

"M-me? How could you forget me?"

"Last I checked, your name's on one of the tickets. So, you're going."

Realization hits me. "Oh, no. I'm very much not going."

"Really? But I bought you a gift to bribe you."

"What could possibly bribe me into this?"

He reaches into his pocket and pulls out a pair of purple sunglasses shaped like flowers. For a second, all I can do is stare at them. They look not only impractical, but like nothing else in my closet.

"What the hell are those?"

"Cute. And for you." He hands them over, and I'm wondering if my best friend lost his mind.

"Uh, thanks. But I'm still not going."

Nate rolls his eyes. "Do you really think that I'm gonna leave you after you just ended your ten-year relationship?"

"Yes, because I told you to."

"Try again."

"Well then. You'll have to stay here, which is also not acceptable because you deserve this vacation."

"So do you."

"I don't—" I shake my head. "A boat and me do not mix. This is a terrible idea."

"Listen, I usually don't push you and water." And he doesn't. All it took was one panicked episode during a summer break and he dropped it. "But I also looked into it. There are pools on only one of the decks. We can totally avoid them. And if you don't want to be on the docks, we'll avoid that as well."

I blink at him. I've never known Nate to do research in his life. He only did it when trying to figure out the qualifications to be a gym teacher. Which means he's serious about me going on this trip.

"B-but I'm fine. I'm literally going on my run right now." I gesture to my leggings and shoes. Even my hair is in its perfect ponytail.

"And what have you been doing up until now?"

I wince, knowing I was sitting on the toilet watching other people get married and crying.

I hate the way Nate can read my mind.

"Why are you doing all of this?" I ask quietly. "You can just take the free trip and run."

The smug look on his face fades. "Do you think I would?"

I regret the words the second I say them. "No, I don't. But you could, and honestly, you *should* take it and run. I'm not gonna be any fun on this trip. You know that, so why do you want me to go on it so badly?"

He pauses, eyes going distant as he thinks about what he's going to say. I can only stare. He hardly ever thinks this hard about his words. "You changed Rob's name on the ticket."

I'd done it right before the deadline, hastily putting Nate's information instead. I had to pay a hefty fee for it too.

"I did."

"Not yours."

"I didn't mean that as a sign or anything," I reply.

"But it's an opportunity for you to join." Nate's fingers tap on his arm as he continues. "And the last few months with the wedding planning . . . it's been stressful for you. And I'll be honest, I was looking forward to this week because I thought we'd be able to spend some time together. Just the two of us, without Rob or the wedding hanging over us."

I blink. Even with the planning, I made time for him. But I knew our hangouts had devolved into me venting about what was happening with the wedding. Immediately, my shoulders slump as guilt hits me.

"I'm sorry," I say. "I'm not trying to pressure you into this cruise. We can just hang out here, and I'll tell my parents the truth."

"No, don't. Jeff and Judy paid a lot for this. I looked it up." He sighs. "I don't want them to lose out on it either."

"So the solution is for *me* to get on a boat?"

"To try it. I'll be there, after all."

"And you think this will go well?"

"Maisie." Nate's voice is soft this time. "It's me and you. We can handle anything, and the boat is so big I doubt you'll even be thinking of the water. But I highly doubt you wanna be alone, and neither do I. So, let's go do this together."

The way this man knows me is still shocking sometimes. We've been in each other's lives since we were children. There were plenty of people who didn't have the dedication to know someone like Nate does.

Hell, my fiancé didn't.

Nate knows he's won before I even voice it. "You have an extra thirty minutes to pack."

"We don't have any extra time. The airport's gonna be terrible."

"Then you better get started." He smiles. "*Before* I start gloating that I'm right."

"Don't even," I mutter before turning to go back to my bedroom. I dimly remember the plans Rob and I made to get to the airport.

Nate's thirty minutes are nonexistent.

My best friend finds me hurling clothes into my suitcase. Once that's done, I throw in all the small toiletries I'd collected over the last few months when I thought I was going on this trip with Rob, finishing it off with the sunglasses I'm pretty sure I'm never going to wear.

"My, my. This is chaos."

"Shut up. I'd like to see if your bag is any better." I'm in the middle of jumping on my bag to get it to close.

"Don't you worry your pretty little head about it, Maisie." Nate walks over to throw his weight on it too. "Mine is *much* worse."

The Nashville Airport is, without a doubt, a fucking nightmare. I'm glad Nate's driving, because after the third near-accident, I'm about to pull my hair out.

"Did people lose all sense in the last few days or something?" I snap as someone stops for a turn so fast that we nearly rear-end them.

"No one with any sense goes near the airport unless they have to." Nate is oddly calm.

I don't know how Rob would've dealt with this. Maybe it's better that I don't.

Nate has surprisingly planned everything out. When I ask about parking, he says he got a spot. When I ask how much I owe him for it, he rolls his eyes and tells me he won't accept a dime.

And then I look up how much it would cost anyway.

"*Nate*," I hiss. "Please tell me this isn't how much you paid."

I turn the screen around and he doesn't even look. "I told you not to worry about it."

"We should have had my mom and dad drop us off," I say as we get out of the SUV. "Sure, they might sit in traffic for two hours, but it would be cheaper than this."

"Jeff and Judy Cohen are the kindest souls I've ever met. I wouldn't do that to them."

"But they'd do it."

"I think being in all of this would send Jeff into an early grave. Besides, I'm getting a whole cruise for free. I think I can afford some expensive parking."

"That, and you'd have to admit you were considering going without me."

"I never considered it at all. I just needed time to figure out how to convince you to go. Unfortunately, you're very stubborn."

"You like it."

I don't expect him to respond, but a slow smile crosses his face as he looks at me. "I do."

I let out a laugh, one of my first genuine ones since everything went down. Nate might be in vacation mode, but he seems more open than usual.

Maybe it's not a bad thing that I came with him.

"We're still gonna make it to the gate, right?"

He checks our tickets and the time. "It looks like you're getting your morning run after all. We gotta go."

That's all he says before he takes off. Nate's legs are far longer than mine and I have to sprint to catch up with him.

"Curse you and your long legs!" I call. "You're about to leave me like Kevin from *Home Alone*."

"You're out of practice," he replies with a laugh, but he does slow down slightly.

It's tempting to grab his hand, but something about the way he avoided touching me just the day before makes me second-guess it. Instead, I push my legs harder to keep up with him.

We barely make it to the gate on time.

Even though we're not in economy, the seats are still tightly tucked together. There's an old man on one side of me and Nate is on the other. When I sit, I have to choose between the old man and Nate.

I choose Nate.

He goes tense the second my leg presses against his, and I frown.

"You okay?" I ask.

"Uh, yeah. This is just very tight." He shifts, almost like he wants to get away from me.

I blink. Does Nate not like to touch people? It's the only thing that makes sense, but how would I have not noticed? Had I been *that* busy with Rob?

"Sorry," I say and move the best I can. Without bothering the other man, all I can do is make it to where I'm not squished against him. I'm just there.

A nervous feeling settles in my gut at my last-second decision to come on this trip. No wonder he doesn't keep his girlfriends around. No wonder he only hangs out with me and no one else. I know I'll do my best to keep my distance if it's what he needs.

Even if I don't love the idea.

I'm not sure when this started. When we were kids, especially when we were graduating high school, touch was always something Nate initiated. Hugs were given freely, and we'd shared a bed more times than we could count.

"Is this better?"

"It's tolerable." His voice is tense and I hate that. My mouth tugs into a frown and I look over at the older man, wondering if I should get friendly with him. "Just . . . tell me what you got up to this morning. Please. Your eyes were red."

I blink. "No they weren't."

"They were. You were thinking about Rob again."

"I was *not*. Mostly. I was crying at weddings in general. Not Rob. I've barely even thought about him."

"Don't lie," he says flatly.

The thing is, when I'm with Nate, I don't think about Rob very much. I never have. Which is why it may be a good thing that I came on this trip.

"A lot of the videos were happy," I say. "And it's hard that it's the day after I was supposed to be happy, and I'm not."

"We'll get you there," Nate says. "I promise." The way he says it makes me want to lean into him, just like I used to when we went on field trips in high school.

But I don't. I settle for a smile.

"Thank you," I say.

Nate's eyes flick to my mouth and then down to my shoulder where we're touching. I remember how much he must hate this. Ignoring the feeling in my gut, I get a few centimeters away from him.

"At least the flight's short," I offer. "Then we're in the middle of the ocean. It's my *dream*."

"It's gonna be fine."

"You and I have very different definitions of fine."

"Massages are included. Along with the sauna. And all the drinks you could want."

"Now you're talking," I reply.

Satisfied, Nate pulls out his Kindle and reads while I double-check the itinerary for the cruise.

We have four stops over the seven days—one in Cozumel, Mexico and three in the Caribbean. I hadn't looked at much of anything, content to survive on the boat without letting Rob see that I hate the water.

Along with all the activities on the islands, Mom had taken the liberty to highlight the things I would enjoy on the boat too. Even though I lied to her, she still made sure I would know about all the non-water stuff available. And it's more than I expected.

It's overwhelming to look at it all. I had a handle on this trip with Rob and a light schedule figured out, but Nate being here throws a wrench in everything I'd planned. I know what he likes, thankfully, and I can easily make educated guesses, but the last few days haven't been the most restful and my eyes feel heavy as I look at everything.

Even though I've only been sitting around, dealing with everything has been exhausting. I've done my best, but the weight of it all and the lost sleep in favor of crying over my blown-up life makes me want to doze right off.

I lie back, closing my eyes for a second.

"Tired?" Nate asks lowly.

"Just resting my eyes." I won't say it, but it's all I can do. I don't have a neck pillow, and I can't rest my head on the stranger beside me.

And I definitely won't on Nate. His other leg, the one not pressed to me, hasn't stilled since we sat. I doubt it will for the whole flight.

I won't fall asleep. I'll just keep my eyes closed and cling to consciousness. I keep telling myself that, even as time goes murky and I feel my head grow heavy. Eventually, my head falls on something warm, and I can't remember why I didn't want this to happen.

As consciousness leaves me, I hear a sigh. "I knew you weren't fine, berry. How much have you been sleeping?"

And I'm gone.

chapter five

"MAISIE. Come on. Time to wake up." I'm being poked at and I groan. I could use a few more hours of sleep. I cling tighter to my pillow. Somehow, it hardens. "Uh, berry." There's a tight voice. "You've gotta . . . I mean, please get up."

That's enough to jerk me awake. I pull my head off of Nate's shoulder, absolutely mortified that I'd let myself sleep on him.

"Oh my God. I'm *so*—"

"Bathroom. I mean . . . I need to go." And then he's gone.

My cheeks burn in shame. I've only barely realized that he has an aversion to touch, and then I go and immediately ruin it?

What's worse is that I *liked* it. I already wish I'd been awake for my time on his shoulder, and I hate the way I feel empty now that he's gone.

"Cagey, that one," a gruff voice says. I turn to see the old man watching where Nate has run off to.

"He doesn't like certain things. It's fine." I shrug. If I say it out loud, maybe it will be.

"Doesn't seem fine. You planning on talking to him about it?"

"Talking to him?" I laugh. "Why would I do that?"

He huffs. "Talking matters in relationships, kid."

"Oh, we're not like that. We're only friends."

"Really?" he asks. "Huh. I could've *sworn* . . ."

"Yep, just friends on a trip. He just likes his space, and there's not a lot of that."

"You're telling me. Extra legroom, my ass." He crosses his arms. "You don't have to crowd the poor guy then."

He's right. I've done enough. No, more than that, and I want to be better. Slowly, I move more to the middle of the seat, where I'm touching the stranger next to me, but at least Nate will have more room. It's awkward, but it'll have to do.

"Thanks," I say.

"Eh, we all have to survive together in these conditions. I feel like a damn sardine." With a shake of his head, the man goes back to his phone, and I only feel a little better.

The cruise sets out tomorrow, and we have one night in a regular hotel room before we set sail. Originally, that room was supposed to be a king-sized bed, but I make a mental note to change that so Nate can get some space.

It only delays the inevitable, but it'll be something.

Nate returns moments later. He eyes where I've shifted to and sits without complaint. He seems more comfortable now that I'm not pressed against him.

I should feel good about what I've done. After all, I'm being a good friend.

And yet, the urge to sneak back closer to him, just to see what would happen, is strong.

What the hell is wrong with me?

Thankfully, I manage to keep my desire to touch him tamped down for the rest of the flight. Once we're in Orlando, I'm too busy getting a taxi to our hotel to think of anything else.

And I'm still busy when we get to the hotel too, because I have to beeline to the front to ask about swapping rooms. I must be lucky, because there's an extra one with two queens that we're able to take.

Nate walks in as I get the key cards. "All set?" he asks.

"Yep." I hand him one of the cards. "Two beds and everything."

He pauses. "Did you originally get two beds? Were you planning on not sleeping with Rob?"

I roll my eyes. "I was able to swap the rooms. I can't do that on the cruise, but at least we can get a little space from each other. The flight was bad enough."

I grab my suitcase and head in the direction of the room so I don't have to see Nate's reaction to what I've said. The last thing I want to do is make him feel bad for a fair boundary.

"Wait up," he says as he catches up to me. "Are you excited to get to the room or something? I've never seen you move so fast."

"I need to reorganize my suitcase, Nate." It's both a lie and not. I *do* need to see what all I brought. Packing was a mad dash, and I already know I'll regret the choices I made.

Nate laughs, and I'm grateful for how easygoing it sounds. "I should've known. I've never seen you be so disorganized."

"Watch it," I warn. "Or I'll organize your suitcase too."

"Trust me, you don't wanna go in there."

I probably don't, but I can still threaten him anyway.

Our room is exactly what I want. Two beds and a bathroom in the back. I let out a sigh of relief when I see it.

"I'm calling the bed closest to the door," Nate says immediately. He flops onto the mattress to make his point.

"Want the ability to make an easy escape?" I ask.

"Something like that."

I walk over to the free bed, ready to make true on my promise of going through my suitcase. I have a bad feeling I can't shake that I forgot something important.

When I finally get it open, I wince. I'm *terrible* at last-second decisions, and what I've packed shows that.

I go through what I have. The dress shirts I've brought are a light material, and if I pair them with the tank tops I shoved in, then that should work. I've brought way too much underwear, a classic for me, and done a decent job of getting all the toiletries I should need.

But as I get to the bottom of my suitcase, I realize that I've forgotten one major thing I'll need.

In my rush, I grabbed a single pair of khaki slacks. And nothing else.

I'm currently wearing a pair of leggings I use for running. Neither of those go with anything else I brought.

Fuck.

"You're panicking about something over there. Wanna tell me what it is?" Nate sounds relaxed.

I slowly turn to him. "So, I forgot shorts."

"Ah."

"This is why I *plan*."

"Sorry I burst your bubble, berry. But we can fix this."

"If you suggest cutting my very nice slacks, I'll—"

"Let's just go buy shorts." He says it as if it's obvious. I stare at him, waiting for the "I told you so" or for him to laugh at me. But that's something I would expect from Rob. Not Nate.

"I'll go. You just got here and that was a long flight."

It's an out I don't want him to take, but I owe it to him to at least offer space after using him as a pillow.

"A long flight?" He scoffs. "It was just a few hours. Come on. We'll both go."

I have to hide the feeling of relief that floods me. Good. He doesn't want to avoid me. Things aren't totally messed up.

We wind up being able to take an Uber to a nearby store. Nate and I bicker on the ride there about who should be covering the cost of getting around town, but we settle on taking turns.

By the time we walk into the store, I've forgotten all about the plane.

Both men's and women's clothes line the walls. I'm tempted to shop for work clothes because they have a sale on more dress shirts and slacks, but Nate shakes his head and leads me to shorts.

And that's when I realize why I didn't pack any. I only have two pairs that I've not put on my body in years. I can't wear them to work, and I opt for leggings on the weekends. My legs haven't seen the light of day in far too long.

It's going to be hot in the Caribbean. I know that, and I need comfortable clothes, but I hate the idea of this.

Nate watches me carefully, and I know he's about to pick up on how little I want to do this.

"Do you wanna look at the men's clothes while I find something?"

"I will later. But now we're focusing on you."

"Yeah, but it's clothes shopping. I'll have to try on a ton of stuff, and I doubt you care about that."

It's a feeble excuse, but a good enough one. Nate might be my best friend, but he's still a guy. Long ago, Rob told me no guy likes to go shopping and handed me a hundred-dollar bill to treat myself with.

Nate turns to me, eyes narrowed. "And why's that?"

"It might get a little boring."

"I'm never bored when I'm with you."

It's such a simple statement, but I blink up at him regardless. It hits me that in all of my years with Rob, there were many times he was very bored of me.

"You're lying."

"I'm not. Even when we're doing something that's not exactly fun, I can always annoy you and it cheers me up."

"Is that why you braided my hair in English?"

He smiles. "You caught me."

I let out a breath, but I also feel my lips turning upward. "Okay, fine. But this'll be a test on how long you can go without being bored."

"This is also a test in how long you can hide the fact that you're nervous about trying on shorts."

My jaw falls open, but then I shut it quickly. "Shut up."

He laughs. "Never. But you'll be grateful for these when you have them. So, pick a few and try them on."

"Fine. But no snide comments when you see me in them." I point at him. "Say one negative thing and I'm spending the trip in my work clothes."

Nate frowns. "Berry, I wouldn't dare."

I pause at his serious tone. "You say my legs are short all the time."

"They're short in a cute way."

"A cute way?" I ask.

"Yeah. You have to hop to keep up with me." He laughs again, and I hurl a pair of shorts his way. He catches it with ease.

"And for that little comment, you're now carrying everything."

"The joke's on you. I was about to offer anyway."

I throw another pair at him, rolling my eyes.

Eventually, I have a pile of nearly every kind. Denim shorts, bike shorts, and shorts that don't go as far down my thighs. I may as well try everything.

Nate carries it all as we head to a fitting room. He sits outside as I go in. As I'm about to shut the door, he calls out, "And you better show me what fits!"

"Fine," I grumble. I put the clothes down and lock the door.

"That's nice." I hear it from the dressing room next to me. "My husband never cares."

My cheeks erupt in flames, but I say nothing as I grab the first pair.

The first two aren't even close to fitting, which hits my self-esteem hard. Andrea was on me every day about losing weight before the wedding to make my dress fit better. I didn't listen, but I can't help but remember her words. How much more had I taken in that damn relationship?

"Maisie," Nate calls from outside. "I was serious about being included."

"I know," I reply. "The first two didn't fit."

I pull on the third pair without even looking at them, and thankfully, they button without a fight. I let out a sigh of relief and open the door.

"Okay, here. What do you think?"

Nate's eyes go wide, as if he didn't actually expect me to show him, but then his gaze travels up and down me, lingering on my legs.

Be normal. It's just Nate.

My skin erupts in gooseflesh anyway.

"T-they're nice." He clears his throat and his eyes meet mine. "Are they comfy?"

I turn and look at the mirror and immediately want to hide again. They're short, coming only to the top of my thigh. Even if they fit well, there's way too much of me on display.

Now I see why Nate acted the way he did. "Come on, man. You could've warned me my ass was hanging out."

"I-I didn't notice."

I turn with a glare. "Don't lie."

The tips of his ears are red. They're *definitely* too short. "All right, all right. I did notice. But is it really a bad thing? This is a vacation, after all."

Yeah, a vacation with my platonic best friend. It's already making me feel like I could melt that he even *saw* me in these. There's no way I'll ever put them on again.

I won't survive if I do.

"I'm gonna try on more." I go back into the dressing room and take a breath when I'm alone. It's tempting to go over his reaction in my head and dissect every clue like a schoolgirl with a crush.

But I don't have a crush. It's just Nate.

The best thing to do is let this go. I want this cruise to be as fun as possible. Making things out of nothing is *not* how I do that.

I throw the too-short pair into the no pile and then go through the other shorts I have. The next set is a pair of bike shorts that go to my mid-thigh, and I feel much better when I come out of the dressing room.

"Those are nice," Nate says.

"And very comfortable. They're good for exploring the jungle, right? Oh! And they have pockets."

"What's with women's clothes and not having pockets?" Nate asks. "Do you think it's a conspiracy to sell purses?"

"Definitely."

"Disgusting. You should get those, though. Fight the anti-pocket man."

"You're ridiculous," I say with a shake of my head, but the second I pull them off after retreating into my fitting room, I put them in the yes pile.

The next pair is a version of the khakis I have. They're the ones I feel the most comfortable in. Nate warns me they might get destroyed, but I get them anyway.

I find one other pair of jean shorts that look decent and go to my mid-thigh before I'm sweaty and desperate to leave the store.

"Just the three?" he asks as he sees what I'm putting back. I wonder if he'll comment on the shorter ones returning to the rack, but he doesn't.

"Yeah. It should be enough. I also have my leggings and pants."

He slowly nods. "Mind if we also go through the men's section?"

"You wanna look at the button-up shirts, don't you?" I spot the multicolored monstrosities from across the store.

"You know me so well."

I roll my eyes. "You're allowed one extravagant shirt per trip."

He perks up. "So I can *buy* one on each trip."

"No, one total. You already have—"

"Too late. I heard I could buy one. I now can't hear anything else." He beelines it for the men's section before I can even open my mouth.

I need to catch up with him, but I find myself pausing and taking a second look at what I'm not buying. Back in high school, I wouldn't have thought twice about the length of what I was wearing, and I'm tempted to try to be that woman again.

But I shake my head. They're not for me.

When I catch up with Nate, he's holding a pink and yellow shirt that hurts my eyes. "Look at this! Does it complement my features?"

"You've gotta be kidding me," I mutter. "It *distracts* from your features."

"Maybe that's how I get all the ladies." He shrugs. "But I do want you to be seen with me, so what about this one?" Nate surprisingly pulls out a blue and green one that's tolerable.

"Deep down, you *do* have a sense of style. Even though you're wearing sweatpants today."

"I was waiting for you to comment on that. They were for the plane, berry."

"And you'll be wearing something normal tomorrow?"

"Now, I can't promise that, but they'll be normal pants."

"I guess that's as good as it'll get." I shrug and eye the checkout line. "Are we ready to go?"

"Yeah, I think so. I need to go grab a set of socks and then I'm good. You go ahead and get in line."

"You forgot socks?"

"I'm ashamed." He sighs and claps his hand to his cheek, which isn't red in the slightest. "You can make fun of me later, but I need to fix this."

"Yeah, yeah." I laugh. "Have fun in the sock section."

When I step into line, I let out a sigh of relief. Things are completely and entirely normal between us. This is what I need.

Nate doesn't return until a few minutes later, and others have entered the line behind me. I wind up paying before him and I wait at the door until he's done.

"Are you a man with socks now?" I ask.

"Definitely. Maybe I have too many socks." He shrugs. "I can never be safe enough. What if I step in suspicious liquid every day on this trip?"

"That's the same logic as bringing too much underwear because you might pee yourself multiple times a day."

Nate eyes me. "And how many did you bring?"

"E-enough."

"Make fun of me all you want. We have the *same* logic."

"Oh, the horrors," I mutter. "At least I didn't forget socks."

"At least I didn't forget shorts."

I'm considering throwing my bag at him when he calls another ride home and holds the door open for me. Once we get back to the hotel, I fold everything in my suitcase and add the new pairs of shorts.

"Hang on," he says as I'm about to close up.

"If you tell me you're out of room in your suitcase, then you're fucked, because you're not using—"

"It's not that. You just have one thing to add."

"*I* just have one thing to add? What could—" I turn, only to see something being thrown in my direction. I barely catch it.

Then I hold it out.

It's the pair of shorts that I didn't buy.

"What? You got these for me?"

"Yep." He says it simply. "You liked them. There was no reason not to get them."

"Nate, they're too short."

"They're not. You looked great, and you deserve to have things you look great in." He shrugs as if it's nothing and turns away.

I stare between him and the shorts.

I always thought I could read Nate like the back of my hand.

Now I wonder if I'm missing things.

chapter six

N ATE GRABS our luggage and I stare at the massive boats in the distance. We're not fully on the dock yet, but my heart's been slowly going up in speed since I first saw the water. It glistens innocently in the summer sun, as if it couldn't kill a human with ease.

It makes no sense. I've never even been in the ocean, but the thought of being over something that I could drown in makes me want to hightail it out of here.

"This'll be fun," I mutter.

"You okay?"

I go from staring at the water to staring at the boat. "It is in fact on *water*. What the fuck was I thinking when I agreed to this?"

"These are the questions I had."

"There's no way I can do this." I shake my head. "You should go and I'll fly home."

"Maisie, nothing bad is going to happen on this cruise."

"And how do you know that?" My gaze cuts to him. "So many things could go wrong. And I can't even swim."

"I'm lifeguard trained."

I blink. "Since when?"

"Since forever. The point is, if you somehow fall into water without a life jacket, which is a big *if* since I'm not planning on letting you get near a railing, I'll be getting you back to safety."

There's something sincere about his words, and his tone feels alien to me. I'm tempted to sink into this moment forever with the version of my best friend who obviously cares so much for me, but he's waiting for me to continue on with all the things that could go wrong.

"What if the boat sinks?"

"I've seen *Titanic*. We would both fit on that door and I would save your ass."

"There's no guarantee we could even get a life jacket."

"I'll fight anyone for a lifeboat and a paddle. And then I'll drag you with me."

Despite myself, I laugh. "You think you could survive in the ocean?"

"Hell yeah I can."

"What if we get stuck on an island?"

"Well, I've watched a *ton* of survival shows. I could provide for you."

It's ridiculous to imagine, but I could see him doing it. When it comes down to things, Nate is fiercely protective of those around him. He'd do anything to keep me safe.

"That helps," I say. "Thank you."

"Once we're on the boat, it won't be so bad."

I nod. "You're right. Let's just get this over with."

We have to check in with security before we get on the boat. That's on land, and waiting in line distracts me. Then we step onto the dock, something I don't love, but it's stable and I can barely see the water, so I survive.

Nate insists we have the porter take our bags, and then we're on the boat.

It's truly a marvel of man-made engineering. I can barely tell we're on water at all. There are multiple hallways and decks to explore.

"When can we check into our room?" Nate asks, and I check the app.

"A few hours."

"We should explore," he offers. "And get food."

Everyone seems to be heading to one of the lower decks. I can see a massive room ahead, something so huge that it shouldn't even fit on a boat.

"Maybe not here," I say. "Wanna find somewhere less busy?"

To get away from the crowds, we decide to see the ship from top to bottom.

There's a running trail on the top of the boat. It goes through hallways and has a decent view of the pools. The second I see it, I'm already planning a run sooner rather than later. I desperately need it after forcing myself on this damn thing.

Below are pools and hot tubs. I stay far away from the water as Nate ventures close. I pretend to take an interest in the bars and chairs, and for once, he lets me get away with it. I'm feeling proud of myself for getting on the boat in the first place. Getting too close to the pool will ruin all of that.

We also find a lounge and other shops. There are plenty of places to sit in the sun, and I know that's most of what I'll be doing on this level.

One more deck down, we find a rich offering of restaurants. Most of them are far slower than the first one we saw, and I immediately drag Nate toward tacos. It's not as good as what I make at home, but it's close enough.

I'm more patient after eating, and when we venture farther down, we find more and more people either eating or trying to find their rooms. We also find a bar and large venues for their shows. The more I see, the more I'm amazed that we're on a boat of all things. Hell, there's even a spa. The second I see it, I know I'll be spending a lot of time there.

Nate wants to explore every corner, and we're walking until late into the day. While I don't like being near the deck of the ship, the rest is . . . fine. Very fancy.

So fancy that I'm not sure how my parents afforded it on their meager salaries. I really owe them a thank-you.

"So, what do you think?" he asks. We're in the elevator heading to the room that we've been assigned. I got the notification hours ago, but let Nate continue exploring.

"My parents went overboard."

"Really? Maybe we should check on them."

I roll my eyes and have to stop myself from laughing. "You know what I mean. This is very nice, and everything's included. I'm honestly glad we're using it. Something like this shouldn't go to waste."

"And this is just the beginning. We have islands to explore. Entire islands."

"As long as I can survive the dock. You might have to go with me."

"You're capable of more than you think," he reminds me. "And even if you can't handle it, we can find something else for you to do."

"I refuse to ruin this trip for you. If I can't handle the dock, then—"

"Then I'll be with you. No questions asked."

My heart skips a beat. I really don't deserve this man.

As we walk down the hall to our room, I'm glad I brought him. He's the right choice.

Our key card to the room is outside of the door. I'm still in a good mood when Nate bends down to grab it before using it.

I knew to expect one bed and a couch. What I didn't expect,

however, was for it to be *this* tiny. Not only is it smaller than I anticipated, it's decked out in roses and champagne. On the bed is a massive pack of condoms.

"Wow," Nate says. "So this is the honeymoon package. I expected it to be . . . bigger."

I shove away my horror. "Never expect a package to be bigger."

At least he's joking. At least *I'm* joking. It means I'm not suffocating in this tiny room.

"There's a couch too. It's basically the lap of luxury."

I eye the thing. It's a modern piece and looks like a pile of bricks with fabric over it. "That couch is a love seat at best."

"I can scrunch."

My eyes immediately narrow. "There's no way you're sleeping on that."

"Well, there's no way you are either."

"I'm smaller than you. It won't be comfortable, but it would work better."

"Still, it's a no from me." He moves his bag to the couch, watching me every step of the way.

"We could just share the bed," I offer.

"No." He says it immediately and with more firmness than I expect. I blink at him, eyes wide. "I mean . . . I wanna give you your space. I don't need a bed."

His light tone feels off, and I realize that he'd rather be uncomfortable for the whole trip than share a bed with me. This aversion to touching might become a big problem.

I move my bag near the bed. "Pardon me, but I think I need to use the little girls' room."

"There's only one bathroom. But have fun anyway. Don't fall in."

I go to shut the door to have a moment to myself, but then I realize something truly horrific.

There *is* no door.

"Uh, what?"

"It's a toilet," Nate calls. "Shouldn't be too different."

"I'm not talking about the bathroom. Nate, there's no door." I don't even have to raise my voice for him to hear me. "Nate, there's *no door*." I have to repeat it uselessly to make sense of the nightmare I just uncovered.

"No way." I hear him walking toward me. "I bet it's one of those pocket ones."

He gets to the open doorway and reaches for the solid wood. He pauses when he realizes that there truly is no way for there to be a pocket door. His hands press flat against the surface as if there's some magical way to make a door appear.

"What kind of place is this?" he asks.

I grab my phone to check the room type.

Apparently, this is a room with a special feature. It's called the *Peeking Suite: bathroom with an intimate view.*

"Oh no." I cover my mouth and show Nate the listing. "It's *supposed* to not have one."

"What are these people into?" he asks.

"Definitely not privacy."

"Great," he mutters. "And your *parents* picked this for you?"

"You know how open-minded Mom can be."

"Still." He runs his hand through his hair, messing up his waves. "This is a—" He stops and looks at me. He knows I'll pick up on his panic. "This is fine." He's trying to be brave, but his voice shakes. I know this isn't ideal for either of us, but especially him, considering all the walls he's seemingly put up over the years.

"They haven't left the dock yet." I need to offer it one more time. "I can leave and you can enjoy this yourself."

Nate's eyes cut to me. "Wait, a missing door is enough to scare you off?"

"No. Well, this is a pretty important missing door. But this whole thing. Maybe it really is better if you do this alone."

"I meant what I said earlier."

"Nate, this room is not just small. It's . . . intimate. And it's different now that we're looking at it."

"But . . . it's us. We can handle anything."

I stare at him. Can we?

Because as much as I want to be completely supportive of his aversion to touching, it's not going to be easy to accommodate here.

"I'm gonna go." I shake my head and step back into the room to grab my suitcase. "This is a terrible idea."

"Maisie, wait."

"No, seriously. What were we thinking? I'm not mentally prepared to be here. And you deserve to have your own space. This is too much . . . even for us."

I'm near the door when he grabs my hand, holding it tight. That finally knocks me out of my panic. His touch is warm. Familiar, even though I haven't had it in years. It sends a jolt up my arm. It makes all my problems fall away. Just one hand—his hand— levels me like nothing else can.

I've missed this. My *God*, I've missed this.

"I want to spend time with you." He says it slowly. "I don't care that this is a honeymoon room. I don't care if this is weird. And I don't care if this is awkward for a little bit. After everything that's happened, I don't want you to be alone. And I also know you want this cruise to be used."

"But you have to hate this. There's no personal space here."

He sighs. "It's not ideal, I'll admit that. But we can make it work. At least try to. Don't just leave." Nate hates it when people leave.

I sigh and close my eyes. "If I stay, I have one condition."

"Is it a blindfold for the bathroom thing? I think I brought a tie we could use."

My eyes pop open. "Why would you bring a tie on vacation?"

"You never know what you might need it for."

I open my mouth to ask, but I get a mental image I don't need.

Shaking my head, I force myself to refocus. "I want to take turns on the couch."

"What? But—"

"I know you won't agree to let me have it the entire time—"

"You're damn right about that."

"But you're way taller than me and it's going to be uncomfortable. I want it half the time."

"That's a lot to ask."

"You want me to stay, don't you?"

"Fine," he grinds out. "I'll *think* about letting you have the couch half the time."

"That's not what I asked for."

"It's as good as you're gonna get."

Honestly, I'm surprised he's even agreed to this. I have my ways of making sure that he lets me take my turn, so I nod.

He lets go of my hand, and I try my best not to wish I was holding it again.

I fail.

"Now you need to leave," I say.

"Wait, what? I thought we worked it out."

"I still have to pee. So get out."

Nate sighs and glares at the door. "Can't I just use the tie?"

"I don't want you to hear the tinkle."

He's laughing. "The *tinkle*?"

"Yes! Some things can't be heard, and this is one of them."

"I don't care about the tinkle."

"Out!" I point to the door. He gives one more laugh before he exits into the hallway.

"Fine. But we're going to the lounge for a drink after this!"

Now that I can agree to. After seeing how we'll be living, I need a drink.

I do my business and then leave the room to join Nate. "What if I heard the tinkle anyway?"

My eyes go wide. "You didn't."

He laughs. "I didn't. Your face was hilarious, though."

I roll my eyes. The door to the room next to us opens and a man walks out, followed closely by someone else.

For a horrific second, I see short brown hair and a wide grin and think it's Rob. I freeze in my tracks, but then a second look reveals it's just a stranger.

Nate sees the whole thing play out.

"Oh, hi." The guy looks at the two of us. "You must be our neighbors."

"That we are," Nate says as I slow my heart rate. "I'm Nate. She's Maisie."

"I'm Aaron, and this is my wife Trixie." He gestures to the woman next to him. "Are you heading out for a drink?"

"We are," Nate says.

"Can we join you? This is all a bit new to us and I'd love to have a smaller group at first."

Nate glances at me, silently asking if I'm okay with this. I'm tempted to say no, but with how things are feeling between us, talking to others isn't a bad idea.

"Sounds fun," Nate says. "Wanna go to the one on Deck Five? That one looked pretty cool."

Aaron nods excitedly, and suddenly, we have plans.

I try to be excited about it too.

"AND THEN, he gets down on one knee and proposes." Trixie's jaw drops even as she retells her own engagement story. "It was *so* sweet."

I take a long sip from the drink in my hand. I must be in my own personal hell because there's no way Trixie sat and immediately started talking about her engagement just after mine fell apart. I know deep down it's not her fault. She has no idea who I am or anything about me.

This is just terrible luck.

If Nate were sitting next to me, he would aim to change the topic instantly. But somehow, he's sitting with Aaron way too far from me, lost in his own conversation. I'm not sure how we got separated, but I'm miserable.

"That sounds amazing," I say, and I do mean it. Trixie's engagement sounded romantic. I bet it was better than my own.

"Then we had the wedding, and here we are." She says it like a wedding is something simple to plan. Like it doesn't take over a woman's life and completely derail everything.

Or maybe it's not supposed to and I just got the short end of the stick. "Congratulations. It sounds like it's gonna be an amazing honeymoon."

"I'm gonna *make* it amazing, if you know what I mean." She laughs and I force myself to join her. "Now tell me about you. I know your name is Maisie, but you've not talked about yourself once."

"Me?" I have to take another sip. "There isn't much to talk about. I'm just here . . . enjoying the views."

"I'm sure you are." She winks, her eyes moving toward Nate.

I frown, fighting the urge to tell her to keep her eyes to herself. But I'm not sure why. She's obviously married and I know people look at Nate with interest all the time.

How could they not?

My phone buzzes in my pocket and I check it quickly during the lull in conversation. My eyes bug out when I see the last person I expect.

ROB

Are you home? I think we need to talk.

Rob hasn't reached out to me since I called off the engagement. I did wind up mailing that engagement ring back to him. They better not have lost it in the mail.

MAISIE

What can we possibly have to talk about?

ROB

I miss you.

Those words should make me feel something, but all that comes is bitterness. Sure, he misses me now. But that doesn't undo what he let his friends call me. That doesn't undo how he talks about me behind my back.

That doesn't undo him wanting me away from Nate.

"Oh, who's that? Is there some drama in paradise?"

At Trixie's words, I press my phone against my chest. "What?"

"Sorry, I'm already a little tipsy and I can be nosy. I really didn't mean to pry. I just saw that it was a guy's name on your phone."

"It's nothing."

Trixie's lips poke out and she looks between Nate and me. "Are you sure?"

I lean away, jaw going tight. I need to get out of here. The last person I want to talk about is Rob when her husband looks just like him.

Just as the thought crosses my mind, I look up and see Nate walking toward me. "Mind if I steal Maisie?" he asks. "She has a short social fuse, and I think she's at her limit."

"Oh, of course. Very chivalrous, by the way." She winks one more time before going back to her own husband.

I want to scream.

Nate waves to them both before we head back to the room. He finally speaks to me when we're alone in the elevator.

"So, was I right? You looked a little done with that conversation."

"You're very right. She was nice, but she talked about her proposal the whole time."

He nods, and I know he understands that proposals and weddings in general are the last thing I want to talk about.

"You know, I bet no one's at the running track right now. Need to clear your head?"

"You're wanting to go running?"

"Want is a strong word. But you enjoy it. And I brought my shoes." He looks at me with a casual smile. It makes my heart flip. "So, wanna race?"

MY LEGS ARE on fire and I can't seem to catch a breath. My runs are never fun, but this is a new level.

"You are . . . a fucking . . . cheater."

Nate laughs, even though he fell onto the ground the second we passed our final lap. "I have longer legs than you, berry."

"Don't use my nickname at a time like this."

"Your face looks like one of those strawberries. I can't help it." I want to throw something at him. The only thing is my hair band. "Hey! Hey! Foul!"

"You're lucky I didn't body slam you."

"You couldn't even if you tried. You're too tired."

"Fuck you." I shake my hair out and it blows in the breeze. The running trail is high up with an incredible view. The sun has long since set and the ship lights are the only thing I can see.

It's almost eerie.

When I look back down, Nate is looking at me.

"Still red as a strawberry?" I ask.

"Yep."

I roll my eyes, but hold out a hand to help him up.

"I got it," he says and slowly gets onto his feet. I stare at my hand with a frown. I was hoping that hand touching was on the table ever since he grabbed mine in the room, but that must've been a one-time thing. A fluke. "We should get back to the room and figure out sleeping."

That pulls me out of my thoughts. "I'll take the—"

"I won the race. I get the couch."

"You won, so you should get a reward." He's already walking toward the elevator. I let out a breath before I push my tired legs to follow. "Seriously—"

"Maisie, it's fine. I know what I want." My bottom lip protrudes a little. "Don't you dare pout."

An idea crosses my mind. "Why not? Is it working?"

"No." He says it too quickly.

I lean in, adding in the fluttering of my lashes. "*Please* can I take the couch? Pretty please?"

Nate leans away, but I can see conflict on his face. "Come on. That's cruel."

"I just wanna be punished for losing." My voice is high-pitched and his eyes are wide. I know how it sounds, but he never thinks that way of me anyway.

And I don't want him suffering on the damn couch.

"Uh . . ." He's still breathing heavily from our run. He must be in terrible shape. "I . . ."

The moment is broken when my phone goes off loudly. I realize that I'm way too far in his space and I back away.

What had I been thinking?

"Sorry, I'll go back to begging in just a moment," I say as I pull out the phone.

"Don't worry about that. I got your message." His voice is low and I don't even know if he meant for me to hear it. I want to ask, but I'm too shocked to see Rob's name on my screen again to say anything.

ROB

I shouldn't have said that about you and Nate.

I blink, my jaw tightening at the words. He'd sworn he had a point, going so far as to let the wedding fall through.

Now he has regrets?

"Why is Rob texting you?" Nate sounds annoyed.

"No idea, but I'm not answering."

"He's apologizing, isn't he?"

"He's . . . trying."

Nate shakes his head. "He always does this. He waits until he knows you're serious and apologizes."

I want to argue, but I quickly realize I can't. Rob and I fought often enough that it's obvious how Nate picked up on a pattern, even if I didn't tell him about every single one we had. I didn't push back on much, but when I did, Rob always dug his heels in.

Until he didn't.

"He let me cancel the wedding."

Nate blows out a breath. I wonder if he's about to drop a bomb on me, but he only shrugs. "Who knows what the hell is going through his head."

"You have thoughts."

"I don't want to get involved in that," he says with a shake of his head. "It's your relationship."

Nate's always been like this. He stays out of everything to do with Rob and me. When I got with him, Nate made sure Rob was a decent guy and then stayed out of it.

The only time he didn't was when he went to the bachelor party.

"What if I want you to get involved?" I ask.

"Why would you want that?"

"Obviously your gut instincts are good with this. Mine are iffy at best."

"Your instincts are fine."

"I'm the one who had no idea how he felt, or that his friends were secretly assholes. I don't trust myself at all right now, to be honest."

Nate shakes his head. "None of that is your fault."

"I know. I've listened when you told me, and I'll continue to listen now. Is there something that I don't know?"

He lets out a long breath. "I'm sure it's nothing, but in the beginning, he came on a little strong. Almost like he was love bombing you. I wasn't sure if I was being overprotective or if that's actually what it was."

I think back to when Rob and I first got together. Nate isn't wrong. Rob did come on strong. He showered me with gifts and attention. And I thought I was living a fairy tale.

"I can see that."

"He also comes on very strong when he knows he's in the wrong. If he's trying to apologize, I don't expect him to give up."

"Shouldn't that be what I want? For him not to give up?"

I see Nate's jaw go tight for all of one second before he forces it to relax. "If you want to get back together with him, then yes. Is that what you want?"

Any other time, the answer would be yes. I'm the kind of person who understands that people make mistakes. But he said it *wasn't* a mistake. It was genuinely how he felt. He didn't want Nate and me to see each other.

"I don't."

His eyes go wide. "You seem so sure about that."

"I am sure about it. I can forgive a lot, but not this time."

"You know he'll try to take it back. He's gonna say that he didn't mean that he ever hated you."

Nate doesn't know that Rob gave me an ultimatum. I'm not sure I *want* him to know.

The elevator tells us we're on our floor, but neither of us make a move to leave.

"Nate, can I ask you something?"

"Always."

"Have you ever hated me?"

"No." He says it the second I've finished my sentence. "And I never will."

Then I should be marrying you.

The thought pops up unbidden and I nearly smack myself; I don't mean *Nate*. I mean someone that feels the way Nate does. And touches me. I wouldn't mind that either.

"And that's the kind of man I should be with. A guy who would never hate me. Seems easy in theory, but hard to find in practice."

"Yeah, hard to find." His voice is quieter than usual.

Before I can ask what he means, he turns to walk toward our room. "I'm still taking the couch."

All other thoughts fly out of my mind. "Hey! You said you would think about it!"

"I did. And I still say no."

chapter seven

NATE SNORES WHEN HE SLEEPS. He woke up before I did yesterday, but this time, I get to steal the moments before he's awake. I have no idea if his snores are because he's scrunched up to fit on the love seat or if it's something that popped up in the last few years.

There's not much I don't know about him.

I'm determined to make it *nothing*.

That's the only logical reason I have for watching him as the sun rises, filling the room with light.

I didn't sleep well the night before. I never do in a new environment. I tossed and turned, trying to find a comfortable position until I settled for watching my best friend sleep.

Shortly after the sun rises, he starts to stir.

"Fuck," he mutters, his voice thick. He can't even stretch out on the couch. "That sucked."

"Have regrets?"

Nate jumps and his gaze meets mine. "I should've known you'd be awake."

"Yeah, yeah. I hate sleeping in new places, but the bed was *so* comfy. You could—" I'm stopped when a pillow hits me right in the face. "Rude."

"Don't gloat at a man in pain."

"You did this to yourself. I'm allowed to gloat."

He flips me off before he slowly stands. "Cover your ears."

I yelp and do what I'm told. For some reason, I also cover my eyes, going for complete sensory deprivation. I give him more than sixty seconds before I peek to see if he's back. When he's done, my cheeks are on fire. "You could have told me to leave."

"And have you move from your comfy bed? Never."

"Joke's on you, I have to leave the bed anyway. I need food and coffee."

Nate laughs as if he knew that was exactly what I was going to say, and then gets new clothes for the day. I do the same and shuffle into the bathroom to change into a longer pair of shorts and a light green shirt.

"Now you look like you're in vacation mode."

"I'm trying to be. I might still go for a run later."

"How the hell are you not sore?" he asks.

"I am. I still do it anyway."

He shakes his head as we walk out of the suite and down to the smoothie bar. I stare at the menu for far too long, trying to decide what to get.

"I guess I'll be basic," I mutter.

"The berry blast looks good."

"It doesn't even say what kind of berries are in there."

He shrugs. "I like berries."

My mind instantly goes to my nickname. Did he mean it in that way, or is the proximity slowly infecting my brain?

"I'm getting something I know I won't hate. Strawberry banana."

"Didn't you burn yourself out on those in college?" he asks.

"Sure did. Still don't love them, but it'll work."

Nate hums as we get close to the front and put in our orders.

Once it's done, we hit up the coffee shop to get two drips, and then find a seat outside. The sun is hot and I have to quickly sip on my smoothie to avoid it melting.

"So, what's the verdict?" he asks.

I taste the strawberries and bananas, but it's muted. It's exactly what I expected it to be. "It's fine."

"Would you like to try mine?" he asks. His is brightly colored, looking almost red in the light.

"What's in that?"

"Still don't know, but it tastes good."

I'm tempted to say no. Usually, I don't like trying new things, but if Nate likes it, then it might not be so bad.

When I taste it, I immediately notice raspberries and blueberries. It's more tart than mine, but I love tart fruits. If it had granola on top, it would be close to my favorite acai bowl I have back home.

My shoulders slump and Nate shoots me a look. "Do you hate it?"

"No," I mutter. "It's so fucking good."

"Imagine that." He laughs as he reaches over. I think he's going for his own cup. Instead, he grabs mine. "I'll take this."

"It's nothing special. I wouldn't even try it."

"Oh, I'm not trying it, berry. I'm taking it. You can have mine."

"What? Why?"

He shrugs. "You like that one more." Nate says it as if it's nothing, and I have no doubts that, to him, it isn't. This is simply the man that he is. He's annoying but caring. I know that he only wants others to be happy.

And he's one of the few who makes *me* happy.

"Thank you," I say. "I should have branched out in the first place."

"You like what you know. Until the moment you know something else is better. I have a feeling you'll be getting that tomorrow."

I can only nod and pull the cup closer. Nate laughs and goes back to his smoothie. His gaze moves from me to other people around. He's people watching. I can't help but follow his gaze. What does he think of the people around us? And why do I want to know so badly?

There's a group of shirtless men in the pool playing with a beach ball. They're yelling and tackling each other as if it's the most important game of their lives. A few women are sunbathing, and others are going up to the running trail.

I finish my smoothie and then my coffee as we watch. Nate doesn't look twice at anyone, but I wonder if that's simply for my sake. He's been glued to my side the entire time we've been here.

"Well, I think it's time for me to take my leave."

Nate's brow knits. "What?"

"I'm gonna head out. I was thinking of checking out the massage parlor."

"I'll go with you."

"This is a perfect day to swim." I gesture at the pool. "Or meet people. You're always good at that."

"Are you trying to get rid of me?"

"I'm trying to tell you that it's time for you to do something you want to do."

"What if I say I want a massage?"

I scoff. "I know how you are about touching."

He lowers his eyebrows. "How am I about touching?"

I lean in and go to put my hand on his shoulder. He jerks back.

"*That*," I say, "is what I mean. I highly doubt you want a massage therapist touching you. So have fun in the pool."

I walk away before he can stop me, trying to feel pleased that I called him out like he does to me all the time.

Instead, there's a distinct discomfort in my breastbone that I try to ignore. It's okay that Nate doesn't want to touch anyone, including me.

Isn't it?

∿∿

It's hard to worry about Nate when I'm getting pampered by a massage therapist. All of my muscles are loose by the time I decide to relax in a sauna.

For a while, I'm blissfully alone, my mind is empty, and it's exactly what I need.

Then the door opens and a woman walks in.

I scoot over for her, determined to go back to my own relaxation. She's older than me, maybe by a decade, and she's in a towel that shows off the nicest pair of boobs I've ever seen. I'm torn between being jealous and cheering her on.

She glances at me with a raised eyebrow and I look down, immediately wishing I'd kept them shut.

"You can look. I might not be into women, but I don't care."

I want to melt into the floor. "Sorry," I say.

"I'm being serious. Plenty of people stare, and I'm too old to give a fuck. At least you were polite about it."

"Honestly, I'm just jealous."

"Usually people get catty when they're jealous. Thank you for being nice instead." She gives me a once-over. "You're not bad yourself. I'd hit on you if I swung that way."

I'm about to hide, but she's smiling at me in the same way Nate does. She must be enjoying this.

"Thanks, but—" I'm about to say I'm taken, but I'm not anymore. "Uh, I also don't swing that way."

She hums. "Are you one of the few single people on the cruise?"

"Technically, yes. I was supposed to be on my honeymoon."

Her blue eyes go wide. "And you came alone?"

"No, with a friend."

"That was sweet of them."

"He's a good guy."

"Guy, huh?"

A prickle of discomfort makes its way into my stomach. I can't handle another insinuation. I just can't. "Just a friend," I insist.

"Is he in the men's sauna?"

"No, he's doing whatever he wants to right now." I wave as if it's casual. I haven't thought about what he's up to, but now it's all I want to think about.

The woman stares at me, and I swear she's looking right through me. I barely know her, but I have an inkling she's not someone to mess with.

"I'm Scarlett," she says as she holds out a hand.

"Maisie." When I shake hers, her grip is so strong she nearly pulls me off the seat.

"If your friend is busy, I don't mind being arm candy," she replies. "I came alone."

"Wouldn't you want time to yourself if you came alone? I don't want to impose."

"Sometimes it's nice, but it's also fun to meet a friend on board, especially one who has such a fun story."

"It's not that fun."

"Did you keep the same suite?" she asked.

"Um, no?"

She laughs. "So, that's a yes. How awkward is it?"

"A little, but we're making it work."

"Interesting," she replies.

"Do you make a habit of finding *fun* stories on a boat?"

"I can't help it, I'm afraid. I'm a therapist and I love a good story."

Oh, great. I'm getting stared down by a trained professional. This is just my fucking luck.

"I'm afraid I'll let you down with mine. Nothing's gonna happen. It hasn't for nearly two decades."

"At the very least, we can talk about the guys. I mean, did you see the group of them playing ball in the pool?"

"They were . . . loud."

"They were hot," she corrected. "Did you not notice?"

"I did." I didn't. I haven't looked at a man since I met Rob. I didn't have a reason to.

Until now.

"Somehow I doubt that." Her tone isn't judgmental, but soft. "How long were you with your ex?"

"Ten years."

"It takes a bit to adjust to being single again, you know."

"I'm guessing you've seen it in therapy?"

"I've lived it. Contrary to what my friends think, I don't try to use therapy talk on everyone." She winces. "Mostly. It slips out. I'm sorry if it has."

"All you're doing is reminding me that I need to talk to someone eventually. I have . . . problems."

"Exes will do that to you."

"How long until I feel normal again?"

"Normal is a social construct. What do you *want* to feel?"

I want to feel like the girl I was in high school. When it was just Nate and me. When he touched me and didn't think about it. Before life got in the way.

"I don't know."

"Let me let you in on a secret. Take it one day at a time. It'll happen before you know it." She winks and leans back, relaxing immediately.

I try to return to the calmness I had before, but it evades me. My mind's eye decides to play the way Nate flinched when I reached for him over and over again.

And I don't know why I'm so stuck on that.

chapter eight

NATE OPENS the door to the room as I'm reading a page of a romance book on my Kindle that I want to throw off the balcony. Usually, romance doesn't bother me, and I like the book club I'm a part of. It's run primarily by Levi's wife, Amy, along with her other friends. I've gotten Quinn to join a few times and we usually swoon over the books together.

But now, I just feel bitter.

I know better than to ever compare a real relationship to a book, but Rob and I didn't even come close. I don't need someone to bend over backward for me, but they should at least do something.

Or even *care*.

"There you are," Nate says. "Did you not hook your phone up to the ship's Wi-Fi?"

"Not yet. Sorry." I turn to him. "Why?"

"I texted you to check in."

I wince. "I'll set that up. But I was just here. Reading this *lovely* book."

"That bad, huh?"

"Let's just say romance is dead to me." I sigh and lock my Kindle.

I finally take him in. He's wearing a damp shirt, and his wavy hair is wet.

"You're dripping everywhere." I throw a towel at him. "Shower, you weirdo."

"Fine," he says. "You better not take a peek!"

"That's the last thing I want to do."

It actually wouldn't be the worst thing. At least Nate isn't ugly. But I'm pretty sure there's a line with friends and getting naked.

Or at least there will be where Nate's involved.

With a sigh, I sit on the bed and work on getting the ship's Wi-Fi set up so he can reach me in the future. In the middle of the ocean, there's absolutely no service, and I didn't even think about being able to talk to anyone. I'm not sure I even want to. Nate's always the exception. I can talk to him whenever I want, but even things between us feel odd on this boat.

Maybe I'm the one who's off.

The shower turns on and I hear him step in. I'm tempted to walk out to the balcony to make sure he has whatever privacy he can get here.

Instead, I look up at the wall in front me ... and directly into the mirror hanging from it.

I nearly scream when I realize it's pointed *right* at the shower.

It's not that Nate looks bad. He doesn't. He's lithe and tall with a form that could swallow me if I let him. And his ass? Well, it's just unfair. I could bounce a quarter off that thing.

But I should *not* be staring at my best friend's ass.

A squeak escapes me as I tumble off the bed. I cover my eyes and dart for the balcony, knowing I should never see that sight again.

When I'm alone, I realize my chest is heaving.

Okay, that was weird. But it was an accident. One that I'll

never think of again. I close my eyes and try to think of anything else.

The first thing I see is his round ass.

"Fuck," I mutter out at the water.

My entire body is hot as I sit on one of the chairs. The breeze does nothing to help the fire spreading through my face, and I briefly consider jumping off the balcony. I hate water and heights, but I'm desperate. It's amazing how the sight of Nate being naked overrides my fear of water. Honestly, that should be studied.

Pressing my palms to my eyes, I try to breathe away the panic I'm feeling. I'm off today, in all of the ways. This is why I don't vacation. Because somehow it leads to seeing my best friend naked, and I don't know if I'll ever get over it.

I'm nowhere near calm when the balcony door slides open.

"Maisie?" Nate asks. "What are you doing out here?"

I should turn to look him in the eye, like I usually would. But I can't manage it. I can't manage much of anything.

"Just . . . chilling," I say. My voice is barely a croak.

"You're chilling while staring at the ocean?" His voice drips with doubt. "What happened?"

"Nothing." I say it way too quickly.

"Yeah, right. Did Rob text you again?"

"No."

"Was the book that bad?"

"No."

"Then, what's going on? Come on. You can tell me anything." His voice now has an edge to it, one that's similar to how he sounded when he showed me the video of Rob. He's worried. There's a scrape of a chair on the balcony floor and he's taken a seat beside me.

And *that* breaks through my mortification.

"The mirror in the suite. The one right outside of the bathroom."

"Yeah?"

"It has a view *right* into the shower."

For a second, there's only silence. Then Nate finally says, "Oh."

I know he's realizing what I saw.

Now I *really* can't look at him.

We always try to say that we're like any other friends, but there are still some topics we don't talk about. Naked bodies is one of them.

Silence settles over us, thick and uncomfortable. I'm not sure why he hasn't cracked a joke about this. It's what he would usually do.

Maybe he hates the idea of anyone seeing him like that.

"Just give me a few to forget." It's a lie. I'm not going to ever forget it.

"Yep. No worries."

The silence lingers.

I can't fucking take it.

"Distract me. *Please.*" Finally, I look over at him. The tips of his ears are red, but at least he's clothed. He's leaned back, looking like he's relaxed. *Almost.* His arms are crossed.

Tightly.

"Distract you?"

"Yeah. Tell me anything. How was the pool?"

I'm determined for things to feel normal, and when Nate looks at me warily, I wonder if they ever will be.

But he must have the same goal as me, because he huffs out a breath and shakes his head.

Just like that, my best friend is back.

"I ran into Aaron and chatted with him for a while."

"Really? How are our . . . friends?"

I'm not sure I would consider Trixie one, but she is nice enough. It's not her fault she doesn't know that my life blew up in the last week.

"There's apparently a group of people getting drinks and food tonight. They invited us."

I blink. I still don't understand how groups of people decide to hang out. I have my few people and that's all I need.

"And what did you say?"

"I said that it's not your kind of thing. I get the idea you don't like Trixie all that much."

"It's not that I don't like her. She just talked about her wedding. *A lot.*"

Nate nods. "I knew I should've stayed with you. Aaron wanted guy time, whatever that means, but next time—"

"I can take care of myself."

"I know, but you don't have to. Not when I'm here."

The words are casual, though they feel anything but. The memory of seeing him with nothing on combines with the warm feeling at the way he cares about me, creating something I can't name. But it's familiar somehow.

"Thanks," I whisper. "But she didn't do anything wrong. And you seem to like Aaron."

"He's okay," Nate replies. "Not as fun as you, though. I seriously would've gone to the spa with you, you know."

"We would've been separated by gender anyway. And you like swimming." I shrug. "You might as well enjoy it. Besides, it sounds like you found some plans."

"Aaron wanted us *both* to go."

"I'm sure you'll find some way to convince me."

Nate smirks. "The bar has burgers. Good ones, apparently."

"I can usually be swayed by a good burger."

"Oh, I'm not done. Apparently, they're playing games." He leans in. "And there's a winner."

Now he has my attention. Neither Quinn nor Rob will ever play anything with Nate and me simply because we're always in it to win. When we aren't teamed up, it's messy.

But when we are? Everyone else is in danger.

"Is there a prize?" I ask.

"To be determined," he replies. "But we can take the pride if there isn't. None of these people know what we can do."

"All right, you've got me." I put my hands up. "I'll go to this game night. But one mention of weddings and we're out. I'm so done with romance talk right now."

"Done." He stands and goes for the sliding door, but pauses before heading inside. "Sorry about the shower thing. Is it forgotten?"

I can still see the round curve of his backside, but I nod anyway. "So forgotten that I don't even know what you're talking about."

He laughs. "Good. The last thing we want is for things to get awkward, berry."

When he's gone, I stare at the place he just occupied and tell myself that I *won't* let anything else awkward happen for the rest of the night. I don't want anything else to be weird between us.

Because I can't deal with the consequences.

THE VERY MOMENT we walk into the room, Aaron stands. "There's our last married couple!" he calls when he sees us.

Nate and I freeze as we both process what he's said. "Did he just call us *married*?" I ask through gritted teeth.

"Give me a second," he says before going to Aaron. I should stay behind. After all, I don't want anything to do with the M-word. But I also need to know what the hell is going on.

"Hey, man." Anyone else would think Nate is being his usual, friendly self, but I can see the tense line of his shoulders. "Uh, I don't know how to say this—"

"Don't tell me you and your better half got into a fight. I know you weren't together earlier, but I didn't want to assume."

Nate only grows more tense. "Listen, I didn't know . . . We're not—I don't think we should be here."

"Why not? Do you have something against a classic game?" Aaron laughs. "I bet you guys will do fine. Maybe not as good as Trixie and me, but you'll try."

I haven't talked to Aaron much, but the second he says I won't be as good as his wife, something flares to life inside of me.

Suddenly, being called married to Nate is the smallest of my problems.

"But we're—"

"Where do we sit?" I ask kindly.

Nate's eyes snap to me so quickly I'm surprised he doesn't get whiplash. "What are you doing?"

"That's the spirit!" Aaron replies. "You can sit at the table next to us. Good luck. The competition is fierce."

I give him a fake smile before sitting.

"Maisie," Nate says immediately. "We need to correct them. And you said—"

"I don't care what I said. *Not as good as him and Trixie?* Yeah, I'm proving them wrong."

"You're willing to let them think we're married to win a game?"

"You aren't?"

Nate's mouth presses together and he slowly sits. "You know I am. But you said no wedding talk."

"So don't talk about weddings," I say simply.

"I can do that." He leans in. "So what game are we playing?"

I shrug just as a cruise employee walks up with a microphone. For a horrific second, I wonder if "games" is code for karaoke, which I will fail at miserably. But then the employee speaks. "Hello, everyone. Welcome to our exclusive night of fun for our newly joined guests. I hope you're all ready for a little friendly competition."

Aaron whistles.

"Try hard," I mutter. Nate hides a laugh with his hand.

The employee laughs. "Exactly what I wanna hear as we go into our game. You better know your partner better than anyone else so you can take home an exclusive prize."

A bag is brought out and Nate and I lean forward. Neither of us care what's in it. We just know we want it.

"Without any further ado, I welcome you to the Newlywed game!"

I immediately snap out of my thoughts. "The *what* game?" I ask.

I take a look at the lounge. Everyone is paired off. Everyone is wearing a ring on their left finger.

Slowly, my gaze slides to Nate, who's frozen in his seat. Then he looks back at me as if I'm a bomb that could go off at any second.

Maybe I am.

"Fuck it."

"Wanna leave?"

"Nope. I want to win."

"Are you sure about this? This is the Newlywed game. In case you're confused, we're not married."

I take a whiteboard with a smile. "You know what would make me feel so much better?"

"A really strong drink?"

"Beating a bunch of married people with my best friend."

He nods, understanding finally dawning on his features. "All right. Fair enough. We should have a plan for if they have questions about romance."

That makes me pause. "Right. Any ideas? You're better at last-second stupidity than I am."

"I wanna be offended, but I can't." He taps his finger on his chin as he thinks. Then he shrugs. "Fake it till you make it."

"Seriously? That's your idea?"

"We've known each other for almost two decades. I'm sure we can guess what the other will say."

"You're putting a lot of faith in us being synchronized."

"Where else am I supposed to put it?" He gives me an easygoing smile that makes my cheeks grow warm. I'm sure he means nothing by it, yet my body reacts anyway.

This entire trip has been weird. There's no other word for it.

"Let's just hope they don't ask who's the better kisser."

"It would be me."

I gasp. "How dare you! I'll have you know I'm great at—"

"All right, everyone!" The employee is back on the mic. "Time to go over the rules and get started."

Reality creeps in and I'm glad we were interrupted. The last thing I need to be doing is arguing about kissing with Nate. It makes my stomach flip just thinking about it.

Instead, I focus on the rules. We would be working in rounds. One partner goes out into the hallway and a question is asked, and then they come back and answer. Whoever has the correct answer written down gets a point.

I'm the first one to go outside while Nate is asked a question. While waiting, Trixie finds me.

"Isn't this exciting?" she asks. "How well does your husband know you?"

I suck in a sharp breath at the idea of Nate being my husband. "U-uh, I think pretty well."

"Aaron can be a little out of it, but he thinks he does." She laughs. "But that's all marriages, isn't it?"

We're called back in and I watch as she practically bounces over to sit next to Aaron. Is that what I would have been like with Rob?

I'm not sure I would have been.

"All right, welcome back," the emcee says. "We'll take turns, but the question was: What's your partner's favorite pizza order?"

I glance at Nate, wishing I could read his mind. He's the picture of ease as he leans in his chair. He knows he got this right.

When it's my turn, I sigh. My pizza order is . . . odd, by most people's standards. I have no doubt he has no qualms about making me say it out loud. "Half pineapple, half Philly steak with green bell peppers."

A hush falls out over the crowd.

"Add why," Nate says. I can *hear* the smile on his face.

"I like both a dessert side and a savory side."

The entire crowd erupts in whispers, and I know they're talking about how weird my order is. Nate chuckles and turns his board around.

My exact words are on there.

"Wow," the emcee says. "Good answer!"

I shouldn't be surprised. Nate is usually the one who orders all of my pizza anyway.

"Did you have to include the pineapple part? These people will never respect me again."

"Oh, I definitely did." He laughs. "It's time for everyone to know your shame."

I want to glare, but it's Aaron's and Trixie's turn, and I notice that he only gets it half right. Despite being outed as a weirdo, I smile. It's nice to be reminded that Nate knows me.

For the next question, Nate leaves and I'm asked who among us is the tidiest. I answer that it's me, adding that it's by a long shot. It's petty of me, but he outed my odd pizza choices, so I have a free pass.

When Nate's asked the question, he immediately laughs. "Maisie's the cleanest. By a *lot*."

I smugly turn my board around. We're once again right.

The rest of the questions are simple. They ask for my coffee order, which Nate knows like the back of his hand, who sleeps in later, and who's more adventurous. We get every single one of them right. We think we have it in the bag, up until the last question.

It's my turn to stay seated and Nate leaves the room. We've

been lucky to avoid any romantic questions so far, but I should have known the other shoe would drop.

"When did your partner fall for you?"

All the muscles in my body tense. This is the one question I can't answer, because Nate isn't in love with me.

He'd said earlier to fake any romantic questions, so I could only guess what he would say.

We have thousands of memories, most of them good. I could choose one of the times we pulled all-nighters and pretended to be asleep when my parents checked in on us. Or the time when he stood up for me when some mean girls in high school were making fun of me.

I don't like guessing. I like *knowing*.

But I have to pick something.

There's one memory that sticks out among all the rest and I jot it down before I can think it through. But as all of our partners are called back into the room, I wonder if I chose the right one.

I'm starting to think I didn't.

Mine is old. Too old. If this isn't the moment he supposedly fell for me, then I'm fucked. I should have gone for something more recent. Something that would make sense.

"Nate? What was your answer?" the emcee asks. Nate glances at me, his smile fading. I know he's trying to figure out which moment to say, even if it is a lie.

He's going to pick the all-nighters. I just know it.

I send up a mental apology as he answers. "I . . . was ten," he begins slowly. "We were in the cafeteria. My mom had forgotten my lunch, and this girl next to me sees me not eating and asks about it."

My hands tighten on my board as I remember the day. Gray walls surrounded us, and I remember seeing him slam his book bag down with a glare. I'd seen him around. He had his friends and I had mine. We'd not crossed paths other than in the hallway.

I was a goody two shoes, and he was the kind of boy who

didn't seem to have a care in the world. We shouldn't have gotten along, and I avoided him because I thought we wouldn't.

I was wrong.

Nate continues on, a small smile on his face. I know he's remembering it too. "And, fuck, I was a little jerk to her. She didn't know it, but I didn't wanna admit that we were too broke for school lunch and Mom had messed up. I asked why she was bothering me. I figured it would get her to leave me alone, but she went red in the face and snapped something right back at me."

"Looks like everything is bothering you," I recall before I can stop myself. "Not just me."

Nate laughs and looks back at me. He looks younger, just like the day he's describing. "She was right, of course. I just didn't expect her to call me out on it."

"You deserved it," I mutter. Back then, I had a little more fight in me, just enough to tell off the boy who was acting like a jerk.

"The plan was to go sit somewhere else, but as she glared at me, she gave me half of her lunch. It was strawberries. *Only* strawberries, which is a fucking ridiculous lunch, by the way."

"I was a picky eater. My parents just wanted me to have something."

"And it was the best lunch I ever had. And that was when I knew."

My cheeks burn. He means he knew we'd be friends, but here, with all these people, I could pretend it meant something else. But it's one of our best memories. It was the start of everything for us, my nickname, our friendship.

Hearing it framed like this makes me feel like I'm lighting on fire.

The audience coos, completely oblivious to my internal screaming.

"Well, Maisie?" The employee looks at me. "What was your answer?"

I turn my board around slowly.

When I shared my strawberries at the lunch table is displayed for everyone.

<h1 style="text-align:center">chapter nine</h1>

THE PRIZE WAS a tumbler with the cruise line's name on it. Not even one of the nice ones either. Nate holds it like it's his most prized possession nonetheless.

"We earned this," he says as we leave the game. "With our blood, sweat, and tears. And that last question—you killed it, berry."

"That was my goal," I say with a laugh. Ever since we'd left the event, I'd felt off, as if my world was tilting.

I'm trying my best not to let it show.

I've never been confused about Nate before. We always were . . . us. Nothing more, and certainly nothing less. But both of us picking the lunch table as the day we fell in love has me thinking things I shouldn't.

"Wow, you guys really know each other." We turn to see that Aaron and Trixie have caught up to us. Trixie gives me the same smile she has ever since I met her. Aaron is eyeing us carefully. When his gaze drifts to my left hand, which has been bare ever since the night of Rob's bachelor party, I hide it. I'm not sure why.

"I told you," Nate says. "This is what happens when you hang around someone for over a decade and a half."

"So, are you a nonconventional couple or something?" Aaron's still watching us. "You're not wearing rings."

"Honey, leave them alone." Trixie rolls her eyes. "Don't mind him. He's a sore loser. I was just happy he picked the right coffee order." As she pats her husband on the chest, I'm prepared to take my leave.

Nate is not on the same page, though. "We're not a couple at all, actually. We're just friends." When he says it, I freeze. I'm not sure if it's because I know Aaron isn't going to like that, or if it's a sore reminder of where Nate and I stand.

But it's never bothered me before. Why is it now? Why is so much on this vacation bothering me?

"What?" Aaron asks. "How? But you're in the honeymoon area!"

Nate looks at me with a raised eyebrow, silently asking what I want to tell them.

"It was just a last-second decision."

"What sort of friends go on a honeymoon cruise together?"

"And why did I never have any like that?" Trixie laughs. Aaron levels her with a glare.

"This is just how we are." Nate shrugs. "And apparently we know each other more than married couples."

"And the whole 'when did you fall in love' question?" Aaron's pressing us in ways I'm not sure I like.

"A lucky guess," Nate answers. I look to the floor.

"I can't believe this!" Aaron says. "And here I was, thinking you two would be easy to beat because you're weird with each other."

That snaps me out of my thoughts. "Hey!" Nate and I say at the same time.

"Go get a drink," Trixie demands. "You're being rude about things again." Aaron huffs and leaves, but she gives us a near-catlike smile. "You two have fun. Within reason of friends, of course." She winks before following her husband.

"Did that . . . seem weird to you?" Nate asks.

"Everything about this is weird to me."

Nate stares in their direction before shaking his head and turning to me. "Oh man. Aaron's *face*. He was so mad."

"They shouldn't have challenged me." I shrug.

"God, I can't wait to tell your parents. They'll get a kick out of it."

It might get a huff of laughter out of Dad. Nate always manages to get those somehow. I just hope he doesn't mention the last question.

Pushing all thoughts of strawberries and lunch tables out of my mind, we head to the room. I use the silence to come up with a plan to get the couch for the night. I know the competition is stiff.

"Hey, Nate. Could you not go into the room?"

"Why?" he asks slowly.

"I need to . . . handle things. And it'll need to air out."

"Oh, God. Why would you say it like that?" He winces. "But fine. Have fun. Text me if you need an air freshener."

"Thanks!" I call. He's heading to the pool deck, and I know I'll have time to do what I need to.

I do have to use the bathroom and freshen up, but then I grab a blanket and pillow and make myself comfortable on the couch. When I sit, I realize that he'll find any reason not to let me stay, so I also grab my suitcase and charger to really settle in.

Nate must not have gone far, because when I text him, he comes back almost immediately.

"It better not be a biohaz—" He pauses when he sees me. "What the hell do you think you're doing?"

"Sitting," I say innocently.

"You did not just kick me out to take over the couch."

I shrug. "You said you would think about taking turns. I'm making sure you think correctly."

A noise erupts out of him that I've never heard before. It sounds like a growl.

My skin erupts in gooseflesh as another memory bursts forth.

Back when we were kids, we would chase each other around to get something. He would steal my water bottle or I would take his lunch when he had one, and then chaos would ensue.

It continued until we graduated.

As I stare at Nate's obvious annoyance, I wonder if I've done enough to push him to start it up again. A tiny cabin on a boat isn't the best place to do it, but those days of us laughing like kids as we messed around with each other were some of the best I'd had.

It hits me that I want him to. Sure, I would laugh and fight back if he tries to drag me off the couch, but it would be something lost to time that we resumed.

Instead, Nate stalks to the bed and I feel disappointment hit hard. "Clever," he mutters. "You got me."

I give myself a moment to feel it. Just a single one, because despite the moments we used to have that are no more, he does know me. He'll know if I'm upset.

I force out a laugh. *Smug.* I need to be smug about this.

"The couch is much more suited to me," I say as I snuggle down. I can't stretch out, but I don't have to be curled into a ball like he had to be the night before. "It's like a normal bed."

"You're lying," he says. "And you'll regret that when we're walking all day for our first excursion."

I bristle. Tomorrow, we're stopping at Cozumel. I've not done nearly enough to prepare for that. I've barely grown used to the cabin on the boat. Now I have to explore somewhere else.

"We should have a plan," I manage to say.

"That's the berry I know and love." My breath hitches as he says it. The gooseflesh is back, and I'm glad I'm under the blanket. "But there's nothing to worry about. I got it."

"You do?"

"Yep. All you need to handle is sleeping on that thing." His lips curve upward. "Unless you wanna give up."

I immediately pull my blanket up higher. "Fuck you. I'm not giving up anything."

"You'll regret that."

"You'll need all the energy you can get tomorrow anyway."

He hums. "Yeah, for when your back hurts and I have to carry you."

"You couldn't if you tried."

Nate's gaze cuts to me and it's heated with challenge. I want to push even harder and make him throw me over his shoulder.

"Get some sleep," he says instead. "Or try to."

The moment's gone and I fight against disappointment.

"I'm pretty sure I'll sleep like a baby." My voice comes out quiet and stilted, but I cut the lights before he can say anything else.

Sleep is definitely what I need. And once I get it, I'm sure all of this will be just an awkward memory.

chapter ten

I DON'T WANT Nate to see it, but the next morning, it feels like I tumbled out of a dryer. That couch is evil and I'm pretty sure it deserves to go overboard.

Nate can definitely tell, judging by the smirk on his face.

Thankfully, he's not a fool because he waits until I have coffee in my hands to bring it up. The entire walk to the coffee shop, I limp like an old lady.

Yeah, the couch definitely deserves to sink to the bottom of the ocean.

"Having regrets?" his smooth voice asks.

"Shut it."

"I was trying to be chivalrous and protect you from this. You just had to be stubborn."

"There's no way that you didn't feel it either. You're like double my size."

He laughs. "That could be an insult or a compliment depending on the way I take that, and I'm going to take it as a compliment."

"Yeah, yeah, you don't get an award for drinking all of your milk. And you definitely don't get one for trying to avoid the question. Is that why you spend so much time in the pool? Be honest."

"The hot tub may have helped a little. And I'm not as grumpy as you are whenever your back is messed up. I can tell this is killing you."

There are many things that are killing me. The deck is bright and the ridiculous sunglasses Nate got me are still sitting in my suitcase. I wanted a smoothie, but the line was so long we had to settle for another place. I've also not been on a run ever since the first one that we did on the night we left port. And with how my back feels, I doubt I should even try to.

But the main one is that the lingering thoughts from yesterday are still bothering me. I want them out of my mind so I can try to enjoy whatever hell is waiting for us on land, yet they still pop up.

Nate and I are different than we were when we were kids. And it's . . . fine. Or it should be.

But it hurts and I don't know why.

I'm hoping that being away from our cabin and out on the town is going to help some of the tension that's growing within me.

"Once we move around, I'll be okay."

"Sure, and I'm also sure that a shitty night of sleep is not going to affect your mood at all."

At the mention of my mood, I glare. I'm eating an omelet I shouldn't be having after a terrible night of sleep. I'm on the edge. "Do you want to ever see the mainland again? Because it's starting to sound like you don't."

"Testy," he says as he eats his own food. "But you don't scare me, berry. You have to be about six inches taller to do that."

I take a piece of bacon and throw it at him.

"Hey, don't waste that!"

"I barely even like bacon," I mutter as I pick it up.

He eyes me as I sit. "Do you want me to tell them to remake it?"

I deflate a little. I had no idea what I wanted, and simply ordered what Nate did. Now I regret it.

"No," I reply. "I'm not gonna be happy either way."

Nate's gaze moves from me to the table next to us. They have a delicious-looking fruit bowl, one that makes my mouth water. I eyed it as we sat, but I hadn't seen it on the menu.

"Hey," Nate says to the two ladies. "Where did you get that?"

"Oh, at the convenience shop one deck up," she replies.

Nate nods and stands. "Watch my omelet, berry. Guard it with your life."

I know where he's heading. He's gone before I can stop him.

A laugh escapes me, and I feel warm in a way that has nothing to do with the hot deck we're sitting on.

Nate knows I'm unhappy and simply . . . fixes it. Without judgment.

I'm determined to be in a better mood when he gets back.

It's not long before I see him strolling down the stairs, fruit bowl in hand.

"Here you go. Pineapple and grapes. With at least one piece of apple."

My mouth is already watering again. "Thank you. You really didn't have to go hunt this down."

"I should've done it the second you got an omelet. What were you thinking?"

I shrug. "I didn't want to delay us any more."

"Come on, it's me. Delay all you want to."

Nate gives me a smile before going back to his food. I dig into my own, much happier with fruit as my main option.

"So, Cozumel, Mexico," I say. "Have you looked into it?"

"You haven't yet?"

"I'll be honest, I was worried I wouldn't make it this far." I shrug. "And any plans that Rob talked about are out the window. I really don't wanna spend my day having an anxiety attack on the beach."

Nate frowns and raises an eyebrow. "And he was okay with you doing that?"

He was. And now that I think about it, I'm not thrilled about that fact. "A-anyway, I have no idea what to do here. What have you found?"

"To be fair, a lot of it is water related."

"That's fine." When Nate glares at me, I clarify. "For you to do, I mean. I can hang out here."

"No."

"Why not?"

"I want to spend time with you." He laughs and shakes his head. "What about that is so hard to get? Whatever we do today, we do together."

"What about what you want to do? I care about your tastes too, you know."

"I do, which is why I let you get away with what you pulled yesterday. But not today. Whatever we do, we do together."

His words are like a balm on my frayed emotions. Him wanting to be around me hasn't changed. At least that's something.

"Fine. Should I look some things up?"

"Way ahead of you. I did a lot of reading, and—"

I fake a gasp. "Wow, I didn't know you knew how to read."

Nate rolls his eyes. "Just because I didn't read at a high school level in elementary school like *some* people doesn't mean I can't do research."

"It wasn't only the reading that was your problem."

"Hang on, berry, I have something for you in my pocket." He reaches in and pulls out a middle finger. "Here you go."

"Now tell me, was that your left or right hand?"

Nate opens his mouth and then shuts it. "I think I hate you a little bit."

"And yet you went on this cruise with me."

"I don't know about you, but arguing with you is fun to me. Call me weird."

"You're weird."

"I have something in my *other* pocket for you—"

I laugh and stop him. "Nate, what did you read up on?"

"Mayan ruins," he replies. "There's an excursion by the cruise line. And they had a few last-minute spots."

"How convenient."

"All you have to do is survive the dock and a bus ride."

"It can't be worse than getting on the boat," I say. "So, is this excursion already booked?"

"It might be. I had a feeling you'd like the idea."

"And how long as it been booked?"

"Since the plane ride."

"Before I was even *on* the boat?"

"I knew I'd convince you. And I did." He throws another smile my way and I'm completely disarmed. I *really* like that smile.

"Y-you thought right," I reply as I force myself to stand. I will not think about the way he looks at me. I won't. "Shall we head out?"

He nods and we throw our trash away before leaving. I knew most people would be heading out, but everyone seems to be doing it all at once. There are enough people to make it hard to keep our usual distance. I'm tempted to shift closer to Nate because he's far easier than a stranger.

But on our flight, that went horribly.

I'm sure that once we get off of the boat, things will get better. We'll both have a distraction, which is what I desperately need to avoid a spiral about the things I'm noticing.

Slowly, we're shuffled off the boat and onto a dock. I feel my usual panic at being close to water, but I manage to keep it hidden and not cling to Nate like a fool. I'm proud of myself as we're loaded on a bus.

Then I see how crowded the bus is.

Everyone is practically on top of each other, squished into rows of seats. I have no choice but to squeeze in tightly with Nate when we sit.

"We should've gotten a car," he mutters.

"Yeah, this is . . . something."

I can tolerate it, but Nate isn't faring well. His shoulders are tense and he stares at the door, as if his will alone could make this end.

My lips tug downward. This isn't the first time we've been on a crowded bus together. Back in high school, we'd gone on a field trip to a local amusement park and sat together like we always did. He was his normal, goofy self.

This version of him is a far cry from that.

"Think you'll make it?" I ask. "I could try to steal another seat or something."

He shakes his head. "No, why would I ask you to do that?"

"You just seem like you hate this."

"Hate what?"

"Having to sit here with me."

His eyes go wide, and for a second, he looks like a deer caught in headlights. Then his shock fades and he shakes his head. "It's not you." He lets out a laugh that seems forced. "It's other people."

"Is it?" I press.

He leans in. "Can you not smell the lack of deodorant here? All I'm catching is onion salad."

Frowning, I take a deep breath of air only to pick up exactly what he's talking about. It's the middle of summer and it's hot, but having that much BO is a crime against humanity.

"Oh, God." I cover my mouth. "Why would you draw my attention to that?"

"You asked."

"I'm gonna breathe as little as possible." I shake my head. "It's the only way I'll survive."

The bus ride takes way too long to get to our destination, and

I'm considering jumping out of the window to save myself by the time we pull into the ruins site.

Nate and I are nearly heaving when we get off the bus.

"It's burned into my nostrils," I say.

"I need ten showers." He shakes his head. "Horrible."

"And we're stuck with them for the tour," I mutter. "Think this place gives out deodorant as a welcome gift?"

Nate looks around. We're in the middle of a parking lot surrounded by tall vegetation. I haven't seen civilization for far too long. "Somehow, I doubt they do that out here."

"At least it'll be pretty," I say. Everyone from the tour is walking through a tree-covered path, and I motion for Nate to follow me. We meet up with a tour guide, who promises to tell us everything we need to know about the ruins. People listen intently.

Nate zones out about five minutes into our walk. Our tour guide is telling us the history of the area. He's decently engaging, but Nate hates listening to someone talk for too long. In high school, he preferred teaching himself rather than sitting in class.

He's putting on a good show, though. Nate is looking in the general direction of the tour guide, but his eyes are glassy and I can tell he's somewhere else in his mind. I can follow just fine, but I'm more worried about him having fun too.

My hand closes around his arm and his eyes go wide. "What are you doing?" he asks.

I immediately take my hand away, trying not to think too hard about the alarm in his voice. I jerk my head to a path behind us and start walking.

"Is this where you drag me off to kill me?" he asks.

"No. This is where we do something else."

"Why would we do something else? You were enjoying that."

"And you weren't." I cross my arms. "This place is cool, but I doubt you're gonna give a flying fuck about ruins if you're bored. So let's go find some and look up the history ourselves."

"Our phones won't work out here."

I pause. "Oh, well. I didn't think of that."

He laughs. "But the gift shop might have something for us to use. Come on." I perk up and follow him. We make it a few feet before he pauses. "Oh, and berry?"

"Yeah?"

"Thanks."

"I'm not the only one on this trip who should be having fun." I'm tempted to bump his shoulder with mine, but I resist the urge. Being physical with him feels so natural, but I don't want to ruin a good thing. So, I hide it and follow him back to the gift shop.

～～～

"Apparently, the steps to this used to be decorated by human faces."

I'm sweating from the hot sun and I can't tell if Nate is joking. I turn to him with a bewildered expression and he shows me the guided map we got from the gift shop.

"It's right here, berry. I'm not making it up."

"Well, this temple is rumored to be to the goddess of fertility," I say. I get out my phone and take a picture. I'm tempted to turn the camera around to me, but I know that I look like death warmed over.

Nate is simply glistening in the sun. It's so fucking unfair. My eyes want to linger on him and I'm not sure why. I already know how he looks.

With us adventuring on our own, we've covered a lot of ground. We've also gotten lost a few times. The sun is high in the sky and I've not seen the main group for a while, but the peace and quiet is nice.

Even if I feel like I could melt.

"I bet the view up there is pretty."

I wipe sweat from my brow. "Climbing ancient sites will get you arrested, Nate."

"Hey, I'm just thinking about it. I would never do it."

I level him with a glare before I go in search of shade. I find it under a tree and finally sit.

"Affected by the heat already? Or was it sleeping on that couch?"

"The air is *wet*. Wet and hot."

"We're from Nashville. We're used to this."

"Not without air conditioning to run to." I sigh. "Is this why you don't mind swimming? Because it cools you off? I think I'd be fine with drowning right now."

"Want me to go find you some water?" he asks.

"No, just sit with me a minute. I need some time out of the sun." I'm going to be a mess of dirt when I get up, but it's worth it to be able to breathe for a second. Nate sits next to me and we're enveloped in a nice silence.

The ship is a lot of moving parts, and while I'm used to that with living in a city, there's something nice about being in a jungle near no one else for a while. Even though it's hot, I'm surrounded with the sounds of nature that are unfamiliar to me, and I can't help but take in every moment of it.

"Is this what the beach is like?" I ask.

"There's usually the sound of the water too, but yeah. Basically."

"It's nice," I reply. "Even though I might melt into the ground."

"Looks like the heat wins."

"It does. I'm a big baby." My eyes shut as I lie back. The hair clip I'm using pokes me in the back of the head and I sigh and sit back up.

"Take your hair down." Nate says it like it's simple.

I immediately shake my head. "No way. It'll be a mess if I do that."

"We're both sitting in dirt on a forest floor. Why are you worried about being messy?"

He has a point, and I bite my lip before slowly grabbing the clip to let my hair tumble down. I know without a shadow of a doubt that I wouldn't do this for anyone else, but here in this moment, I'm safe with Nate.

My dark hair falls in waves around me, but I'm able to lie back. Nate chuckles before going quiet. I lift one eyelid, seeing him gazing at me.

"What?" I ask.

"It's rare to see you with your hair down these days," he says. "You've even had it in a bun to sleep. I'm not sure how your scalp can take it."

"Worried about my hair's health, are we?"

"It just looks . . ." He trails off.

"Frizzy. Or it gets in my face. It's okay, you can say it."

"Berry, it looks beautiful. It always has."

I feel a heat that has nothing to do with the weather rush through my body.

"It's just in the way."

"Fair enough. You used to wear it down more when we were younger. Before Rob."

I close my eyes, hoping that I can keep my face straight. "He made a comment about it once or twice."

"Asshole," he mutters. "You know you can do what you want, right?"

"I do. And that's why it's down right now."

"Good," he replies. "It's gotten so long."

This should be casual, but it doesn't feel like it. I know Nate's eyes are still on me, and I hope he's staring right at my hair. I don't know why I want him to, but it's satisfying.

I let him watch me and I settle in. Slowly, I relax.

There's no telling how much time passes, but Nate lets me

lounge. It might be the first time I've truly felt calm on the whole trip. I'm pretty sure that I doze off a few times.

The sun eventually moves and I can feel it burning my exposed leg. That's when I finally sit up.

"This is nice, but I don't want a sunburn."

Nate has laid back too, covering his eyes with his arm. "Ugh. Ten more minutes."

"What time is it anyway?"

"No idea."

I hum and pull out my phone. It's late in the afternoon.

"Hey," I say. "Do you know when the bus is supposed to leave?"

Nate slowly moves his arm with a frown. "Um, no."

"Do you know when the ship is supposed to pull away from the dock?"

"Four, I think."

Slowly, I turn my phone around. Nate and I share a moment of panic before we scramble off the ground.

chapter eleven

Getting back to the ship is chaos. But Nate thrives in chaos, so somehow, we manage it. It's still at the dock when we both tumble out of the taxi he hired, and we make a run for it.

"Made it," he says. "Just in time."

"That was . . ." I'm still trying to catch my breath. "The *worst*."

"You're a runner."

"*Slow* runner," I remind him. "I don't do it for speed."

He laughs and leads me onto the boat. The best part of being so tired is that I couldn't care less about the dock.

We stop in our room for a moment to wash up, and then hunger hits me. I skipped lunch, and only having fruit was a terrible idea.

Nate must know I'm starving because he already has plans.

"Are you sure the steakhouse is where we should go?" I ask as we walk up. "We're still kind of a mess."

"So is everyone else."

"We're not even dressed for it." He's in a half-buttoned-up shirt and shorts. While it's nicer than what a lot of guys wear, it's not steakhouse level. I'm in one of the new pairs of shorts and a tank top. My hair is trying to escape the clip I've wrangled it into after taking it down at the ruins, and I know I'll have a hell of a time getting it under control later.

"No one else is. This is a cruise."

He has a point, but I can't tell if I'm grumpy because I'm starving or if this place is too crowded. I sigh and give in. He smirks as we step into the line.

It's loud, and I didn't miss the rocking of the boat. I'm trying to get my bearings while also contending with the fact that I might eat my own arm when someone runs up to us.

Trixie pulls both Nate and me into a hug, squealing the whole time. I try not to grimace.

"Are you guys eating here too?" she asks. "What a coincidence. Aaron is just up ahead." She points him out; he's almost at the hostess stand.

"Hi," I manage to say with a fake smile. "Nice to see you again."

"Wanna join us for dinner? I'm sure Aaron wouldn't mind."

Nate and I look over at him. He's watching us, and I'm pretty sure he's still mad about us taking him down at the Newlywed game earlier.

"That's okay," Nate says. "You two should get some time to yourselves."

"Oh, we got plenty earlier. We stayed in our room." She winks, and I get the implication immediately.

Nate coughs. "Ah, well."

"Come on! We'll be getting a table quicker anyway!" She grabs both of us and takes us to Aaron. Now my face is red at the idea of what they did earlier *and* for her letting us cut in line.

"I brought us some friends," she says to Aaron.

"Hey, guys." He nods. "Enjoying your cup?"

"Still mad we won it?" Nate parrots right back.

"Kind of. But you guys are weirdly in sync." He shrugs, seemingly more relaxed than he was the day before. "How was Cozumel?"

I tell them about the island, grateful for small talk, as we move up in line. Trixie loves all the photos and ribs her husband for not wanting to go, but it's decent conversation.

By the time we're led to our table, I'm hopeful for the dinner. Maybe having it with other people is a good thing.

Nate gets my chair for me and I give him a smile without thinking.

Aaron and Trixie see it. "So," she begins after we put our drink order in. "What's the deal with you two?"

"What do you mean?" I ask. "We're friends."

"You're the closest friends I've ever seen," Aaron remarks.

"We're not," Nate adds. "We're just normal. Platonic." He says it casually, but there's an edge to it that I've not heard before. I glance at him and I'm only pulled away when Aaron speaks again.

"Why?" he asks. "You guys could probably work together."

"Definitely work together," Trixie adds.

"That's just not how we are." Nate has a lot of practice saying this. He has for years. He said it to my parents, to Rob, and to Quinn. It's simple enough.

It's just not how we are.

Because that's what it is. It's a simple fact that we're . . . *friends.*

"Exactly," I force out. "We're happy like that."

I don't feel happy about it, and I hate that I don't. But I'm also supposed to be married right now, and here I am on a cruise with my best friend who won't even—

Pushing the thought out of my mind, I stand. "Excuse me. I never went to the restroom when I got back."

I keep it together until I get through the door. Then my breaths turn shaky.

We shouldn't have left the boat. That already had me messed up, and now I'm having to explain my friendship to strangers, which I haven't done in *years*. Being with Rob cemented the fact that Nate and I will always be friends, and only friends.

Now I don't have that.

I've never liked having to explain Nate and me to people. We simply . . . are. And I'm fine with that. No one else needs to know anything else.

But I'm far from fine in the bathroom. And I need to figure out why.

One of the stall doors opens and my gaze falls to my hands. I'd slipped away from the group to have a moment to myself, but now that I'm standing in the bathroom not needing to use it, I try to get my breathing under control while washing my hands, pretending I have a reason to be in here.

"You okay?" I know that voice.

My gaze snaps up to see Scarlett. She looks gorgeous in a tight red dress. Her hair is straight and falls over her shoulder.

"Uh, hi."

She gives me a half smile as she washes her hands. "A bathroom isn't a great place to have an emotional moment."

"I-I'm fine."

She raises one single eyebrow that tells me I'm full of shit.

Right. She's a therapist.

"Are you?" she challenges.

"No. Not really."

"Wanna talk about it?"

"I thought you were off duty."

"I am, but that doesn't mean I can't help a fellow gal who's nearing a panic attack."

My shoulders slump. "Just bill me later."

She laughs. "This is what I consider community service. What happened?"

"I think . . . coming on my honeymoon with my friend was a poor choice."

"I see."

"But not for the reasons you think," I rush to say. "Nothing is happening with him. Not at all."

Scarlett stares me down. "Really?"

"No. We've been friends so long that I can't . . . I *won't* do that. I'm just confused. He's got these walls I never noticed until now, and then other people are asking about us and I . . . I hate it. I hate all of it."

Scarlett is quiet for a long moment and her lips press together. "It's safe to assume that your friendship is very important to you."

"Yes," I say. "So important to me."

"I'll be honest with you, there's a lot to unpack there. More than should be dealt with in a bathroom, but I will say this. You've had a lot of change, right?"

"Too much," I say. "And I hate change."

"Then there's going to be discomfort." She says it slowly. "But that doesn't mean anything's wrong. It means you're changing. Sometimes it's a good thing."

I think about it. Am I changing?

Hell, I'm on a ship *willingly*. I'm branching out. Or trying to. And I'm getting time with Nate that I could've lost. The alternative was letting Rob separate us.

"Is it possible that things changed between Nate and me because of my ex?"

"Definitely," she says. "And now you have to find your footing without someone else in your life. The biggest question is where you'll end up."

"We'll be friends."

"Fair enough, but what kind of friends is the question." I don't know if I want to answer that. "Give it time," she says softly. "And maybe enjoy the boat while you're at it. Have you been to the pool? It's where I'm heading next."

I flounder for an excuse. "It's a little late."

"It's the middle of the summer and there're lights for after dark. There's plenty of time." She waves her hand. "You don't have to spend the whole time mulling in your friendship. Have some fun." She winks at me before leaving the bathroom.

I sigh when I'm alone. I have no idea if I know how to have fun on a boat in the middle of the ocean.

But I need to try.

By some miracle, I manage to make it through the dinner without any more incidents. The talk with Scarlett helped more than I can say, and I feel a little more levelheaded in her presence.

It also helps that Nate must have said something while I was gone, because Trixie and Aaron drop the subject of us and talk about other happenings on the boat.

The food is delicious, and I'm happily full as we retire to our room for the evening.

"Feeling better?" he asks.

"I was fine the whole time."

"Oh, you mean when you lied about having to go to the bathroom? You went right when we got on the boat."

I gulp. "You caught that?"

"I catch everything. Also, next time you make an escape, choose a place where I can follow you. The ladies' bathroom is a terrible place for me to try to make you feel better."

"Sorry," I say. "I really needed a minute alone."

"Was it what Trixie and Aaron were saying? They barely know us, berry." He waves it off. "And they know how we are now. It shouldn't happen again."

I think about what Scarlett said about finding my footing. She was the only one who didn't make things out to be more than they needed to be.

And I let myself feel uncomfortable.

"I know," I say. "It's just been a while since we had to deal with it. People got quiet when Rob was around."

"We're too old to worry about what people think about us." He says it like it's simple. "We're both happy as we are, right?"

The answer should roll right off my tongue. *Yes. Of course I am.*

But that's not true, is it?

I'm *not* happy.

It's not because Nate isn't good to me. It's not because he doesn't care. But there's something missing. Something I want more than anything else.

Nate waits patiently for my answer, but my silence makes him narrow his eyes.

"Hello?" he asks. "You there?"

"Oh, um. Yes. Sorry."

"You must be tired. You're slower than usual."

"I thought I was always slow because I had short legs."

Nate smiles. "You said it, not me."

"You thought it."

"Is it a crime to have thoughts?"

"It is if it's about me."

"Put me in jail, berry. I think about you a lot."

My gaze cuts to his. There's no way he knows how that sounds. I open my mouth to continue our usual banter, but find . . . nothing.

"I'm . . . feeling a little off, actually." All I can say is the truth.

He raises an eyebrow and my entire body tenses. I should talk to him, but I'm way too scared to.

"We did a lot today for me. And I'm feeling bad that you didn't get to see the beach."

"I have the pool."

"Which you haven't been to today."

"And you're feeling off. I'm not going swimming and leaving you alone."

I'm a total idiot, because a suggestion escapes me that I should *not* be offering.

"I guess I could go to the pool deck."

He pauses. "What? Are you serious?"

"I won't swim," I clarify. "Obviously. But I know someone who'll be there. And I could watch you in your element."

A slow smile spreads on Nate's face. "You're being very nice. Are you hiding something from me?"

Shit. "No, of course not! You're just doing a lot for me. And I wanna return the favor. You know, like a good friend does?" I say. Nate hums as he considers me, and I know I'm close to convincing him. "And I think the pool deck might be slow."

"You have a point there. Are you sure you'll be okay on the deck?"

I laugh as I prepare to lie through my teeth. "You know me. Fear never stops me for long."

chapter twelve

NATE LOOKS like a kid at Christmas after we head back to the room, so I know I've made the right choice. I manage to snag a chair that's a safe distance from the pool, and I pull out my Kindle.

My lie is mostly paying off, even if I feel like I could bolt at any second. When I got out here, I scanned the area for Scarlett, only to come up empty.

Maybe she went to bed instead.

I wish I'd done that. After exploring an island and having to run back, I'm exhausted.

Nate doesn't seem to share the same sentiment. He immediately jumps into the pool. When he comes up, he gives me a wave. I return it before smiling.

"Ah, you took my advice." I turn to see Scarlett in a navy-blue swimsuit.

"There you are. I thought you'd changed your mind."

"I move slow on vacation." She smiles. "Mind if I sit?"

"I won't be much fun. I'm just reading."

"I love reading." She pulls out a paperback. "It would be nice to have a buffer in case some idiot tries to make a move on me."

They definitely would. "I can fight them off. Or pretend to be your girlfriend. Whichever works."

She laughs. "I love a good fake date. And you don't even have to feel bad about it. You *are* single, after all."

"That I am. Even if I don't feel it yet." Scarlett's eyes meet mine and she has a pensive look on her face that tells me she's trying to figure out a deeper meaning to what I said. I bristle. "Ten-year relationship, you know?"

"The best part of dumping someone is the rebound."

My eyes widen. "You're a therapist. Shouldn't you tell me to be single for a bit?"

"I don't always follow my own advice. And you don't even have to have a rebound, but you could always *look*."

"I looked at you."

"And I appreciate that." She preens at my compliment and lifts her book up to start reading. Casually, she adds, "But you could also look at *men*. You know, the gender you're presumably attracted to?"

"I don't . . . I barely notice them."

"Because you feel like you're taken. You're very much not." She leans in. "Look at that one."

My eyes land on a man with bronze skin and an eight pack. "He's not bad," I say.

Scarlett gestures for me to continue. "There has to be more than that."

"He's . . . buff. Maybe too buff? I don't know."

"What about the guy reading?" She points to a man with a book on a lounge chair. He has thick glasses and he's kind of cute.

"Okay, maybe he's not so bad."

Another woman walks up and gives him a kiss. "Oh, he's taken. All the good ones are."

I huff out a laugh. "I have a feeling I'll run into that a lot here."

"Maybe, but you're noticing men. Which is the first step to getting over your ex." She looks over the pool deck. "There's one for me." She peers over the top of her paperback and her eyes are narrowed.

I look over to see a guy around my age or even younger making his way toward the metal ladder at the edge of the pool. He's tall with longer hair that he throws over his shoulder as he gets out.

"He's . . . young."

"A toxic trait of mine," she says with a sigh. "I love them immature."

"How do you know he's—"

One of his buddies tackles him into the water. I wince. When he comes up, he's sputtering, but laughing.

"Come on! Gimme a warning before you rail me!" he yells.

"He's . . . uh, not worried about how he sounds?" I ask it slowly.

"You can judge me," she says back. "And I'm not going after him. Trust me, I've learned my lesson about younger men."

I raise an eyebrow to ask about how she's learned it, but then her eyes widen and her jaw drops.

"How did I miss *him*?" She slaps my arm as she sits up. "Jesus Christ."

"Who? Where?"

"Dark hair. Getting out of the pool. This is eye candy for *both* of us."

I turn. I *do* see a man with dark hair getting out of the pool. My mouth goes dry as I see a lithe frame glistening with water. He's laughing as he gets out, and I swear time slows as my heart kicks into gear.

But I'm not looking at a stranger.

I'm looking at *Nate.*

"Uh, Scarlett?" I manage to say. "I . . ."

"Shh, Mommy's watching." She's fully sitting up. "I hope he's not married."

I look back at Nate.

Sometimes I forget we've both grown up. And over the years, I've definitely not noticed that he's . . . hot.

So hot.

I need to rip my eyes away, but his muscles are hypnotizing. All of him is.

Should his swim shorts be that low? And what's hiding underneath?

Oh, God. Am I thirsting after *Nate*? The one who's my best friend? The man who doesn't even want to be near me?

"Oh, shit. He's coming this way. I have a rule to stay single here. So don't let me do anything."

I can't say anything. My brain is fried from the thoughts of Nate's . . . everything. Now that I'm having the thought that he's hot, I can't *stop* having it.

Even though I need to tell Scarlett who he is. *Desperately.*

"Maisie." Nate's voice is now in front of me. "Did you make a friend?"

His voice is deep. God, it's like velvet.

To my side, Scarlett slowly turns to me. I have no doubt she knows *who* Nate is now.

"U-uh. Huh?"

"You okay?" he asks slowly. "Did being near the pool fry your brain?"

Scarlett finally composes herself and clears her throat. "Probably. Sorry, are you the friend she came with?"

"That I am," he says, eyes finally turning to her. I rip mine from him and try to gain my bearings.

"I've heard a lot about you." Scarlett has entirely pulled herself together, which is more than I can say for myself. "It's so nice of you to be her plus-one. I ran into her at the spa the other day and we talked for a while."

"Oh, that makes sense. It's a little hard for this one to get away from me." He laughs good-naturedly and eyes me again. His smile fades. "Are you sure you're okay? Do you need water?"

I need to get out of here. *Now.* "You know what? I totally do. I'm gonna get that right now!" The words come out as a squeak and I rush off. I don't think water is enough. I need a lobotomy. I'd forget about Nate if I couldn't think at all, right?

I manage to make it to the bar and order a water as I try to get my wits about me. It's like seeing him naked all over again, and I can't get it out of my mind.

A hand lands on my shoulder and I yelp. "You did *not* warn me."

It's Scarlett. I know it the second she touches me.

"Sorry, I was busy being an idiot." I mutter it as I take another gulp of water.

"That man is the friend you brought? *Him?*"

"Yep."

"And you didn't think to stop me from thirsting after him?"

I can't meet her eyes. "Ah, well . . ."

Scarlett gasps. "Wait a minute. Was I not the only one?"

"Shh," I hiss. "He's worried about me, which means he *will* be coming over here."

And sure enough, he is. Scarlett grabs my arm, her grip tight. I wonder if she's gonna make a move, but when I look at her, she's watching us excitedly.

"Don't—"

"Just be yourself," she whispers. "I need to witness this."

"Hey, don't get your therapist rocks off to us."

"But you make it so easy!"

"Did that help?" Nate asks when he gets to me. "You still look red as hell."

"Sunstroke. I'm not used to being outside this often." I fan my face.

"Oh, come on." Scarlett's grin is feral. "Tell him what we were really doing."

I glare. "No."

"It's not a crime," she says, and then she leans. "And I won't mention *who* either."

"Scarlett, it's embarrassing."

"What?" She laughs. "He's your friend. I'm sure he wouldn't be bothered by us objectifying men."

My face is on fire.

"Wh-what?" Nate asks.

"I was just reminding her that she's single and there are plenty of guys to look at." She shrugs. "You found a few, right?"

I glare. Then I realize she's not looking at me. She's looking at *Nate* to gauge his reaction.

My anger fades. I immediately want to do the same thing.

Nate's eyebrows are high and I can see the slight hint that he's uncomfortable. His lips press together before they turn into a smile. "Care to share who?"

It's such a Nate response.

I shouldn't have gotten my hopes up.

"Scarlett likes the surfer bro that got tackled into the pool."

"Hey!" she hisses. "I never said my type was *good* for me. And you liked the nerdy guy."

Thankfully, she doesn't mention how he pales in comparison to Nate.

"He's married," I say with a shake of my head.

"We're just checking out the menu. Not ordering. Unless you want a rebound."

"At least a nerd is better than Rob," Nate says pointedly. "Pick a guy with less of an attitude next time."

He orders a water too. And I can feel a frown forming. He's absolutely fine with me looking at other men. Of course he is.

I turn to Scarlett, wondering if she's as disappointed as I am. She's still watching us like we're her favorite TV show. My eyebrows pinch. She should've picked up on his dismissal. Why hasn't she?

"I'll do my best. I'm afraid my taste is garbage."

"I can vet someone next time." Nate gulps his water and I do *not* look at his throat bob. I simply don't. "What do you say, berry? The next guy has to go through the best friend test?"

"I can agree to that."

"You two are just the *best* of friends, aren't you?" Scarlett is still smiling. "Love to see it. I'll let you two *friends* enjoy the rest of your night. I'll see you later, Maisie." Scarlett walks off with a wink, leaving me with only Nate.

"She's . . . interesting," he says.

"She's single," I reply. "She says she's staying that way, but you could try."

I ignore the ball of cotton that makes its way into my chest.

What's happening to me? Maybe I do have sunstroke.

"Nah, I'm fine. Glad you made a friend, though. She kind of reminds me of Quinn."

I shouldn't be relieved at that. But I also shouldn't have found Nate so hot earlier. Yet I did. I glance at him, hoping it was just a moment of madness.

It's not.

"Are you sure you're okay?"

"I think I need sleep," I say quickly. "We did too much in one day."

"Now that I can agree with. Ready to fight for the bed?"

That puts images in my mind that I'd rather not have.

"You know what?" My voice is too high. "You can have the couch. I'll let you be nice to me."

"Really?" he asks. "Who are you?"

"Just seeing sense." I return to my chair and frantically grab my things. "Ready to go? Because I sure am. I can't wait to sleep!"

I'm running to the elevator before he can say anything else.

chapter thirteen

"HOLY *SHIT*." Nate is panting when we finish the run. "I didn't know you could actually move that fast."

I regret it. Immensely. But I knew more than anything that I could *not* stare at his back while we were running.

Sleep didn't do anything. When I woke up, I saw Nate's strong legs dangling over the couch and had a full-body reaction. A ridiculous shudder pulsed through me and I knew I was still in trouble.

That was when I got up to go for a run.

And Nate woke up just in time to join me.

The second I stop, I fall onto the deck. I can't even worry about how dirty it must be—I just need to be horizontal.

A water bottle appears beside me and I take it from Nate, guzzling it without a second thought. "Thanks," I manage after a moment.

"You pushed yourself a little hard there, berry. It's almost like us humans have limits."

"Fuck you." I'm still heaving, and it takes effort for me to talk. "I just wanted to prove that I'm not slow."

"Oh, you proved something all right."

"What? That I'm capable of beating you?"

A slow smile spreads on his face. "I wasn't even sprinting."

"Are you *kidding*?"

"Nope. But you did prove that you have issues. So many issues."

"Look, I have something in my pocket for you."

"You don't even have pockets." He gestures at my leggings.

I flip him off anyway.

"Now you're stealing my jokes. Get your own sense of humor."

"We've been around each other too long. We basically have the same sense of humor at this point."

"Or you've just stolen all of my material. Rude." He huffs, but holds out a hand. I take it and slowly get up.

The second I'm upright, he pulls it away.

Now I'm unnerved that he's so hot *and* disappointed that he's not touching me more.

I really am losing my mind.

"Are you really all right?" he asks. "You don't run like that unless something is bothering you."

"I'm still feeling off," I admit. "I'm trying not to be, but I am."

"That's okay," he replies. "We both thought this week would be different. Hell, I never expected you to be on a boat like this *ever*."

I laugh before sobering. "It would have been terrible to have Rob here, by the way. I'm glad it's you."

He gives me a half smile. "I'm glad it's you too."

A moment passes between us, one where I think he could mean something more. But I shove that away. I'm not ruining this by letting whatever has come over me make me question him.

"We're on Grand Cayman today, right?" I ask. "Should we get breakfast before we explore again?"

Nate looks down at the sweat covering his body—something I

definitely did not notice—and winces. "I think I need a quick shower, but yes."

A shower means seeing his ass.

Which I cannot do.

"I'll just tidy up in the pool deck bathroom then," I say. "And check in with everyone back home!"

The high pitch in my voice is back, and Nate frowns.

"Are you—"

"Yep! Bye!"

I GROAN when I flop onto a pool chair. I'm still in my running outfit, but I refuse to be anywhere near a naked Nate. My leggings and sneakers will have to do.

Pulling my phone out, I finally open the messaging app. Since I've been with Nate, I've been so focused on us that I've not looked at a thing. I have a few unread messages waiting for me.

QUINN

Hey, just checking in. Want to hang out?

Haven't heard back from you. Call me when you see this?

The second I see the message, I video call her.

"Maisie?" she answers. "Thank goodness. How are you?"

"I'm okay."

"I should come over. How about a girls' movie day? I need it after all the drama with my birthday party and . . . other things."

I grimace. I feel even worse for what I'm about to say. "I would say yes, but I'm not home. Nate convinced me to go on the cruise with him."

She goes quiet. "I thought you said you didn't want to go."

"I didn't, but he made some good points about how I shouldn't be alone. It's . . . fine, I guess. Hard to complain about life when you're surrounded by water, right?"

It's a bald-faced lie, one that wouldn't work on Nate.

Thankfully, I'm not talking to Nate.

"Well, that explains a lot." She lets out a laugh. "We were all worried about you when Rob went by your place and you didn't open the door."

I blinked. "Rob went to my house?"

"Yeah, he wanted to talk it out. But when you didn't answer, I figured I would check in on you. Not that you have to answer for him, of course. I'm on your side here, but usually you do."

Suddenly, I'm glad I'm on the boat. I'm not sure how I would have fared if I were home and saw Rob on my front porch.

"Not this time."

"He's really trying to make it up to you."

"He is?"

"Not that you have to accept! But as the days go on, he's getting more and more serious about it."

I wish he wasn't serious at all. He said what he said.

And I won't take an apology this time.

"You don't need to be in the middle of this, not with your party coming up. Just tell him I need space."

"I'll try. You know how he is when he's determined."

I do. And now that I'm away from him, I'm not sure I like it.

That determination was the main thing I liked when he asked me out. He showered me with gifts and attention. And with the information that he just wanted to fuck me, all of it is shallow now.

Does he want me to take him back because he's sorry, or is this a challenge for him?

"I do, but that's his issue to deal with."

"Fair enough," Quinn says. "How is the cruise, though?"

"Great," I lie. "I mean, I'm with Nate. What could possibly go wrong?"

"That's fair. You two always manage to have fun." She laughs. "Enjoy it. And take pictures!"

I promise her I will before I see Nate on the pool deck looking for me. He must have taken the shortest shower ever.

With a deep breath, I stand and wave at him. No more of the weirdness. I'm determined to be normal.

TEN MINUTES INTO BREAKFAST, I mess it up by mentioning Rob.

"He went to your house?" Nate asks slowly. The grip on his fork seems to tighten.

"Yep. Thank goodness I wasn't there."

Nate's only answer is a hum. He doesn't look like himself and I hate the frown that's made its way to his face.

"Nate, I'm sure he thinks a pathetic apology will be enough, but it won't be. Not this time."

His gaze flicks up to me and back down at his cup. "Yeah, sure."

I narrow my eyes. "What? Do you have a different opinion?"

"It doesn't matter."

"I think it does."

He lets out a long sigh and takes a drink of his coffee. "Do you really wanna do this?"

"I do."

"Fine." He leans forward. "Do you remember the time he didn't talk to you for two weeks straight? It was three or so years ago."

I *don't* like to think about it, but of course I remember it. Nate and I were hanging out, and I was in a bad mood but not sure why.

That was when I opened my text chain with Rob and he'd completely ghosted me.

"Yes," I say. "And I gave him hell for that."

"You did. I remember you saying you'd rather be single than ignored, if memory serves."

I wince. That was harsh, but now that I think about it, it might have been better to stick to my guns. I'm not sure why I didn't. But I remember Rob calling. He promised to be better. And over time, that anger faded.

He proposed less than a year later.

"He whittles you down. Slowly makes it seem like *you're* the one overreacting. No one tries harder than Rob when he's messed up. If you ask me, he should be trying every single day." The words are coated with a bitterness that I can't explain, and it unsettles me.

"Are you . . . annoyed that I stayed with Rob for so long?" I ask.

"Why would you ask that?"

"You have a weird tone." When he stares at me warily, I laugh. "Come on. You're not the only one who knows their best friend. I know you too, remember?"

"Right," he mutters. "And when you were happy, no. But it wasn't fun seeing him screw things up and get unlimited chances."

I stare at Nate. Is that what I did? Give Rob unlimited chances when he hurt me?

Would I have ever seen it if he hadn't gone after Nate?

My stomach churns and I'm not sure I want to be eating anymore. Now that Rob's gone, I'm not missing much. My life hasn't changed in a dramatic way.

I don't even miss him yet.

So why did I give him chances? Why did I let his gifts and attention win me over?

My phone buzzes with a text and I flip it over.

ROB

I'm guessing you went on our honeymoon.

A flare of defensiveness hits me and another one comes through.

ROB

You probably need that time. Enjoy it.

As I read them, I can see where I would have taken those words at face value. He seems like he regrets it. He seems sorry.

This is when I would soften.

"There he is," Nate says with a laugh. He finishes off his drink. "I knew it wouldn't be long. I'll let you decide what to say to him."

He sounds resigned, like he knows what I'm going to do. With a smile that doesn't reach his eyes, he stands and walks away.

My jaw tightens as I refocus on the text. I still remember what he said about Nate and me. It still burns when I think about it.

Instead of softening, I poke the bear.

MAISIE

Thanks. Nate and I are definitely enjoying it.

Rob texts back immediately.

ROB

Are you serious? You went on OUR honeymoon
with him?

I huff out a humorless laugh. Whatever his deal is with Nate, it's still there.

It'll *always* be there.

With a long sip, I finish my own coffee and shoot off one more text before I stand and follow Nate.

MAISIE

Of course I did. What else are best friends for?

chapter fourteen

When I finally catch up to Nate, he seems determined not to talk about Rob. He smiles and hands over my flower sunglasses, giving me a half-ass excuse that I'd need them. Judging by the way I've squinted all morning, I'm inclined to say that it's the right choice.

"This isn't a massive island," he says. "But there's a botanical garden."

I can still see the tense line of his shoulders, and the way he doubts I'll stay away from Rob hurts.

But my bravery is waning. I pushed things by asking Nate what he really thought. And now I regret it. I want today to be fun, and I'm determined to get rid of the lingering awkwardness between us.

"That sounds fun," I say. "Shall we get in line?"

He nods. It's later in the morning and there are less people getting off the boat this time, yet the line seems to be slower. I'm mostly focused on Nate and wishing I could start some sort of banter to completely melt any remaining tension.

I haven't given the island a second thought, but when we get to the front of the line, I realize I've made a massive mistake.

The water glistens below and I see a smaller ferry waiting for us. It rocks in a way the larger ship doesn't as people are walking on to sit. Looking out, I realize there is no port. We're in the middle of the ocean still, and we have to ride the dingy little thing to shore.

Oh *fuck* no. I've grown used to the sight of water, but the cruise ship makes it feel farther away, so much so that it doesn't feel as dangerous. But the tiny thing looks like it's *in* the water, barely above it.

"Shit," Nate says. "You okay? I didn't know there wasn't a port here."

I wish him being within just a few inches of me would cure my fear, but I'm still about to board a tiny boat that I can barely trust when I can't fucking swim.

Nothing feels scarier.

All I can do is jerk my head side to side. Words are impossible.

His hands land on my shoulders. He moves us to the side so others can get on the boat. I'm worried he'll let me go the second we're out of the way, so I grip his wrists to keep him close.

He's warm and real.

"Okay, here's what we can do." His green eyes meet mine. "We can stay here and find something else to do for the whole day. Or I can help you onto the boat. But either way, you're in control, and I'll make sure nothing happens to you."

"It's just . . . small." At least I can talk. He doesn't take away the fear, but he helps.

"I know. And I should've looked into it further. What do you know? I actually *am* bad at reading. But we can walk away now."

I study the planes of his face. This close, his eyelashes curl against his slightly tan skin. He's got a little stubble; he must have forgotten to shave this morning.

Usually, he's far enough away that I can't see these things.

And that distance has been bothering me.

I hate this. I hate that there's any tension at all between us. It feels wrong after being friends for so long without it.

We're fine when we're busy, which is why we can't stay on the ship.

Slowly, I gulp in air. "I want to go to the shore."

"You sure?" he asks.

It sounds like a death sentence, but I nod anyway. "Can you just . . . stick close? You were serious about saving my ass if I somehow fall in, right?"

"I am." He says it quietly, but the curve of his brow tells me he's unsure about something.

Is it me asking him to stay close?

"Come on," he says. "Let's try to board."

Nate is kind enough to keep one firm hand on my shoulder as we walk toward the tiny boat. My teeth grind. Now I wish he were closer *and* I'm scared out of my mind.

It's not a great combination.

Slowly, we get on the tiny thing. It rocks with the movement of the ocean and my fists tighten. Nate and I sit next to each other. It's so crowded that our thighs are pressing together. I know he hates it, and I turn away from him so I can't see his expression.

Through the other people who are also finding their spots on the boat, I can see the water. My knuckles go white as I glare out.

I can't help that I don't have good memories of swimming, and it's not the ocean's fault that things are different between Nate and me, but it's the only place I can look where he won't see me and worry.

The terror in my gut settles with the way I miss him. It turns into something hotter and sharper, and I try to push it away.

I don't want to be angry that Nate's put distance between us. It's not his fault.

But I *am*.

I want to be able to link our arms without a second thought. I wish I could focus only on how terrifying this boat is without feeling guilty that I'm making him be near me. Back when we were kids, none of this was an issue. And I want that again.

The boat starts moving when I'm not prepared for it. It's a sudden jerk that nearly topples me over.

Nate steadies me with an arm around my shoulders. "I've got you," he says.

"Thanks." I force a smile before I look back out at the water. His arm slips from my shoulders, just like I knew it would.

Everyone else seems so comfortable being on this thing. Too many eyes are gazing at the water with wonder, and I don't understand the appeal of it.

I can still feel what it was like to go under. My limbs flailed and I breathed in water when I shouldn't have. My chest burns as I picture it.

And here I am. Near it again.

A hand closes over mine. At first, I go to yank it away, but then my brain catches up. It's familiar.

"Take a breath." Nate's voice is soft.

Slowly, I turn, unable to believe he's actually touching me. But it *is* his hand, and it stays there, even when I expect him to pull back.

"You're still tense as hell, berry. You'll hurt yourself if you keep this up."

Right. He wants me to breathe and loosen up. It feels impossible, but the way his face contorts into a frown that's so unnatural to him makes me want to try.

I force myself to let go. My hands go lax, and I realize I've pressed my nails into my palms hard enough that they hurt. My muscles nearly cry with relief.

"Sorry," I say. "I just can't wait to be on land."

"We're almost there. It's close." It doesn't seem close enough at all, and as I look at the water behind him, my grip on him tightens. "Hey," he says softly. "You were doing good. Don't ruin it now."

I nod. Any second now, he'll pull away and the cycle will start again. I know he can't tolerate this for long.

Instead, his hand stays. He's a lifeline. There're only a few minutes left in the ride, but when I tense up again, he tells me that I'm okay. I need his words to survive.

Finally, we come to a long, wooden dock that stretches to the island. I nearly jump up, eager to get off the boat. There's a second where I freeze up, but Nate gets off first and he helps me step over the water.

"Thank fuck," I mutter. "Would it be weird if I kissed the dock?"

He laughs. "How good is your immune system? You already exposed yourself earlier to the deck. Who knows what's been on this dock too."

I wince at the thought. "Okay, maybe not. But I'm glad that's over. Thank you for . . . you know."

Nate is back at his usual distance, but he nods as if it were nothing.

And I already want more.

I force the thought away. If I made it on that tiny boat, I'm enjoying this damn island. I'm not thinking about Nate or the fact he doesn't like to be touched anymore.

"Botanical gardens," I say as I turn to him. "That's where we're going, right?"

"Yes. Our car's waiting."

I nod, knowing my delay back on the ship didn't help our timing, and he leads me to a tiny cab that's idling. As we take off, I watch the sights. Many of our shipmates are shopping with local vendors or getting on a bus for their tours.

After our experience the day before, I'm glad to not be doing that.

The drive is longer than I expect. We have all day on the island, so I know we have plenty of time, but this is an excursion that would take up all of it. Nate knew that, and he was willing to walk through a garden with me rather than stay on the beach.

And I've been worried about what I don't have with him.

This is why we need to be on the mainland. I can think

straight. He's one of the best friends I have. So what if he doesn't want to touch me? That's not a requirement for friendship.

I feel more like myself when we're dropped off. Not even the sight of the water through the car window is enough to dispel it.

"I call paying!" I announce. Nate loses time because he's in the middle of saying goodbye to the driver when I run inside.

I slap my card down in front of the poor woman running the ticket counter before he catches up. "Too slow," I say with a smirk.

"I thought you were still traumatized by the boat. My mistake."

"I'm on land now. You've got your best friend back."

"I'll remember that." He huffs. Once we have our tickets, we enter the gardens.

I didn't realize how much I missed greenery until it's in front of me. Everything is lush around us. Palm trees stretch toward the sky and all kinds of island plants sprout from the ground. The air is hot, but there's plenty of shade.

"Wow," I say. "This is gorgeous."

"And so much slower than the beaches," Nate adds. "I don't think many of the tourists from the ship are willing to venture this far."

"So, that was your plan, huh?"

"We've been surrounded by people a little too much," he replies. I can't disagree with him. I much prefer the sound of birds in the distance to the white noise of the ship.

I'm able to remember Mom wants pictures of all the adventures we're on, so I make sure to get a few of the new plants and animals around us. The gardens are beautiful, and I know I'll have plenty to show her. We go over wooden bridges and see massive floral arrangements.

There are a few people here, most of them couples who are taking pictures together. Even I can admit that everything feels romantic in a way it shouldn't. Rob always went on the hunt for the best places in town, and if I could've gotten him here, he would have used it for some kind of sappy confession.

I wait for Nate to crack a joke about it like he always does. The tension I'm determined to ignore is waiting at the edges of my consciousness, and I can't tell if it's because of Rob or if it's the way something feels like it's missing from this walk.

Finally, we come to the most extravagant part. The arch above us is covered in purple flowers. The air smells sweet. Ahead of us, couples are taking adorable shots with it as the backdrop.

I watch, an uncomfortable feeling settling in my chest at the sight. At first, I think it's because I know I won't have those sorts of moments anymore, not after I dumped Rob.

But it's something else. Something I can't name.

Instead, I walk toward it. "Mom would love this," I say. I turn my phone on me, eager to get one photo of myself. The purple flower glasses look cute when I have them on, but my hair is a mess from the wind of the island, baby hairs going everywhere. I'm tempted to tamp them down, but a hand appears behind me, forming rabbit ears.

I still snap the photo before rolling my eyes.

"If you're gonna photobomb, then at least be *in* the photo."

"Hey, I only go where I'm invit—" He's cut off when I grab him by the collar of his light blue shirt and yank him into the frame.

"Consider this your invitation. Smile!" He laughs right when I take the photo. His face is full of fondness, an expression I've missed. "There we go. One of us both. She'll leave me alone now."

"Us," he reminds. "The last thing we want is for her to ask if we fought."

He shakes his head and walks off. I follow, but bring the photo up on my phone.

I *love* the smile he has here. It's wide, and I can see the goofy expression he always shares with me. It's something I don't see with anyone else.

"Berry?" he calls back. "You coming?"

"Y-yeah, sorry." I jog to catch up, locking my phone.

"What's got you so distracted?"

You, I want to say. *I keep thinking about you.*

But that's not what friends say.

Instead, I only shrug and ask if we have a car to get back to port.

THERE'S a line to get on the boat back to the cruise ship.

"Here we go again," I mutter.

"Feeling nervous?" Nate asks.

"Oh, you know me. I *love* standing over water while waiting in line to get on a tiny boat. My favorite."

Nate's eyes go to my hand, but he doesn't reach out for it. "Let me know if you need me."

I hope not to need him.

But I probably will.

People pack in together way too tightly. I can tell most of them are eager to be back on the boat, and some have no issues cutting in line. A few times I get shoved, but I'm determined not to reach for Nate's hand, even as a few people get in between us. I should call out for him, but he seems to hate being close to me so much that I don't want to make him miserable.

I'm probably safe in the sea of people, and I can't see the water as well since I'm short. I keep my eyes on the transporting boat, determined to make it through this.

And that's when it all goes wrong.

"Hang on!" someone calls just before the crowd lurches. "I gotta catch up to my wife! She's way ahead of me!"

Someone pushes my back and I lose my footing. I fall right in between two people who are at the edge of the dock. We're near the boat, just where the water gets deeper. There's nothing there to catch my feet as I tumble, feeling like I'm in free fall for all of a second.

And then there's water *everywhere*.

It stings my eyes and gets into my mouth. There's no way to see, and both the water and my fear are choking me. I have no idea which way is up and which way is down. Panic claws at my throat and I don't know what to do. My feet and arms are useless as I flail around, desperately trying to get to the surface.

But just as quickly as I fell into the water, I'm out of it. I'm pulled against a strong body, their hand curling around my waist as I suck in air gratefully.

I'm a mess of coughs as I try to clear my lungs. My hands lock around whoever was brave enough to save me, and I know I won't be letting go any time soon.

"I've got you," a familiar voice says. It's meant to be calming, but I can hear the tightness in it. "You're not going back under."

It's Nate. Of course it's Nate. He had to have been nearly at the boat, but the second he heard me fall, he came back for me.

All I can do is hold onto him as I try to catch my breath. My arms wind around his neck as I let him get us to the edge of the dock.

"Take her first," I hear Nate say, and suddenly, I'm being pulled. I make a noise, trying to keep Nate with me, but the arms grabbing me are too strong, and I'm out of the water and on the dock a moment later.

Nate is hoisted up next, and I'm reaching for him before I can think twice about it. Instead of flinching away, I'm the first one he runs to.

His hands are on my face, rubbing my cheeks as he checks me over. "Are you okay?" he asks.

I don't know how to answer. My body is hopped-up on energy I didn't know I had. My eyes hurt. I can't catch my breath.

And I also can't let go of Nate.

"Are you on the cruise?" someone asks. A crowd has formed around us. "There's a nurse's station on board."

"We are," Nate says. "That's where we're going."

I yelp as he hoists me up, but I don't mind.

The ride to the medic is a blur. I can't panic about the boat because all of my energy was used when I was underwater. Nate hovers like a mother hen. Dimly, I wonder if I should fall into water more often.

"What happened?" the nurse asks.

"She fell off the dock. She may have inhaled some water. Some idiot ran right into her."

My eyes widen at the sound of his voice. Nate doesn't get angry.

Until now, I guess.

The nurse turns to me. "What a day. Is all that true?"

Slowly, I nod. "I think I'm fine. Unless I'm in some form of shock."

"It can happen. Let's make sure your breathing is okay and check for anything else." She gives me a smile. "Luckily you had someone there to get you out."

I glance at Nate. "Well, he said he would be there to save me."

"Always will."

The words fill me with a warmth that chases away the last bits of fear.

After looking me over, the nurse gives me a clean bill of health and says I can leave at any time.

My fists have been clenched. I know that the feeling of water invading my nose is going to haunt me, and he's going to witness every bit of it.

But the second we're alone, Nate slumps.

"Fuck, that was terrifying." He shakes his head. "I can't even imagine what it was like for you."

"Yeah, it wasn't my favorite way to spend an afternoon."

"God, when I heard you fall, I—" His eyes close. Then he does the last thing I expect.

He pulls me into a hug.

I'm pressed against his chest and he's got me in a tight grip. I don't think about what could come of this with my newfound feelings. I just know he's *here* and he's the only thing I need.

My arms wrap around him and I hold him as tight as he's holding me. I have no idea how long he'll tolerate this, but I'll steal all the seconds I can.

It ends too soon.

Nate pulls away, and I expect to find the usual distance. But instead, he hovers just away from me, his hands on my shoulders.

"Talk to me," he says. "How are you feeling? Are you okay?"

I take it all in. "I'm cold and I smell. I *still* can't swim and might have sunken into that nasty water . . ."

Nate lets out a harsh breath. "I wouldn't let that happen to you."

"I know. Thank you."

"Still, maybe I shouldn't have pushed you to come on this cruise."

I frown. "What? Why?"

"You've been miserable this entire time, and then you got pushed into the damn water by an idiot." He shakes his head.

"*I* was the one who originally planned this whole thing. And you were right. We need this time together. That wasn't fun, I'll admit. But it didn't ruin anything."

"You just had to relive your biggest fear and it didn't ruin anything?" He raises an eyebrow. "Are you sure about that?"

I am. I know it immediately. Falling into the water doesn't erase the moment in the ruins from the day before, where we simply existed in each other's space, or the photo I now have that I want to print out and put on my wall.

But if anyone had asked me a few months ago, I would have said falling into the water would've ruined anything.

I was a different person then. Hell, just a week ago I was. That version of me hadn't dumped Rob, hadn't gotten on a boat with Nate.

I always thought fear ruled me, but I'd just fallen in the water. I'd lived.

What else could I do?

"I think I am. But I'll feel even better when I have a shower."

He looks down at me and then himself. "Yeah, we're both really gross right now. Who knows what was in that water anyway?"

chapter fifteen

IT TAKES me way too long to shower away all the grime from the day. It doesn't help that the water pressure is terrible and that the shower is tiny. When I'm done, I'm huffing and annoyed, but I tell Nate it's his turn and flop onto the bed.

He lingers. "You're not gonna take a peek at me, are you?"

"No. I'm staying right here."

"Are you still okay?"

I mostly am, but when I recall the terror of having fallen in, it doesn't feel great.

"I'll survive while you shower. Then I might need you again."

"Got it," he says. "I'll make it quick."

"Quick but thorough! I can now say for certain that ocean water sucks."

I hear him laugh as the water turns on. I can't hide my smile as I open my newly cleaned phone. I'd hastily washed it in the sink, thanking my lucky stars that it was water resistant. It didn't take any damage in the fall, and I need the distraction so I don't turn around and look at Nate in the mirror.

I send Mom a few photos from the trip, letting her know we're having fun and leaving out my adventure in the water. Then I scroll social media until my eyes shut.

The second they do, I'm in the water again. I can't move, I can't breathe—

I jerk awake, trying to catch my breath.

"Maisie?" Nate's voice is soft. I turn to see that he's done with his shower and is fully dressed.

"S-sorry. Must not be as over it as I thought." I shake my head and sit up. "How was your shower?"

"It was serviceable," he says with a half smile. "I'm more worried about you, though. You saw it again, didn't you?"

I wince, but know this isn't the first time. When we were eleven, I pushed myself to go to the pool with him. I dipped one foot into the water, panicked, and had nightmares for weeks. "Yeah. Just like last time."

"Has it happened more on the trip?"

I shake my head. "No. I think it's being *in* the water that starts it."

"What helped last time? You had one nightmare, but I can't remember if you had any more."

The memories are fuzzy at best, so I don't blame him for not remembering what happened.

But I do. And I doubt it'll happen.

"Don't worry about it." I wave my hand, knowing better than to even try to lie to him. "It'll go away."

Nate gives me a flat look. "Did you just tell *me*, of all people, not to worry about you?"

The words make my heart skip a beat. He means it in a friendly way, but it feels like more. "Yes, I did."

"Not happening. You know what'll help. You just don't wanna ask for it." His eyes narrow as he walks to the bed. "What is it? Do you need me to find you a plushie? Or sing you to sleep? I've been told I have a very nice voice, you know."

Oh, I can believe it. "No, nothing like that. It's . . . Well, it's not something you'd enjoy very much. And I won't ask it of you."

His brow furrows. "What? There's not much I can't handle, berry."

I look away. "Seriously, I'll be fine."

"Tell me, or I'm calling Judy and asking her what happened."

I jerk my head to him so fast I worry I'll give myself whiplash. "You wouldn't."

"I would. Try me."

"Fine," I hiss. "It was you, okay?"

"Wait, me? What did I do?"

"You spent the night, just like you usually did, but it was quiet because you felt so bad about taking me to the pool. I woke up with a nightmare and you . . ." My cheeks are on fire as I say it. "You crawled into bed with me and stayed there."

"O-oh."

"Mom and Dad had a rule about that. You could be in my room but not in the bed. That was the first time we broke that rule."

And it wouldn't be the last. We'd break it all the time.

My body aches at the memory. Just like when we hugged, I didn't know how much I was missing. All of those times of him holding me as I fell asleep, I never imagined there would be a last time.

Nate is still staring at me, brow pinched as he thinks about it too. I know what he's going to offer, so I shake my head.

"Anyway, we aren't those little kids anymore. I'll be fine." I turn to my side, rolling over to look out the window. I'm sure looking at the ocean after falling into it isn't going to help my dreams, but it's better than facing Nate after what I've admitted.

Then the bed dips with weight.

"What?" I turn to see Nate lying down.

"Come here," is all he says. I stare, waiting for him to flinch or move away. When he doesn't, all I feel is *relief*. I nearly scramble to get into his arms, and it feels like coming home.

Nate lets out a long breath, and I wonder if he'll tense up as I make his shoulder my pillow. Instead, his arms wrap around me, pulling me into his side.

If I thought his hugs were good, cuddling with him is even better. He's everywhere and I don't want to leave. My leg hikes up on his and I can't resist the happy sigh that escapes me as I sink into him.

"Thank you," I say. "I needed this."

I expect him to crack a joke, which is what he would do any other time. Instead, I feel him sigh, and I'm pressed tighter into his chest.

It feels like my heart could explode.

"Get some sleep," he says softly. "You need it."

As I drift off, I know I will. This is what I've been missing for . . . years.

And I have it back.

When I wake up, I'm being drowned in the best way.

Nate must have turned to his side at some point during the night. My back is pressed tightly to his chest, and he's curled around me like a comma. There's never been a doubt in my mind that he cares for me, but this really puts it into perspective.

For once, I feel well rested. I didn't have a single bad dream while wrapped up in Nate's arms. It seems like what worked all of those years ago still works to this day.

I'm tempted to get out of bed and go get him a coffee as a thank-you for what he did for me the night before. But as I try to move away from him, he grumbles in his sleep and pulls me closer. His hips were slightly angled away from me just moments ago.

Now every single inch of us is pressed together, and I can feel something against my ass.

Something *very* hard.

Immediately, it feels like I'm back in that pool again, watching Nate step out as I realize my body wants his. I didn't think I would ever consider the idea of sex for a long time after Rob, yet here I am.

It's bad and it's wrong, but my body heats up. My brain nearly goes offline, and I'm tempted to trace the outline of his cock. To wake him up with a completely different sort of thank-you.

From what I'm feeling, it'll be a treat for us both.

But my logic hangs on by a thread and I stay still while I figure out what to do. Luckily, I don't have to do anything because Nate wakes up. At first, his hands rub up and down my side, and I'm starting to wonder if I have a fever. Then he tears away from me like I'm on fire.

My eyes slam shut and I feign sleep. There's no *way* I can face him, not after what I felt.

"Shit," he mutters. "I knew I shouldn't have . . ." He trails off and goes to the bathroom.

I knew I shouldn't have? Shouldn't have what? Slept in the same bed as me?

Slowly, I sit up, my body growing cold. The night before, I tried to catch any signs of discomfort from Nate about our position, and I hadn't caught a thing. Had I been wrong?

Yes, feeling his hardness was awkward, but it wasn't the end of the world. Men get boners. They're rarely sexual first thing in the morning. It was very possible it had nothing to do with me. It was simply friction.

The thought didn't make me feel any better.

Maybe I had pushed him too hard. Yesterday was scary, but that's no excuse for me putting him in a position where he's uncomfortable. With a sigh, I wait for him to come out of the bathroom. I purposely don't look at the mirror, giving him as much privacy as I can.

Ten minutes later, he walks out.

"Maisie," he says. "You're up."

Me faking sleep must have worked. I know it's a good idea for us to talk about it, but the idea of what he could say is terrifying. I want to get better about facing my fears, but ruining things between us might be my biggest one.

"I am. Hopefully last night wasn't too miserable for you."

"It was . . . something. It took me a bit to get to sleep."

We both know it took no time at all for me to fall asleep. I'd let myself be selfish by asking him to stay.

I shouldn't have.

"Thank you," I say. "No more nightmares. So that worked."

"Good."

My jaw tightens as I realize that things are now awkward between us. Again. I wish I'd never brought up what worked all those years ago.

Clearing my throat, I stand. "I'm gonna get changed and then I'll get us both some coffee. I think we need it."

"I can come with you."

I shake my head. "You obviously got less sleep than I did. It's the least I can do."

I brush by him a little closer than I would have the day before. He takes a healthy step away from me. That's when I know we're back to where we were yesterday. The whole cuddling business was a one-time thing, just like saving me from the water was.

My disappointment stays off of my face as I grab my last pair of longer shorts and a shirt. It only shows when I'm in the bathroom. I give myself five seconds to feel it, and then I put my clothes on and walk out of the room.

Nate lets me.

chapter sixteen

WHILE GETTING COFFEE, I try my best not to agonize about the way Nate talked about sleeping next to me. The closer we get, the more uncomfortable he becomes.

And it's killing me.

I'm still in a bad mood when I get two to-go cups and head back up to the room. When I get there, Nate is not only dressed, but is in the hallway talking to Trixie and Aaron.

No sign of the discomfort is on his face. At least he's moved past it.

"Coffee delivery," I say as I walk up.

"Hi!" Trixie greets me. "We were just talking to Nate about our plans. Are you excited about the port today?"

I haven't even thought about it.

"Yeah," I reply. "Which one is it again?"

"Montego Bay," Aaron says. "It's got the clearest water. I was seeing if Nate wanted to go snorkeling with us, but he mentioned you two have other plans."

"Boo," Trixie says. "We'd love to have you join us, but Nate mentioned water isn't your favorite thing or something."

"Which is weird because we're on water."

155

"Right," I say. "I don't always make sense, but no need for Nate to miss out on something like that. You should go."

"What?" he asks. "But—"

"I'm gonna hang out here," I reply. "Catch up on some sleep."

Nate frowns. "I can still hang out with you."

"I'm good. Really. Some time alone would do me good. Have fun." I take my coffee and turn on my heel to go into the room.

He follows me. "Maisie, what the hell?"

"What? You should go with them."

"I said I was spending this time with you."

"I don't need to be around anyone right now," I say. And it's mostly true. I feel raw over how we woke up, but I don't want to fight. "Yesterday was . . . bad. I need time to myself. So, please go have fun. You like Aaron and Trixie."

"You really need time away?"

I make myself nod. "Yeah. It'll be good."

Nate's frown deepens and I don't understand why. He should *want* this space away from me.

"Fine. Just stay in contact."

"Will do. Now go catch up with them." I open the door for him to go and only let my shoulders slump when I'm alone.

It's for the best. By the time he's back, I'll have my head on straight.

I try to sit on the bed and pull out my Kindle, but everything in this room is a reminder of how I woke up. When I have to reread the same page for the fourth time, I groan and decide to leave.

THE SPA IS open even though we're at port, and after still struggling to read, I waste no time going inside.

I'm a creature of habit, so I get the same package I did the last time I was here. As I get a massage and go into the sauna, I wait for the moment that I forget about Nate.

It doesn't come.

Frustration blooms within me as I sit in the warm air. I'm tempted to go back to the room and sleep it off when I discover I'm not the only creature of habit on the boat.

"Okay, this is getting weird." Scarlett puts her hand on her hip. "Are you following me?"

"Not intentionally."

"I'm surprised you're not out on an excursion," she says. "Or that your friend isn't here."

I shrug. "He can't really be here. And he's out with some friends."

"You sound happy about that."

"I'm the one who sent him," I say. "I'm fine with it."

Scarlett hums and sits next to me. I know she's having thoughts, ones I probably don't want to know, and I try to keep from asking.

"Did you hear that someone fell off the dock yesterday?"

I freeze. I hoped she would change the subject, but she came to the *worst* possible topic to discuss.

"Uh, yeah. I definitely did, considering it was me."

Her jaw drops. "What? It was you?"

"Yep. Another trauma to add to the list."

"I heard someone had to rescue you."

"That was Nate."

"Oh my God. Was it as heroic as people said it was? I heard he dove in after you and everything."

"I was trying not to drown, so I have no idea."

"Can you not swim or something?"

I grimace. "Uh, no. I can't. I'm terrified of water, actually."

"Hang on a second." Scarlett blinks at me. "You're scared of water and you're on an island cruise?"

"Yeah. Not my finest choice ever. This whole thing was for my ex and I regretted it the second we weren't together. Nate promised me he would make sure I was safe, which is why I came. He did his part."

"He really did. So, when did this fear of water start?"

"I was a kid. I almost drowned in a pool. Probably the typical way to develop a fear."

"You'd be surprised," she says. "Some people just have an innate fear of things. I can't believe you're even here, to be honest. Being afraid of something and facing it? I usually have to push my patients for it."

"I'm not facing anything."

"Are you not scared at all?"

"I am."

"Then you're working on it." She smiles. "Which is more than most people do."

"There's no work. I'm just scared every time I step on a dock. God, it'll probably be worse now." I sigh. "Great."

"Fear doesn't mean you're doing anything wrong."

"I'm pretty sure that's exactly what it means."

Scarlett twists her lips. "Do you take your fear as a warning, Maisie?" Her voice is deeper now, and I wonder if this is how she sounds when she's with a patient.

"That's what it means, right? It's to protect us."

"Historically, yes. But these days, it sometimes spirals out of hand. Our brains want to protect us from things that are perfectly normal to experience. Like water."

"I can't swim," I remind her. "I have a real reason to be afraid of water."

"Absolutely, but you could learn. Water might pose a risk, but it's not always dangerous if you learn how to handle it."

"There's no way I can learn how to handle water." I shake my head. "I just can't."

"I'm not saying you have to. But other than this cruise, do you avoid the water?"

"Like the plague."

"Is there anything else you avoid when you're scared?" she asks.

Her words slice right through me. There's a lot I've avoided. My issues with Nate. My issues with Rob. I couldn't even *face* Rob after I dumped him.

"A-are you sure you're not gonna bill me? This seems like a therapy session."

She blinks, her cheeks coloring. "Oh, sorry. I don't mean to pry into your life. I kinda went on autopilot there."

"No, it's okay. I don't think you're wrong. It's just hard to hear."

"Still, consent is important in therapy. When people come to me with issues and sit in my office, that's at least more of an agreement than I've gotten from you. I really don't mean to go into therapist mode."

"My problems are just irresistible, huh?" I ask.

"A little, but I'll leave you alone now." She turns away from me and the conversation ends.

My mind still circles on what she said, though. Despite me wanting to move on, I can still remember how awful it felt to be in the water. I can remember the helplessness I had as a result of me never going near it. I hate to even think about going back, but avoiding the water like I have my entire life put me in danger.

I'm not sure what would've happened if Nate hadn't pulled me out.

Nate isn't always going to be around me. Hell, I'm pretty sure he doesn't even want to be. So, I need to know how to save myself should I ever be in that kind of position again. I've spent my life avoiding the things that terrify me.

But am I any better for it?

"Scarlett," I say quietly. "Should I be facing my fears?"

Her eyebrows raise. "Do you want to?"

"I don't know. But avoiding them clearly hasn't gotten me anywhere. And I mean that with . . . a lot of things in my life."

"Like what?"

"Like my ex," I say. "I didn't confront him. I let things go when I should've thought about it. And now I feel like I wasted a decade of my life. I don't want that."

"Then you could try facing something. Try getting past it."

I consider it. "Maybe I should try to learn to swim."

"Oh, wow. You're going for that one." She laughs. "Is that the easiest one?"

"All of them are bad. But I'm on a boat with a ton of pools. It's like fate wants me to deal with this one. And Nate knows how to swim. He'd love to teach me."

"Do you feel safe enough around Nate to face a fear with him?"

"Yes," I say immediately. "He's the only one I could do this with."

"Interesting."

Glancing over at Scarlett, there's a smile on her face. It's *the* smile, the one Trixie had.

"Please, no. Not you too."

"Do you know how you two look?"

I wince. "I do, but it's not like that."

"Maybe it isn't. But is that because you don't want it, or because you're scared?"

I shake my head. "Scarlett, we've always been friends. That's what we'll always be."

"You don't only have friendly feelings," she says. "I was there when you realized it."

"I'm over that."

She rolls her eyes. "You are *not*. Look at me right now and say you feel nothing."

I don't even try. I know I'm lying.

"He doesn't feel the same way," I reply. "I know that."

"And how do you know that?"

I think about this morning and how upset he was waking up

with me, and the way he slips and lets me touch him, but it makes him tense every time. "There're a lot of signs. And we're supposed to be using this trip as time together. I keep ruining it with these thoughts."

"He's really important to you, isn't he?"

"*So* important."

She pauses, and I wonder if she's about to do the thing that everyone does—tell me to get over it.

"Then I get it."

I blink. "Really? That's all you're gonna push?"

"Nothing good comes from forcing someone to see what you want them to see. And you do know about your feelings. That's the first step, and the hardest one. There's only one thing *to* do."

"And what's that?"

"Not be dense to what he feels."

"There's no way I could be. He's making it clear."

Scarlett purposefully keeps her face level. "You know him best." I have a feeling she sees it a different way, but she's wrong. There's no way he thinks anything else. "So, you're facing your fear of water." She changes the topic with ease. "Think you'll be going in?"

"No idea. I don't think I can without a swimsuit."

"Well, we *are* at a port that's known to have shops."

"Really? But I'd have to go on the dock and then deal with people."

Scarlett laughs and sits up. "Maisie, I'm inviting you to go shopping with me. If you don't want to, fine. But at least let me down gently."

"Oh," I say as my cheeks heat. "You know what? That would be nice. But we'll have to go slow. I might freak out."

She laughs. "Good thing I'm a trained professional. I won't judge you. As long as you don't judge me for how much money I'm about to blow."

GETTING off the boat isn't fun, but it's not terrible. I find myself missing Nate, but Scarlett is nice enough about it and holds my hand without immediately letting it go.

We're able to walk to all the local shops and find one that's dedicated to swimsuits. The second we step inside and get to a fitting room, she goes wild. It gets hard to see her through all the swimsuits she has piled on my arms.

"You do know I only need one, right?"

"Oh, my young padawan, you're new to shopping for a swimsuit. It's like a war. You have to find the needle in a haystack."

"Did you just reference *Star Wars*?" I ask with a laugh.

"Hot people can be nerds too. Let me guess, you and Nate love it?"

"Nate does. So does my other friend, Quinn. I don't get the hype."

"Excuse me?" She raises an eyebrow.

"How about we pretend I didn't say that. I can't handle another lecture about *Star Wars*. Ever."

"I should be on Nate's side here," Scarlett mutters. "At least you're cute."

My answer is cut off by her tossing another one at me. "I think my arms are gonna fall off," I complain.

She sighs. "Fine. But this might not be enough."

"We have nearly everything in the whole store."

"I stand by my statement. Now, to the fitting room. And keep your underwear on. There may have been other people's coochies in these."

I nearly trip over my own feet. Nate and I don't talk about this, and Quinn's always been uncomfortable with me discussing it since I've been with her brother.

"Right. No coochie sharing. Got it."

"Not with strangers, at least." She smiles before she pushes me into the dressing room. I have to take a moment to gain my bearings.

Once I pull the first one on, I see why she got a ton. "Are they supposed to be this . . . tight?" I ask.

"Let me see," she says and I open the door. "Oh, wow. Look at those boobs."

I shift awkwardly. "They're practically falling out."

"Yeah, and not in the sexy way. It needs to be tight, but not too tight. This isn't the one."

I sigh. "Great."

"Chin up, my dear. This is a battle we all have to have eventually."

"But you look so hot all the time. Is there anything that looks unflattering on you?"

"Oh yes." She says it immediately. "So many things. I just know how to find what works."

I wind up going through half the pile and don't like any of them. Scarlett wants to see each one. She never outright says I look bad, just that I need to find something that complements me better.

It's nice. It makes me wish she lived in Nashville so I could spend more time with her.

Eventually, I pull on an orange bikini that I think is more of a threat than an option. It's barely a swimsuit, and half of my ass hangs out. The only thing saving me is keeping my nude underwear on.

"This one's a no," I say immediately.

"Wait, I wanna see!" she says.

"It doesn't fit right."

"That hasn't stopped you before. Come on. I won't say anything bad."

With a cringe, I slowly open the door, stepping into her appraising gaze.

Way too much of my skin is on display, and as she stares at me, I wonder if she's seeing the cellulite on my legs or the way that the skin and fat jiggle as I move. That doesn't even include the way my entire top half is nearly hanging out.

This would be a thing that Rob would immediately turn down.

But Scarlett sucks in air. "You think this doesn't fit properly?" she asks. "Girl, you're gorgeous."

"I'm not. This is . . . way too much skin showing."

"There's no right way to wear anything. If you want something more modest, that's totally fine. I do think it looks great, though. Especially if you do this." She reaches up and takes my hair clip out. When my hair tumbles down, I no longer see the version of Maisie I've been. I see someone else.

"I used to dress differently," I say. "I never had a swimsuit, but I wore crop tops and short things a lot when I was in college."

"What made you stop?"

I take in a breath and then let it out. "Rob said I needed to cover up. I needed to look grown up."

Scarlett frowns. "I'm sorry. He told you to cover up?"

"Yeah. He pointed out things that made me want to over time. I want to think I look good, but when I look at myself, I'm remembering all the things he made me notice."

"First off, fuck your ex."

"You're a therapist. Should you be saying that?"

"I'm off work right now. Trust me, I think it often. Usually about men. Your partner gets no say in what you wear. *You* do. And making comments on your body? Absolutely not."

"You're right."

"What does Nate think?" she asks.

"I don't talk to him about this kind of stuff."

"But does he ever make any comments like that?"

"Oh, God no. He would never."

Scarlett raises her brow and I realize she led me right to her point.

"I didn't think about all of it. Not logically, at least. I avoided it."

"Sometimes the body knows what the mind doesn't, even if you're afraid. Don't ever doubt the power of denial. We all have it every now and again."

"At least I'm not a total idiot."

"You're not. And you're out of that relationship. No one will make a comment like that again, and if they do, punch them in the face."

"You're advocating for violence?"

"Absolutely." She laughs. "Especially to idiots. Now—" She leads me to the mirror. "What does Maisie think about this outfit?"

I look away from all the things that Rob would've pointed out. I can see the slight olive tone of my skin, pale after being hidden for so long. I may be shorter, but I like the curve of my hips and the way my boobs look because of the underwire the bikini has.

"I . . . like it. Even if I'm nervous."

"There you go," Scarlett says. "So, we're getting this."

"Which means we're done, right?" I don't like the idea of cutting this off here, but we accomplished what we came for.

"Absolutely not. I saw some dresses at the shop next door we *both* need to try on."

I perk up immediately. "That sounds fun. But I don't need a dress."

"Every lady needs a hot dress. You included."

"Will we make it back to port in time?"

She pulls out her phone. "Close enough. But we have no time to waste. Let's go."

chapter seventeen

WE BARELY GET BACK on the ship in time. The second my phone connects to the Wi-Fi, I have multiple texts from Nate asking if I'm okay. I curse when I see them and immediately run back to the room, dragging my bags with me.

Nate's on me from the second I open the door. "Maisie, what the hell?" he asks. "Where have you been?"

"I may have gotten off the boat for a little bit."

He blinks and finally notices that I have bags with me. "Seriously? You said you would be here." His voice carries a hurt that stabs me like a knife.

"I did say that. But then I ran into Scarlett in the spa and had a very good conversation about life, and then we decided to go shopping."

"In the spa?" he asks. "I thought you needed time alone. Or was that just time alone from me?"

"No!" I say immediately. "I thought time alone would help, and then it didn't, so I went to the spa. Which is mostly alone. Running into Scarlett was a total accident."

Nate's jaw tics and he speaks slowly. "And throughout all of that, you never sent me a text?"

"I didn't think about it. And you were busy." The excuse sounds weak to my own ears. It hits me that we're fighting and I have *no* idea what to do. The only experience I have with fighting is with Rob.

"Right," Nate says. "So you not only told me you'd keep in contact, but you went onto the same island as me and didn't consider I might want to come? Really nice, Maisie. I love that."

Tears immediately spring into my eyes. My stomach is in my ass. I've never forgotten him like this before. "Nate, I'm *so* sorry. There was really no plan for any of this, and I should've stopped for a moment and considered you."

It comes from the heart and I do mean it. But when people are mad, apologies take a while. I fully expect Nate to snap or tell me he's too mad to talk and to walk away from me to calm down.

But at my words, he takes a deep breath and his shoulders loosen.

"I was really worried about you, berry. Can you please try to communicate next time?"

I blink. That's it? We're having a fight and he's not continuing it? He's simply asking me to do something different if it happens again?

If only Scarlett were stalking us. I'd love to get her opinion on this.

"Of course," I say. "Seriously, I'll be better. That was on me, and I wasn't thinking clearly. She offered for me to try something . . . scary with her, and I was more focused on that."

"Something scary? Like go on the dock?"

"That, and shopping for something for a new goal of mine." My hands tighten. "But you're still mad at me, so we can talk about it later—"

Nate holds his hand up, which makes me shut my mouth. "I don't stay mad long. Not at you."

"You should. I feel terrible about it."

"Which means you probably won't do it again." He gives me half a smile. "You'd never hurt me intentionally."

"Hopefully not unintentionally either," I add. "I would feel awful if I did."

He pauses for a moment, eyes going distant as he thinks about it. "That . . . is a part of life, berry."

"Wait, have I? When? What did I do?"

He shakes his head. "It's nothing you can control. Trust me, it's not."

"But—"

"All I ask is that you please don't avoid me. I can't take that."

I nod immediately. "I won't. I promise. And what I want to do involves you anyway, so it definitely won't happen again."

"And what do you wanna do?"

"I want to learn how to swim."

Nate rears back. "What?"

"That's what Scarlett and I talked about. Water is a thing I'm gonna have to deal with. And you're not always going to be there to catch me if I fall."

"I'm a little insulted after I saved you yesterday." The tone I don't like is back.

"Not like that. I know you'll always catch me if you're around, but when I was in there, I was *helpless*. I didn't know what I was doing or how to get up."

"You were scared."

"I don't wanna drown because I'm scared," I say. "I want to be . . . brave and see if I can beat this."

He pauses. "You want to intentionally traumatize yourself to be brave?"

"Fear isn't always a bad thing, but if you hadn't saved me, I would have drowned. I'm not saying this'll be fun, but I need to know how to save myself. I can't keep avoiding things."

"Is Scarlett putting you up to this?"

"Not really. She asked me if I felt up to it, and honestly, I never will. But I can do it when you're with me. Which is why I'm asking you to help me."

"Me?"

"You're my safe person. If anyone can get me out of my head and into the water, it's you."

He considers it, but his eyebrows are pinched. "It didn't go well when we tried before."

"We were kids," I say with a shake of my head. "This time I'm choosing it."

Nate sighs. "Yeah, I see why you blacked out this afternoon and didn't text me. You're really considering this?"

"I even bought a swimsuit. I'm serious about it."

Nate's eyes widen. "I can tell."

"Please at least consider it."

"I am. But we need ground rules. This is . . . a decent idea, but I'm worried about what this is gonna do to you."

Considering the thought of facing my fear makes me want to run for the hills, I still nod. "I know. It's not gonna be pleasant for either of us. And I'm not saying that I try to conquer it immediately, just take steps to. Like getting close to the water to get used to it."

"So, going slow. That I can agree to."

"Yes!"

"*But*," he says slowly. "I don't want you to feel like you did yesterday, okay? That was . . . I can't take that again. Or the aftereffects."

The aftereffects. Like me cuddling with him.

Ouch.

I push the thought away. I don't need to spiral again when I've already messed up enough for one day. Instead, I nod. "I'll stop before I get afraid."

"You'll be afraid the whole time."

"Okay, true." I cross my arms. "What if we have a safe word? Like if it's too far, I say it and we stop."

He goes pale at the mention of a safe word, but eventually, he nods. "All right. That's also a decent idea."

"If I say the word . . ." I consider it. "Obi Wan, then we stop."

"Your safe word is a *Star Wars* character?" He shakes his head. "If Scarlett is the one who made you see the light, I'm gonna be pissed."

"She didn't, but a safe word should be something that never comes up in conversation, and I would *never* bring *Star Wars* up."

"Yeah, I know." He rolls his eyes. "But that's a good word. We'll do this."

"How tired are you?" I ask. "Because we could get started right now."

He sighs. "Snorkeling is not for the weak, but I'm alive. The panic is what got me."

"Sorry," I say again. "We can wait."

"No, let's do this. I have enough energy to spare."

I eye him. "Are you sure about that?"

He *does* look tired. I wonder how tiring snorkeling could actually be. "Today was a day, but I wanna spend time with you. And that includes helping you conquer your fear, so let's go." Finally, he smiles at me and gestures to the door.

My body nearly melts in response. I can't stand it when he's mad. I'd much rather have this side of him.

"Good. I can't believe I'm about to say this, but let's go to the pool."

～〜～

MY BRAVERY WANES the second we're on the pool deck. I can see the bottom, and the water's clear—already seemingly better than what I fell into the day before—but just the sight of it sets me on edge.

"We can turn back at any time." Nate hasn't even pulled his

shirt off yet. I have a feeling he doubts that I'll get close. "There're plenty of other things to do on the boat, you know."

"I'm doing this." I take a shaky breath. I have to force my feet to move. The pool deck is decently busy, especially since we're about to leave port.

Within a few feet, my body starts to lock up, so I stop and stare at the water.

"You're doing good." Nate's voice is soft, and I have no doubt that he's his usual distance away. With his long arms, he could easily reach me if I fell in. But I still want him closer.

No. I'm not thinking about that right now. I need to focus on my fear of the water and getting over it.

There's a nearby lounge chair, so I walk over to it and take my shoes off. When I get done with that, I slowly creep toward the edge of the pool.

I'm only at the shallow end. Even though I can see the bottom, the water looks like it could be endless. My fists tighten and my breathing speeds up. Suddenly, this seems like a terrible idea.

But being afraid doesn't mean I need to turn away. I have to remember that.

Nate's hand lands on my arm. "Obi Wan?"

"N-not yet. Let me get closer."

"This is the closest you've ever gotten to a pool since we were kids. It's a big step."

"I can do more."

"Would it help if I go with you?"

Nate's hand is still on me, and I know without a shadow of a doubt that it would. I don't want to admit that I need him because it's going to hurt when he inevitably puts distance between us again.

I give him a jerky nod and he moves from being behind me to by my side. His hand stays on my arm as I inch closer to the pool.

"Try sitting," he offers. "It's a little less scary when you're not standing over the edge."

I back up before sitting on my butt and scooching toward it. Nate's right. It's marginally less scary, but I still feel like I'm inching my way toward my own death.

I have to stop when I'm sitting cross-legged at the edge of the pool. That's more progress than I've made in many years.

"Would it make it worse if I got in?" Nate asks. He put on his swim trunks when we came out here just in case he had to dive in to save me. I knew I wouldn't be going far, so I gave the excuse that I needed to wash mine, so I'm in my normal clothes.

I shake my head in response and he finally lets go of me to hop into the water. He does it like it's natural, with no fear of what could happen. The water doesn't even come up to his hips, which makes me feel like an idiot for being so terrified of this.

Nate's nearly at eye level and his face interrupts my stare at the water.

"You good?"

While looking at him, I am. That's the power he has over me. The power I don't know how long he's had. "I'm okay. This is just a lot worse than I thought it would be."

"You've done a lot. More than I thought you'd be willing to. I'm really proud of you, berry."

I know he has his reservations about this, but I also know he'll let me do whatever I need in order to get over this. That's the thing about him. He can push, but he can also offer quiet support.

Keeping my eyes on him, I decide to go one step farther. I slowly uncurl my legs and look him in the eye as I dip my feet into the water.

"Holy shit. You good?"

"I'm fine." My voice shakes. "Freaking out, but fine."

"Look at you go."

The pride in his voice makes me tempted to continue. I like it when he has that warm tone to him. But I know I'm at my limit. Even the water being over my feet is terrifying.

It's warmer than I expect. And having my feet completely

submerged in it feels odd. I don't know how my own limbs work or how to make sure I move correctly in water. That's how I've almost drowned far too many times.

My moment of triumph is interrupted by a group of guys at the other end of the pool.

"Cannonball!" one of them yells as he launches himself into the water. Ripples erupt from where he disappears and I yank my feet out.

"Obi Wan," I say. "That was enough."

"They're rowdy," he says with a sigh. "You still did good, though."

"You could stay," I say. "You just got in."

"Surprisingly, I've had enough water for the day. Mind if I shower and then we get dinner?"

"Dinner sounds good. And I can hear about how snorkeling went."

He laughs. "That will be one hell of a story."

chapter eighteen

NATE, of course, waits until I'm mid-drink to tell me the worst part of the day.

"So, the only person who could pee on his leg was me."

I nearly shoot my water through my nose. "I'm sorry, *you*?"

"Yes."

"You peed on Aaron's leg."

"Unfortunately."

"After he got stung by a jellyfish."

"He begged me to," Nate defends. "Turns out, peeing on someone *isn't* what you're supposed to do. We got an earful from the nurse on board." He shakes his head, lips pressing together. I have to cover my mouth. I want to laugh so badly. He knows. "Don't you dare."

"It's kinda funny, though."

"Pissing on a near-stranger's leg is *not* funny."

"How hard did he beg?" I can't stop the smile now.

"Maisie," Nate warns.

"I'll stop." I still have a smile on my face. "The last thing I want to do is . . . piss you off." Nate glares. "I hear you already did that to Aaron, though."

"I hate you," he says.

My laugh escapes me at the pure misery written across his face. As I let loose, he slowly lowers his head to the table.

"Okay, okay. I'm done. You were very brave."

"Apparently, jellyfish stings rarely happen. *Rarely.* Am I cursed?"

"Maybe I'm just your good luck charm. It's too bad I'm still too new at swimming."

He sighs. "No more excursions with them. I felt like the third wheel until I had to pee on him."

"It does sound pretty bad." I let out a sigh. I do want to make it up to him then. Guilt still follows me around like a shadow. "Would you like it if I watched a *Star Wars* movie with you?"

He perks up. "I'm sorry, what?"

"I owe you for worrying you earlier. And you had to pee on someone. It's the least I can do."

"You better be serious about this, because I'm watching *Revenge of the Sith*."

I groan. "But that one's so sad."

"You owe me."

"Fine. But I'm getting ice cream first."

MY EYES GO glassy by the time Yoda is on the screen for the first time, but I keep my mouth shut.

"You're bored," he says as Padme and Anakin talk on the balcony.

"I'm fine," I say. A yawn betrays me.

He laughs. "You've done enough. We can change it."

I immediately shake my head. "I still feel bad for earlier, and you're owed one movie for it. You'll just have to deal with me being bored."

"I'm serious, Maisie."

"I am too. This isn't the first time I've suffered through Revenge of the Fifth."

"It's Sith, and you know it."

"Do I?" I tap my chin. "I guess I've forgotten things. I'll have to refresh my memory."

Nate rolls his eyes and goes back to watching the movie.

I have other reasons for not moving. For once, Nate and I are sharing a couch and he doesn't seem upset about the closeness between us. I'm nowhere near on top of him like I had to be on the plane and the bus, but it's something.

Even though this is one of Nate's favorites, the day has taken a toll on him. I can see him shift until he leans on the arm of the couch. He slouches over for just a few minutes before his breathing evens out and he's fast asleep.

We haven't even gotten to Order 66 yet.

I should take advantage of this and end the movie early. I couldn't care less about this part anyway. But I promised him I'd finish it, even if he fell asleep early.

Still, between my attention not being tied up with the movie and the subtle rocking of the ship, I'm gradually lulled to sleep. I don't mean to, but my eyes slip closed a few times as the sound of blasters firing fades into the background. Eventually, I slump over too, finding the warmest pillow I can.

Dimly, my mind tells me there will be repercussions for this.

My heart tells me it doesn't care.

WHEN I WAKE UP, I'm still on the couch. My head is still on Nate's chest, and I'm curled into a ball on top of him. He's asleep too, head tilted back on the couch, arms wrapped around me.

This is very possibly one of the best ways I've woken up in a long time.

For all of a second, Nate is relaxed. He doesn't know I'm here, and when he doesn't, he keeps me close. It feels right when it's like this.

I should pull away and give him space. He won't like this when he wakes up. He'll run the second he sees me, but I *want* this. I know it without a shadow of a doubt. It's not fair that I do, and one day, I'll put all of it in a box and be the friend he wants me to be.

But I don't know if I can today.

Nate starts to shift, and his entire body stiffens when he realizes I'm here.

"Sorry," I say as I sit up. My muscles protest, but I ignore them. "I must've dozed off."

"What the fuck?" he mutters as he rubs his eye. He immediately moves closer to the edge of the couch and away from me.

I knew he would do this. He's consistent in his desire to be away from me. But seeing it hits me *hard*.

Nate catches the second it does and he sits up, no doubt to try and make me feel better. But I don't want him to try. It's obvious that he's uncomfortable. That's not going to change. The only thing that can change is allowing myself these slipups.

"You know what?" I stand and turn away from him, determined to hide the way I feel like my insides are mush. "We should brave the smoothie place. I really need one of those right now."

"Berry, wait. I—"

I hold a hand up, which stops him. "It's okay." I take a breath. "That was a total accident. I should've let you be nice and slept on the bed. It won't happen again."

With that, I go to my suitcase to get clothes for the day. I have to re-wear a pair of my longer shorts. The ones Nate got me are tempting, but I feel too emotionally raw to even consider it. Nate goes out onto the balcony while I change, and I think I can almost handle seeing him once my loose shirt and shorts are on.

But when he walks in, he steps in front of me. "I'm sorry if I upset you by moving away."

"It's . . . fine. You have nothing to apologize for." And he really doesn't. He can't help it if he doesn't like touching people. He shouldn't have to push against it just because I'm having different feelings now. "Let's head out. We'll both feel better after eating."

I give him a smile that's almost real and then turn to the door. As we walk, I focus on keeping our usual distance as we chat about our plans for the day. I want to make more progress on the pool, and Nate seems happy to give me that.

Things almost seem normal when we have our smoothies and sit in the lounge. My heart still feels sore, but maybe I can do this.

That all shatters when we head back to the room and run into Aaron in the hallway. Our friend's leg is bandaged up, and when he spots us, I wonder if he'll be embarrassed.

Instead, he *runs* at Nate.

"There's my guy!" he says, tightly hugging my best friend. Nate goes stiff, eyes wide.

"Uh, hey." He awkwardly pats Aaron on the shoulder.

"I *so* owe you one for yesterday, man. That was so scary and you kept it together." Aaron's arms tighten. "You're a real friend."

I wait for Nate to get a mirror expression of this morning. Panic should set in at any moment, and I know the way that looks all too well. Nate considers Aaron for a long moment and then . . . stays. He doesn't look thrilled. But he doesn't look like he does when it's me touching him.

The door to Aaron's room opens and Trixie comes out; when she sees the scene, she sighs.

"Oh, Aaron." She walks to her husband and pries him off of Nate. "Sorry about that. He's clingy when sick."

"It's fine," Nate replies. "Yesterday was . . . something."

Judging by the sinking feeling in my gut, I think today will be *something* too. "I heard about what happened," I say. "I'm so sorry you got stung."

"It's so unfair." Aaron sniffs. "We were all in the water and *I'm* the one it decided to get freaky with?"

"Come on," Trixie says as she leads him away. "Let's not cry on our friends. Remember the buffet? We're heading there!"

"Yay . . ." Aaron mutters as he walks down the hall.

I want to run and hide in the room. I want to forget that Nate seems far more comfortable with Aaron than me.

But I don't.

"Is that how he acted yesterday?" I ask with a laugh.

"Yeah. He was very needy."

"Wow. Poor guy."

Nate shrugs before looking at me. "So, the pool?"

I'd honestly rather jump off a dock again, but just the thought of hurting Nate like I did the day before makes me push aside what I've just seen and smile at him.

"Yep. We're heading to the pool. What could possibly go wrong?"

chapter nineteen

T HE BEST PART about having a fear of the water is that no one has ever seen me in a swimsuit.

When I get to the pool deck and see that's about to change, I'm tempted to scrap the entirety of this idea and go back to bed.

I'm already slightly wet, since I did a quick wash of the swimsuit before I came out here and didn't have time to dry it. And my discomfort makes it even harder to take off my clothes and expose myself.

"Are you ready?"

"No." I say it immediately. "What if you get in first?"

"And leave you to do it all by yourself? Absolutely not."

It was worth a try.

"Fine," I mutter as I finally take off my shorts and tank top.

The first thing I feel is wind. It hits the skin of my stomach and legs, and I'm tempted to curl inward to avoid it.

But I refuse. I know I look good in this. I'm not chickening out now.

That's when I notice Nate's watching.

His eyes have gone wide and he's looking at every single inch of me. This isn't the fond gaze he gave me when I took my hair down. This is *hungry*, like he wants me.

My stomach flips just as he shakes himself out of it.

"Shall we?" he offers. His voice is off. It sounds breathless.

I stare at him for a second, trying to make sense of his reaction. He doesn't want to touch me . . . but he looks at me like *that*?

I'm confused.

"Berry?" he asks again. "Are we swimming today?"

"Uh, yeah. Let's do this."

My confusion is the only reason I'm able to get to the pool without panicking. This time, I move to the edge before I remember what I'm doing and how much I hate the water.

But when it starts, it takes over. I freeze almost immediately.

"How are you feeling?" Nate asks. "If you need to pull an Obi Wan, I'm sure we can find something to do."

I need to pull an Obi Wan on my whole brain at this point.

"I'm terrified. Why do people do this for fun?"

"No idea. I think humans are very prideful. They love to do things that can kill them."

I let out a shaky laugh and reach out to grip the handrail. Oh, this is going to be *terrible*.

"Go slow," he says. "There's no rush here."

My life would be so much easier if I could shove all of my fears into a box to get over them. That goes for things that aren't just the pool. But my fear makes itself known, so I pause and stand just two steps into the water.

"You okay?"

"Y-yeah." My hand tightens on the railing. "Thank God this is an adults-only cruise. I think kids would have pushed me in by now."

"What is with kids and loving pool stairs?" he asks. "It's so funny."

I force myself to laugh before I look back down at the water.

"This is way worse than I thought. It looks like the pool I—" My breath hitches as I think back on it. I can't even say it.

"Hey." His voice is soft.

"I want to do this," I remind him. "Please don't tell me to turn back."

"Okay." He grabs my hands, making my heart skip a beat. "We're gonna try something."

All I can do is rely on humor. "If you throw me in, I'll take you with me."

He shakes his head. "I'd never do that. Did I tell you about the end-of-year dodgeball match that got me yelled at by admin?"

I blink. Just what is he going for? "You didn't. Are you keeping secrets now?"

"Not intentionally. That was when wedding planning was on your mind." He shrugs. "Now's as good a time as any."

He tugs me a little farther in and I squeak. I hold onto him so tightly that it feels like I could break his hands, but he doesn't complain. "Okay, tell me about it."

"Most of the kids were stressed with finals. Actually, all of us were. Have I ever told you it's bullshit that I have to have some kind of final?"

"You have," I reply. "It's up there with the fact that you have to wake up early every day."

"Exactly," he says. "But you know how much we enjoyed dodgeball when we were kids."

"*You* enjoyed it. *I* got hit in the face and you yelled at Terrence McKay for it."

Nate rolls his eyes. "Asshole had it coming. Anyway, apparently you can do something dodgeball-esque with foam balls and different rules. The kids loved it. The administrators didn't. Wanna know what I called it?"

"What?"

"Cabbage Catch Kids."

I sputter out a laugh. "*Nate!* That is such a dad joke."

"They all thought it was so stupid. But they had fun. And no one got injured."

I can see it now. A bunch of kids throwing foam balls at each other while yelling. It brings a smile to my face.

"Has anyone told you you're a great gym teacher?"

"Most people think I'm mediocre at best."

I roll my eyes. For as much as Nate likes to keep it light, he *does* care about his job and the kids he teaches. "Well, I would've loved to have you as my teacher."

"As fun as that sounds, I prefer having you as my best friend. And if I were your teacher, I wouldn't have been able to yell at Terrence."

"True. I did enjoy that."

"Oh, and berry?" He leans in. I lick my lips, unsure of what could possibly be on his mind. "You're in the pool."

I look down and realize he's right. He's slowly been tugging me farther and farther in. I was so focused on him that I barely noticed.

"Oh my God." The fear chokes me up, but I push it away. My feet are on solid ground. I'm fine. I hate this, but I'm okay. "You're a genius."

"You love my stories from school. And you needed a distraction."

"Well, no distraction is enough to make me forget the fact that I have no fucking clue what I'm doing." I let out a sound between a laugh and a sob. "So, is this the part where you teach me how to swim so I don't die?"

"This is the part where I try. Are you ready?"

"Absolutely not. What's the first step?"

He shows me the way to move in the water. Most of the time, I feel like I'm fighting every molecule around me, and any time I move my legs or feet, I don't get anywhere. Nate has to touch me to guide me into whatever position I'm supposed to be in, but being moved in the water usually makes me cling onto him like a fool.

Luckily for me, he's a good sport about it.

"You're doing good," Nate says hours later.

"I feel like a rock. A rock that's trying to sink to the bottom of the pool, and I'm failing miserably."

"You've not sunk to the bottom of the pool once."

"But I could, at any moment."

"That brings us to our next lesson. How would you like to learn how to float?"

I narrow my eyes at him. "You mean there was a secret to floating this entire time and you didn't tell me? What is it, some trick where you take a bunch of air in your lungs or something?"

"Not like you're thinking," he says with a shake of his head. "It's where you can float on your back. You just have to position your body right and not move."

He lies back, somehow staying above the water. I stare at him, wondering how he makes it look so easy. He only floats for a moment before he sits back up.

"The trick is to keep your feet elevated and your chest up. You'll move a little bit up and down while you breathe, but it's not as hard as you think."

I grimace. "My face would be very close to the water."

"I know. Are you feeling brave enough?"

I bite my lip. *Am* I ready for this? I'm not sure.

"Stay close to me."

"Every time, berry." He gets down in the water. "Just stay relaxed."

There is not a future where I will ever be relaxed in the water, but I take a deep breath anyway.

"How do we do it?"

He shows me the movements before gently guiding me. I promise myself that I'll be okay and then slowly lean back.

I almost think I have it and that I'll be able to do this, but then water invades my ears, just like it invaded everything when I fell off the dock, and I spring up.

"Obi Wan! Obi Wan!" I flail in the water, and I'm pretty sure I'm about to go under when strong arms wrap around me.

It's like the moment I was pulled out of the water all over again. I don't have logic as I tighten my hold on Nate. I just want him close.

"Hey, it's okay. You didn't go under." His voice is soft with a tone that's like a balm soothing my erratic mind. "I caught you."

"I—sorry."

"It's fine. You stopped when it went too far. That's good."

Slowly, my mind comes back online and I realize there's way too much of my skin pressed to his. Hugging while clothed is something he's not a fan of. He has to *hate* this.

I pull away abruptly, wiping the splatter of water from my face. "I think I need a nap," I say. "And a shower. How about you have fun here while I do that?"

Nate's brow furrows. "But we're supposed to be hanging out together."

"There's not a lot of space for naps in the room. And you like being here. Just give me a few hours."

I can tell he doesn't like it, but I refuse to accept any other answer.

None of it makes sense. He wants to spend time with me, but the second I get too close, he pulls away. It's frustrating, and I don't know how to begin to parse through what's happening.

What I really need is to get the fuck away from the pool and actually rest.

Then I can handle whatever the hell is going on.

SLEEP DOESN'T FIND me and I'm annoyed at myself. Rather than clearing my mind and dropping off the face of the earth for a few hours, I doomscroll on my phone and send pictures to Mom.

I'm so frustrated, but I feel like I've won the lottery when she video calls. I need a distraction, *badly*.

"There's my favorite daughter!" Mom says.

"I'm your only daughter."

"Still! Jeff, look at Maisie!" She shows me Dad, who's doing a crossword. He gives me a glance before he returns to his puzzle.

"Huh. Your hair's down," he says.

I immediately run my fingers through it. "Uh, yeah. Vacation mode, right?"

"Looks cool."

"I think it's gorgeous!" Mom turns the phone back to her. "You've always had the best hair. And it's so long!"

"Thanks," I say. "I'm trying something new. And my scalp is feeling better."

"Are you by yourself?"

I resist the urge to wince. I don't want to think about Nate. "I am right now, but not overall. Nate's at the pool."

"I'm so glad you took him!" Mom laughs. "Are you having fun?"

"Y-yeah, of course. It's just a little awkward."

"How so?"

"You know, the honeymoon suites don't have *doors*."

Mom blinks. "No doors? Why would it have no door?"

"I told you that's what the Peeking Suite meant, Judy." Dad's voice is flat, and my face immediately heats.

"*Anyway,*" I say. "We've made it work. Even though Nate has a thing against people touching him."

Mom pauses. "Hates when people touch him? Is that a new thing?"

The pain in my chest is back, but now it's expanding. "I . . . I don't think so."

"Really?" She hums. "You know, I've never noticed it before or anything. When did this start?"

"I mean . . . it's been a while." I don't have a date for it, but the fact that I don't remember when it started tells me a lot. "Like years."

"But he hugs me at every holiday party. And he always does the awkward hug your father does."

"It's manly," Dad gripes.

I feel like I've fallen into the pool again. "Oh. Maybe he's just in a weird mood then."

"Maybe your mother just doesn't know how to take a no. She's blind to other people's emotions, you know."

"Rude." Mom huffs. "Just ask him. And tell me if I'm accidentally making him uncomfortable, please. I'd hate to keep bullying him into hugs if he doesn't wanna touch people!"

"Y-yeah. I'll ask."

"I won't take you from your trip for long. Have fun and tell Nate to call me."

I force a smile onto my face as she says her goodbyes.

But her words stick with me. I think about holidays when Mom is waiting by the door to give us all hugs. I'm usually first, but Nate is always the second one she goes for.

And Mom's right. He never jumps away from her. He didn't jump away from Aaron.

It's just me.

I go through all of our photos on my phone. Most of them are with Nate, since he goes to almost every event with my family.

In family photos, he stands next to Mom or Dad. He seems to always have an arm slung around their shoulders as if it's the most casual thing in the world. I have a few pictures of him with other people. Some are the girlfriends that he didn't last long with. And some are with Quinn.

And in every single one, he stands closer to them than he does me.

My heart feels like it's being pierced.

As I go through more and more photos, I realize that Nate doesn't have an aversion to touching most people. In fact, in all of these photos, his smile is easygoing and happy.

It's nothing like how he looks when I try to do the same thing. And as I swipe through more, going back years and years, I realize that it's a pattern. It's not that he hates touching friends, and from what I've seen, it's not like he hates touching strangers either.

He hates touching *me*.

A text comes through from Nate telling me that he's heading up. I immediately close the message, knowing I can't face him until I get it together. I have *no* idea how to handle this. I just know I can't at the moment.

I grab my bag and run out of the room, sending the fastest message to Scarlett.

I need a distraction and she mentioned dancing.

And I need to take her up on her offer. Anything is better than the realization that Nate doesn't want to touch me.

Anything.

chapter twenty

Change of plans. Found Scarlett and we're gonna hang out for a bit. Maybe it's time for you to check out the spa or something. See you later!

MY TEXT IS NOT SUBTLE at all, but it's the best I can do considering the swirl of messy emotions inside of me.

"You're serious about not talking about this?" Scarlett asks. "You're not even giving me a hint as to why you burst into my room and begged to get drunk and dance with me?"

I wince. "It's just Nate drama. I know you're tired of hearing about it."

She crosses her arms. "Are you assuming right now?"

Right. She can see through bullshit. "I just got confirmation that Nate really doesn't like me like that, okay? I need some space to process and move on before I go back to being his friend."

Scarlett's face falls. "Oh, babe, I'm so sorry."

"It's okay," I reply. "It really will be. This whole trip has me out of sorts, and hanging out with you helps. Even if we're not talking about every little thing that's going on with me."

"You know that talking about every little thing is my job, right?"

"You're on vacation," I remind her with a smirk.

"Which is the only way I'm letting you get away with this." She points at me. "But if you change your mind and need a shoulder to cry on, I can lock back in."

"Even after drinking?"

"Oh yeah. I'm flexible like that."

I laugh and follow her. One of the gathering rooms is meant for drinking and dancing, and every night, people flock to get wasted and have a fun time. I never thought I would be here, but Scarlett walks in like she owns the place, leading me right to the bar. I order something simple and try to adjust to the loud pop music playing.

The lights are low, illuminated by a disco ball and sparse colorful lights. People dance like they don't have a care in the world.

I know I need at least two more drinks before I can join them.

Scarlett has no reservations, though. She joins the dancing like she's meant to, and she looks like a natural out there. I wonder if she'll get lost in the sea of people, but she lingers at the side, like a silent invitation.

I join after my second drink.

Scarlett moves her hips easily, raising her arms as she dances to the beat. I'm not drunk enough to completely lose all inhibitions, but she grabs my hands and gently moves me with her.

"Everyone here is either drunk or too invested in their own little world. Let loose, Maisie."

She says it right when a song ends, and I glance around the crowd. True to her word, no one is looking twice at me. I can tell who's drunk and who's not, but the sober people in the crowd are too busy talking to their own friends.

I want to let go of everything and live. I *have* to.

When the next song starts, I follow Scarlett's movements. I

have no idea what I'm doing, and I probably look like a gazelle with a broken leg, but all that matters is the music. Scarlett's face brightens and she cheers me on as one song turns into two and then three.

I'm tempted to go get another drink when I see her eyes catch on someone who's near the door.

"If you see a guy, go for it!" I yell in her direction.

"Oh, no. Not for me." Her hands land on my shoulders and she turns me around. It takes me a minute to see him, but right near the door stands Nate.

I blink, trying to make sense of it. *Why* is he so worried about me? Why does he follow me wherever I go when he can't even stand to be near me?

"You should talk to him." She urges me forward. "Enough running."

I glare at her. Just the sight of him brings back all the hurt and fear that surrounds him. Instead of going right to him, I stop by the bar and get another drink, which I down immediately.

Then I go face him.

The third drink hits me harder. My head is spinning, but I feel like I can face things.

"Nate," I say. "What are you doing here?"

"What are you wearing?" he asks, eyeing me up and down. I glance at myself. I'm in the teal dress I impulse bought with Scarlett. It's not as short as her red one, but it's a spaghetti strap, and I realize I'm in less than I usually would be.

"Just something new." I shake my head and nearly topple over. Nate goes to steady me, but his hands stop before they touch me.

The sight nearly sets me off.

I was hoping drinking and dancing would make me forget all that's happened, but now it's concentrated, and my common sense is off the boat. It's just me.

And my hurt has turned into something ugly. Nate's not in the wrong. He doesn't *have* to touch me, but the way he jerks away from me like I'm on fire has festered. And I hate that it's like this. I hate that he feels this way about me.

So, I do something stupid. My hands lock around his wrists, and I finish the movement for him.

He jerks away. "What was that?"

There's a part of me deep down that hopes I imagined it all.

I didn't.

"Just go back to the room. You get a night off from me."

"What?" he asks. "Maisie, what's going on? You sent me a text saying you're going dancing with Scarlett out of nowhere when you were supposed to be napping. What the hell happened?"

"I changed my mind. I'm fine."

"Then why won't you look me in the eye?"

I know that if I do, I'll lose it. I can't put all this in a box, especially not when tipsy.

But maybe I can't when sober either.

"Don't worry about it. I'm going back in there." I crave the feeling I had before I saw Nate. I crave the person I was before I knew he had shown up.

Turning to leave, I'm ready to get back to the dance floor.

But Nate grabs my hand.

And it sets me off.

"Don't," I hiss, yanking my hand out of his. "Don't you dare touch me."

He steps back, green eyes wide. "Maisie, I—"

"You don't have to force yourself anymore."

"Force myself? Who said I was forcing myself to do anything?"

My eyes squeeze shut. I'm still angry and I want to cry, which is a dangerous combination. "Just stay away from me."

"What did I do?" he asks. "Tell me and I'll fix it." He says it urgently, and I know he'd try.

If I were more selfish, I'd ask him to get over it. To try and be closer to me. But I know he hates it.

"You can't fix how you feel," I mutter. "So don't worry about it."

"How I feel? What do you mean how I feel?"

As much as I don't want to do this drunk, I also want this over with. Once he's aware that I've caught on, the faster I can be away from him and move forward.

"Nate, I know."

"What do you know?" He has an edge of panic in his voice. He's terrified of being caught.

I don't blame him.

I'm terrified of saying it.

"Maisie, *please.*" He's begging me. His voice is close to breaking. "What do you know?"

My eyes grow wet as I prepare to say it. "I know that I repulse you. So much so that you don't want to be near me."

My words hit their mark. Nate lets out a sound like I've punched him. A single tear escapes my eye and I shake my head. The last thing I want is pity. I don't want his stammered apologies. I want to cry into a pillow.

I'll go for a run. Pull myself together. Be normal.

I know this'll be harder than any other time. Nate isn't like Rob. He's not even like when I lost Grandma. This is the kind of pain that might take me out. This is the kind of realization that is going to stick with me.

"I thought you didn't like touching anyone," I say. "And you did with me when I needed you, but you didn't like it and couldn't wait for it to be over. But then I saw you with Aaron this morning. And then Mom reminded me you hug her all the time. I looked back at the photos, and I realized that I'm the exception. *I'm* the only one you don't want near you." I take another breath, trying to keep it together. "I shouldn't have made you touch me." I say it softly. "I'm sorry about that. And I'm sorry about all the times before. I'll stay away. I just need some time to accept this."

The plan is to get back to the party. There's no way for me to dance, but I might be able to find a corner to cry in. Scarlett will find me and I'll beg to stay in her room on the couch until I can pull myself together. Eventually, I'll be able to pretend that this doesn't absolutely gut me.

But my plan crumbles when Nate's hand wraps around my arm, and this time, I'm yanked to him. Instead of just pulling me a few inches, he's pressing me into his chest so tightly that I can feel his entire body shaking.

I'm so shocked that I don't pull away. I don't think I can.

"I'm sorry," he says into my hair. "I'm so fucking sorry. That's not . . . Maisie, you could *never* repulse me."

"B-but I do."

"You don't. I swear to God you don't." He tightens his hold on me. I'm not sure if he's trying to hug me or *absorb* me.

But I'm not complaining. I could never complain about this.

I need to pull away and ask questions. I need to clear more up, but the smell of his body wash, a mix of citrus and woods, is everywhere. I could pretend dancing would help. Or that drinking would numb the pain. But the only thing that could make me feel better is *him*.

Tears escape before I can stop them. What had started because of pain quickly turns into relief.

He doesn't hate me. This is a misunderstanding.

I can take Rob hating me and move on. I can take almost anyone else feeling the same.

But not him. *God*, not him.

Nate's hands go to the back of my head. He curls around me as if he could envelop me entirely.

And I'd let him.

"I'm sorry, Maisie. So sorry." He's said it already, but the repetition is what I need to hear. He continues to say it, even when he doesn't have to.

We must look like fools to anyone around us. But I can't bring myself to care.

"Why?" is all I can ask. My voice is as raw as the emotions inside of me.

He swallows. "You . . . chose someone else."

I tug away, a frown forming on my features. "I did *not*—"

"Maisie," he says it calmly, but firmly. "You were with Rob. That changed things."

"It didn't have to."

"Yes, it did. Rob was never okay with how close we are. No one else either. And I didn't know how to stop other than . . . stopping it altogether."

What he said makes sense logically. But I can't wrap my head around *anyone* being important enough to come between us. "But you're my friend. That's important to me."

"And we've always been that. Just with . . . space."

My heart tells me that I don't want space. I've never wanted space. Not from him.

"Is there some happy medium we can find?"

He blinks. "I don't know. The issue with me and you is that I don't think either of us knows when we go too far."

The words make my breath catch in my throat and I wonder if everyone else has been right the entire time. Is there something more between us?

I open my mouth to ask him just that. But then it closes before I can. Things go wrong. If me asking him if there was anything more ruined our friendship, it would be like the feelings I just felt, except so much worse.

I want to be brave so badly, but I can't let things fall apart between us. Not after what's just happened.

"Okay." The word hurts, but I say it anyway.

Nate frowns. "Okay?" he repeats. "What does that mean?"

"It means I get it. This may not be what I want, but that's okay."

"And what do you want, Maisie?"

"Anything you're willing to give me." It's true. I'd take being one inch closer to him than where we were before.

Nate's jaw drops. "Are you serious? Maisie, I don't think you know what you're asking for."

"I do know."

"No, you really don't."

"You wanna touch me, right?" I ask. He blinks and his ears go red, but he nods. "Then do it."

"What happens when I go too far?"

"I think it'll probably be me who goes too far." And it's true. With all the things I've thought about him, I wonder if platonic touches will *ever* be enough.

"Don't challenge me," he says lowly. "This'll be the one you'd lose."

I know I'm the one losing here, so I only shrug. "It's better than you acting like I burn you every time we touch."

"That's not . . . entirely inaccurate," he says, eyes going distant as he thinks about it. Then he focuses back on me.

I feel like a walking bruise. I want *so* much, and I have no idea what he's willing to give me.

But then Nate reaches out, tucking one strand of hair behind my ear. He doesn't jerk back. He doesn't tense up.

It's just him.

"Do you know what you look like right now?" he asks.

"A mess?"

"God no. You look like the girl who thought I'd spiked the punch at homecoming junior year, right before she dragged me outside to yell at me."

"Nate," I groan. "Are you ever gonna let that go? I was wrong about that. You didn't spike it. You just helped them get it in."

"You called me out on something stupid." His hand moves down a long lock of my hair. "Your hair looked like this too."

My heart is doing somersaults in my chest. "Is that a bad thing?"

"No, you lost a lot of your fight when you were with Rob. I missed this side of you."

"I missed it too."

A soft smile crosses his face. "We should figure out new boundaries about all this. I promise I won't shut you out this time."

I nod, relief hitting me like a truck. "Thank you."

"But not when you're drunk."

"I'm only tipsy."

"Which means you're gonna be tired soon," he adds. "Tell me, are your eyelids feeling heavy yet?"

I sigh. "Only slightly."

"Then we're on borrowed time. Do you wanna go back in there?" He looks at where the dancing is happening. "I might need to catch up with you on drinking, but I can dance if I want to."

I look back at the room.

"I think I want food and to go to sleep early."

"I could also go for those things. As long as I get to be with you." The words are said casually as he puts his hands in his pockets. But it feels anything but casual to me.

"Let me say bye to Scarlett," I say as I step away. "I'll be right back."

He gives me a nod before I find my friend. She's near the door, still dancing, but easy to find.

"Hey. I'm gonna head out."

"Oh?" She turns to me with a smile. "Did talking work?"

"You know it did," I reply. "Thank you so much for giving me a safe space to just be for a little bit."

"No problem," she replies. "But I better get to see you again before this cruise is over."

"You will." I pull her into a tight hug before leaving.

After a quick dinner, we finish *Revenge of the Sith* from the last scene that Nate remembers while I plan how to broach the topic of where we're sleeping. He gets ready for bed first while I lounge on the couch.

"So, I guess it's my turn," I say when he comes out of the bathroom.

"Your turn for what?"

"Getting the couch."

His eyes narrow. "No way. You're not taking the couch."

"After how you slept last night, you have to be sore, and I'm not." I don't say it's because he's a good pillow, even though I want to. "Plus, you can have space if you need it."

"You think I want space?"

"I'm giving you the option. It's up to you."

He huffs out a breath before his gaze lands on me. I wonder if he's annoyed, but I see one corner of his mouth quirk upward, and I sit up straighter.

That isn't annoyance. That's mischief on his face.

Which is terrifying.

"What are you planning?"

He doesn't answer and walks over to me. I'm about to ask again when he grabs my legs and *pulls*.

"Whoa!" I yelp as I'm launched toward him. He leans over and makes sure I don't hit the ground and then drags me to the bed. "Nate, what the fuck."

"Show, don't tell. You're not sleeping on the couch."

I kick at him, trying to free myself. "I can do what I want."

"Not this time."

I manage to get free enough to scramble to my feet and make a break for the couch. He grabs me by the waist to stop me, but my foot is under his, and both of us topple onto the hard surface. I land underneath him, and the air is knocked out of my lungs. Luckily, Nate mostly catches himself so I'm not completely crushed.

But I also can't move.

"Ow," I hiss. "Why are you so heavy?"

"Why did *you* take my foot out? This is your fault, berry."

I huff. "You told me what to do."

"So, you did it harder?" He rolls his eyes, but there's a smile on his face. "That's my girl." I pause. I like the sound of being *his*. "Uh, I mean—"

I cut him off by trying to squirm out from under him, which only makes things worse. It makes *my* situation worse. He's everywhere.

And I don't mind it.

Nate's body is rigid, and I swear something pokes me before he's gone in a flash and in the bathroom.

I stare in shock. "Did I actually win?"

"Don't flatter yourself," he calls back. "I just need a minute."

Had he gotten hard? I blush at the idea, but I'm determined not to ignore the thought that he's attracted to me.

Scarlett is right. All the signs are there.

"I'm serious about you not sleeping on that thing," he says as he comes out of the bathroom a few minutes later.

"One of us has to," I remind him. "Unless we share the bed."

"That's what I was trying to get at." He crosses his arms. "Or was me dragging you to it not clear enough?"

"It was not. This is a time when telling *does* work."

"Would you have listened?"

"Maybe after a fight."

He laughs, but gestures to the bed. My body tenses. I still don't know what I'll do in my sleep. When Rob and I shared a bed, I didn't have too many issues, but I'm starting to realize that I didn't care about Rob like I do Nate.

"I'm a bed hog," I warn. "You may not get any sleep."

"Like I'll get great sleep on that couch." He rolls his eyes. "And I know you hog the bed. You did it all the time when we were kids. You hog blankets too. Actually, you're pretty inconsiderate all around." I throw a pillow at him. He takes it and puts it on the bed. "Listen," he adds, "I don't want you to ever feel like I'm repulsed by you ever again. And this is the most logical solution. That being said, if you don't feel like you wanna do this, I completely understand. I still won't let you take the couch, though."

I consider it. I enjoy Nate's openness. He wouldn't be too angry if I woke up cuddling him. He would probably run back to the bathroom, though.

I can deal with that.

"Fine, but you don't get to act like you won this one."

His lips stretch into a smirk. "That's exactly how I'm gonna act."

"Then I'll stay on the couch."

He groans and then shuts his mouth. That's when I finally get up.

The bed is a queen, the same size that we used to share when we were kids. In my house, I'd quickly upgraded to a king-size bed, so it still feels small to me, especially when I'm sharing with someone else.

When I was with Rob, it felt like I couldn't get enough space from him. He snored loudly and was more of a blanket hog than I was. As Nate lies down next to me, I realize I don't need the space. In fact, I don't need anything else than this.

He turns the light off. "Just like old times, huh?"

Back then, being in the same bed was a need. Graduating high school was a dark time in both of our lives. And the only way we survived it was by sticking together.

Tonight isn't just for survival. We could sleep separately and be fine, but we're choosing this. Both of us.

"It's not exactly like old times," I say.

"Yeah, being on a boat is different."

The dark makes me brave. I grab his arm, which is resting on his side, and drape it on my hip. "There. Now it's like old times."

Nate is silent for a long while, and I wonder if he'll tug away or make an excuse for space.

But instead, he laughs. "You're right. I forgot the most important part."

"You're like a weighted blanket," I say. "It's nice."

"Seriously? Are you objectifying me right now?"

"Shh." I turn only so I can put my hand on his face. "Blankets don't talk."

Nate scoffs as I roll back around. "This was all a ploy to get me to be quiet."

"And it's *still* not working. You're lucky my parents aren't here. You know you're the reason we kept getting caught when we were kids, right?"

"Me? I seem to remember you reading me your entire *Nancy Drew* book."

"You asked!"

"You didn't say no." His arm that's draped over me tugs me closer. "And we're adults now. We can do what we want."

My lips tug upward as I let myself think about all the things I do want. I snuggle into him, feeling even better about finding a way to tell Nate I want more.

I'm tired, more so than I expect. Even though I have more snark to throw, being in bed with him is already making me want to fall asleep.

Nate lets me, and I can hear the sound of his breathing. It's better than any sound machine I could buy, and I'm drifting off in seconds.

chapter twenty-one

CONSCIOUSNESS SEEPS IN SLOWLY. I know before I've even opened my eyes that I've slept *hard*. I have no idea what time it is or how long I've been out, but I'm pretty sure we could've hit something and I wouldn't have known.

Light spills through a crack in the drawn curtain, so I know it's sometime during the day. I try to move and get my phone only to realize I can't do anything.

When I dozed off, Nate's arm was slung over me and I was barely grazing his chest with my back. It was close, but there was some semblance of space between us.

Not anymore.

There's no indication of who moved throughout the night. All I know is that there's no way I can go anywhere without waking him up.

At some point, I moved to my back. Nate rolled over, planting his head right on my chest. It can't be comfortable with his size, and his feet are definitely hanging off the bed, yet he's still fast asleep.

I want to be worried. But this feels natural. I want to run my fingers through his waves, just enough to wake him up so he looks up at me with his adorable green eyes. Then, he would lean up for a kiss.

My cheeks go red as I wonder what kissing Nate would be like.

It's not the only thing I'm curious about.

Nate's eyebrows furrow in his sleep as he reaches out. His fingers graze my ribs and I go tense. Is he waking up?

Instead, his arms tighten and he presses his face into the nook of my shoulder and neck. I feel like I could combust, but I don't dare move. His leg hikes up, and that's when I feel it.

He's hard. *Very* hard, and his dick is pressed into my leg.

My eyes squeeze shut and I take a deep breath. Just the feel of that does more to me than Rob ever could. I would be working with far more than I ever had before.

Would he be more caring than Rob was? Would he give me time that I had to steal from Rob? Would it feel like all the songs and books said it should?

Nate's cock presses into me one more time. I resist the urge to push back. He's asleep. We've not talked about *anything*.

But I want this.

So bad.

Still, I try to pull away.

"U-um, Nate?" I say. "Hey, could you—"

His eyes open in a flash. He's much faster at putting the pieces together than I was, and he's off of me before I can even finish my sentence.

"Shit," he mutters under his breath.

I'm suddenly cold. I blink slowly, trying to get my wits about me.

Nate stares at me with a stricken expression before he's gone and in the bathroom. I'm tempted to use the mirror, but it's obvious he wants the only privacy he can get in this tiny room, so I let out a sigh and flop back onto the bed.

A heavy silence settles in as I give him a moment. My cheeks burn and I can only imagine what he's thinking.

It takes a long time before he emerges. I'm still lying on the bed, trying to parse through my emotions. It's so easy to take him running off the wrong way, but I'm trying my best not to go down that path.

"Maisie, I'm *so* sorry about that." He says it slowly. "That was so inappropriate, and I know I made you uncomfortable."

"You didn't. It's fine." The words come out strangled, mostly because I'm resisting the urge to pull him right back into bed with me. To make him see that I was fine with what was happening. We just need to talk first.

"Don't lie," he says. "You can't even look me in the eyes right now."

I blow out a breath and slowly sit up, looking him right in the face. The desire I felt in the bed meets the fear that him running away was a rejection, and it sparks something new. It makes me defiant, something I am with so few people. "See? Fine."

Nate doesn't look convinced. He doesn't look anything other than guilty. His arms are crossed, his shoulders hunched. "I think we need better boundaries. No more sleeping in the same bed."

"Wait, *what*? I'm not agreeing to that."

"It's for the best. We said we were figuring out what works for us, and we found that sharing a bed does not."

"Speak for yourself. I slept great."

"And then woke up to me going . . ." He sighs. "Way too far with you."

"You just got hard. It's not the end of the world or anything."

"Are you being serious right now?"

I make sure I don't look away. "I am."

He blinks and I know I've convinced him. "Why are you not more freaked out by this?"

"You're acting like I'm blind to the fact that you're a man. Men get hard."

He only stares. "You didn't think that was . . . overboard?"

"Overboard. How the hell does morning wood equate to

falling off the side of the boat? I'd say you need to get your fears in order." I make myself smile.

He still looks at me like I'm a bomb about to go off. "Was that a joke?" he asks.

"Kind of," I reply with a shrug. "Water safety is no joke to me, obviously. But I could entertain some jokes about the hard member that woke me up, if you're . . . *up* to that."

Nate blinks, and then *finally*, he huffs out a laugh. "Maisie, was that a double joke?"

"I'm a woman of layers. What can I say?"

"You're being shockingly calm about this."

The thing is, he's right. If this had happened a week ago, I would have panicked just like he is now. But I've come to terms with my feelings and I know that they're real. I know that there's no avoiding them.

"Contrary to popular belief, I can be calm."

"That's news to me."

I give him a glare. "I can pretend to be upset if you want me to. *Oh no, your dick. It's hard. What will I ever do?*" My acting voice is purposely terrible. The second I'm done, Nate is laughing.

"All right, all right. I can see you're not faking it this time. The vacation must finally be working on you."

"Right before we get back too. Just my luck. I'll have to travel more often to chase this. Or maybe you could get hard again. That might work."

The tips of Nate's ears go beet red. "Really? That's your next joke?"

"What? Was it bad?"

"New rule. No more jokes at my expense before coffee."

"What? *None?*"

"Just none about my dick. I can't process this yet."

"Fine. I'll stop. I was just making sure your little *buddy* is ready to face the public."

Now he glares. "You're pushing. And don't use the word little. You'll hurt a man's pride."

I bite my tongue. I want to tell him there's nothing that should hurt his pride, but I know I need to toe the line.

Nate can see it. "At least you're finally listening. Let's go."

Half an hour later, we're at the lounge sipping on lattes. I know I'm still thinking about this morning, and Nate is too, judging by how he keeps glancing at me when he thinks I won't notice.

I'm not sure how to broach this. With Rob, everything was done for me. He's the one who made massive displays to prove how much he cared.

Nate isn't like that. He's quietly there, like a support system I can't live without.

This morning was the first time we did something that wasn't like what friends do.

"So, today's the last excursion," Nate says as he's halfway through his drink. "Then it's back to real life, huh?"

That, I dread. "Yeah, I guess so."

I haven't put much thought into life on the shore, but I'm not excited about seeing all of Rob's family when I go to Quinn's birthday party. Before the cruise, it was a nebulous concept, an issue I didn't have to face. Now, I do.

It's tempting to hide, just like I did when I called the wedding off.

But Quinn wants me there and I've never missed one of her birthdays before. I *have* to be brave and face this. I don't want fear to stop me.

"So, we're in Nassau for the day." Nate's looking at his phone. "There's not a lot to do for someone who doesn't like swimming."

"That seems to be the theme here," I say with a sigh. "But it's our last full day on the water. I think I could go for an attempt at swimming in the ocean."

Nate blinks. "Really? That's a tall order."

"Is it?"

"There are waves," he says. "Though, they're pretty small here. And you did get an experience with the ocean on this trip that wasn't so good."

"I'd like an experience with the ocean that isn't traumatizing," I say. "And I get to use my swimsuit again."

"Yeah, that."

Nervousness settles in my gut. "What? Do you not like it?"

"No!" he says immediately. His fingers start tapping on the table and he can't look me in the eye. "It, uh, looks very nice on you. You and Scarlett picked that out?"

"Yeah. Our shopping trip was . . . enlightening."

"Tell me about it."

"You can't possibly want to know the details of a shopping trip."

"I love hearing you talk about what you get up to. Tell me everything."

If it were anyone else, I'd think they were lying.

"Fine."

He perks up as if I'm handing him his favorite candy. And I can't help the grin that takes over my face as I tell him about how Scarlett made me try on each and every one in the shop.

"I like her," he says. "Where does she live again?"

"No idea, but not in Nashville." I blow out a breath. "I'm kind of sad about it, honestly."

"We can travel to see her."

We. I like the sound of that.

"The one I got I almost didn't buy," I continue. "Honestly, I thought it was a little . . . showy."

Nate raises an eyebrow. "And that's a problem?"

"Not really," I reply quickly. It's hard to sit still. "But I guess I've gotten used to some things that were said to me about wearing things like that."

"By who?" Nate's leaning forward, brow pinched. "If I did

anything that made you feel like that, feel free to smack me. Or tell me off."

I hold a hand up. "Not you, I promise."

He lets out a sigh of relief before he's focused again. "So, who did?"

Nate will be able to guess it. Quinn would never. Neither would my parents. "Rob made a few comments about me needing to be more modest because I didn't have the kind of body that looked good in certain things."

I expect Nate to roll his eyes and call him an idiot. That's what he is. Instead, his whole body goes tense. He's so close I can *feel* it.

"Excuse me?" he says.

"Y-yeah." I shake my head. "I'm working on unlearning that."

"He should have *never* spoken to you like that. If I'd known, I would've—" He trails off, shaking his head.

He's angry *for* me, and it's yet another way I know he cares.

My hand lands on his arm. "I know," I reply. "Thank you."

Nate blows out a breath before he glances at me. I see him push his anger away and he relaxes. "Good. You shouldn't have to put up with him like that."

"And I don't have to." *Mostly.* It would be cleaner if I could never see him again, but I know that's not how everything will work out. "At least not in the same way. The only time I plan to see him is Quinn's birthday."

"I'm going too," he says.

"But I thought you hated her family."

"I do, but I'm not letting *you* deal with it alone. So, I'll be with you. If you'll have me."

My hand tightens on his arm and his skin is warm. "I'll always have you. It's one of my favorite things about being your best friend."

chapter twenty-two

I END up changing into my swimsuit and layering my clothes over it before Nate and I head onto the island.

The ship is pulled up to a wooden dock. I feel better about being near the water, but I'm in no way comfortable with it, even now. While we're in line to leave the ship, Nate's hand intertwines with mine. It doesn't completely erase the fears and haunting memory of falling into the ocean, but it helps.

"Would you jump into the water again if I fell?" I mutter as we move. I want to be casual about how I'm feeling, but my hand tightens around his. I know he's aware of how nervous I am.

"Every time," he replies easily.

We take it slow and stay away from other people. Thankfully, no one pushes me off the dock this time, and I make it to land unscathed. When the ground is solid underneath my feet, I let out a long breath of relief.

"Still wanna see the beach?" Nate asks.

"I think I saw something about a staircase that people tend to flock to. It's historical or something. Can we see that first before we go to the water?"

"Of course."

We wander the shops and find the staircase I mentioned, but it doesn't take long to check out those and the adjacent waterfall before moving on to the next thing. Eventually, my fear from the dock has entirely faded and I'm willing to be near water again.

I'm already feeling overheated as we find public beach access and rent an umbrella. I can see why people are so gung-ho about getting in the water when the weather is so warm.

As I gaze out to an endless sky with picturesque blue water underneath it, I understand how this is relaxing for some people. I still can't deny the bubble of nervousness it gives me, though. Falling off the dock set me back quite a bit. I can still feel the salt stinging my eyes and burning my nose.

Nate is watching me closely, and I can tell he's about to ask if I'm okay.

"I'm adjusting," I say. "But I'll be okay, I promise."

"One mention of the safe word and we'll go back to the boat."

After one more deep inhale to steel myself, I say, "Let's do this."

We make it to where the edge of the water is. It's calm today, but there's a gentle push and pull of the water I'm not expecting. My throat closes up and I forget about anything else.

"Take your time."

"I wanna get in there eventually."

"If you just get your feet in, that's a win. Don't put so many expectations on yourself, berry."

My life would be so much easier if I could shove all of my fears into a box to get over them. It would make life infinitely easier.

But my fear is here. It tells me this is dangerous, that I should run and hide.

The water rushes at us and I nearly topple over. Nate catches me.

"Still good?"

"Not good, but okay. Could you distract me again?"

"Did I ever tell you that I think one of the teachers has a crush on me?"

"What? No, you didn't." My voice is high, and I'm not sure if it's because of the water or if it's because I want to go stake out the school he works at the second they reopen for the year. Nate works with a lot of women who are our age. Before I realized my own feelings for him, I always thought he would end up with someone from work.

"She's been hinting at it for a while," he says. "She's always coming by the gym with some excuse and she wants me to do all of her heavy lifting. It's flattering, really."

"I bet it is." I try to say it lightly, but it comes out all wrong. "Have you heard from her over the summer?"

"No, she's not one for phones. She's a face-to-face kind of gal."

"Oh. Do you . . . like that?"

"Sometimes, but you know there's one big thing I didn't mention about her."

"She's super hot?"

"She's seventy, berry."

"*Nate!*" I can't help the guffaw that escapes me. "You had me thinking the worst!"

"The worst? Is a woman liking me the worst?"

"It . . . could be." My cheeks are turning red. I just know it. "Either way, you should've led with the fact that she's a harmless old lady."

"I don't know about harmless. She's persistent. I'm about to bring you in just to get her off my back."

I raise an eyebrow. "You think I'd get her off your back?"

"Oh, yeah. You always do."

I blink. Do I do that? I've never intentionally tried to, but I've always made sure his girlfriends know I'm his best friend.

They always disappeared after that.

Shit. That's exactly what I've done.

"Earth to Maisie," Nate says, waving a hand in front of my face.

"Wh-what?" I ask. The gears in my mind are still grinding. I should apologize for . . . being close to him? I'm not sure what.

But I know I've been hiding from it. I don't like thinking about Nate with other women. I never have. Up until this trip, I always explained it away. I would say that I didn't want us to lose time together, or that who he was dating wasn't right for him.

And those things were sometimes true. But now I know that I've always seen Nate as . . . *mine*.

Even when he isn't.

Fuck.

"You're in the ocean," he says.

Suddenly, my surroundings come rushing back. I'm waist-deep in water. Just like that.

"Oh." I blink. "I guess I am."

"Was my distraction that good?"

"You sent me right into my own head." I'm not sure I'm fully out of it. "Do I really scare women away from you?"

"That was a joke. Don't worry about it."

"Do I?" I ask again.

He sighs. "It's not a huge deal—"

"Nate." I say it urgently. "I never meant to."

"And you don't. Not really. But most of them want me to cut down on time with you and make more for them." He shrugs. "It was never an option for me."

I freeze. They wanted the same thing Rob did.

And Nate chose *me*.

"I—"

"Maisie," he says. "You wanted to get in here and practice more. Why are we talking about my exes right now? You're in the ocean. And you're mostly okay."

"Right. Sorry."

"I'll know to distract you with another high schooler I caught smoking weed next time."

I roll my eyes, but my lips tug upward. "Those stories are boring."

"I guess I'll have to hope for more interesting kids this year." He pulls me a little bit deeper. "Are you ready for more practice?"

I groan, the smile slipping off of my face. The ocean is both the same and different from the pool water, but I try to avoid anything getting in my eyes so it doesn't sting. Nate is as patient as he was yesterday, though it's easier to focus on swimming and not him now that I know he doesn't hate touching me.

Hours go by as I try to figure it out. I'm not a decent swimmer by any means, but as the late morning slips to the afternoon, I feel like I could save myself if I fell into the water.

"We have a little bit of time before we need to be back at the boat," Nate says. "We could head back now or keep practicing."

I consider the water for a second. I wouldn't say I'm having fun, but I'm getting used to it. "Can we try floating again? I think I might be able to handle it."

"Whatever you want," he says. "Want me to help you?"

"Please," I nearly beg. "I'm gonna hate this."

He laughs, but shuffles closer. He has to remind me how to get into position with his hand steady at the small of my back.

When I try again, the panic of the water getting in my ears is back, but thankfully my face doesn't go under. Nate's hand hovers on my back and his fingers press into my spine gently.

I'm weightless and I can't hear a thing. It's terrifying, but I stay in place. The water is so different from the air in the way I move and in the way I float.

Nate's hand feels like a thread keeping me grounded. I have no idea if I truly enjoy this, but I can tolerate it.

Eventually, I'm done with it. I try to sit up and nearly go under when Nate pulls me up.

"Well, that wasn't elegant," I mutter.

"You did so good," he says. "Seriously, that was great."

I feel like a wet rat. I probably look like one too. My hair is sticking to my forehead, and I have no idea how it's laying. But Nate's looking at me like I'm the universe. His smile is wide and I can feel his pride even though he isn't saying it.

I feel proud too. I can't believe I did that.

"I didn't come out of it very well." I'm out of my element as I try to move my hair from my face.

"Don't worry about that. It's just something you have to learn. But you did it. Even though you were scared."

Fear has always been something that I've avoided. After all, I always thought it was telling me that I shouldn't do something. But as time goes on, I'm starting to realize that I can do things while scared. And it's good for me to do them too.

I nod and then look between the water and him. "I think it's time."

Nate pauses. "Time for what?"

"I'm gonna try to go under the water."

Nate knows how big this is for me. Going under is the main thing I'm scared of. Falling off the dock had been miserable, but being stuck under the surface when I was a kid was even worse.

But I want to be brave, so I'm going to try it.

"Are you sure?"

"Yes, as long as you'll be right here."

"I'll always be right here."

I take a shaky breath and prepare myself. Then I try to go under, only for my legs to lock up.

"Nope. I can't."

"Berry, I know it's scary." Nate has a hold on my hand. "But this is the first time you get to go under the water and be in control. And that's huge."

"And once I do that, I won't be as scared anymore, right?"

"Maybe. Or maybe it's more of a process. But you'll have done it. And that's the goal."

I wish I could guarantee that I'll never be scared of the water again, but Nate's right. I'll probably always hate swimming.

But I can face this. I can at least learn how to deal with it.

This time, I force my legs to relax. And I go under.

It's awful. Water is everywhere and salt makes my nostrils burn. I last all of five seconds before I'm back above the surface, sputtering as I try to get my hair off my face.

But when I finally feel like I can open my eyes, Nate is grinning at me.

"You did it."

"I did it."

"Was it fun?"

"Fuck no." I rub my eyes. "Everything burns now. And my hair is so sticky. Can we be done? I might be done."

"You didn't even have to use the safe word," he says with a laugh. "I'm proud of you."

It only gets worse when I'm out of the ocean. Even though it's the middle of summer, the air is still cold on my body, and the minimal fabric of my swimsuit is shoved into places where the sun doesn't shine.

"I need to dry off," I mutter the second we're on shore. I do my best to make sure my hair and body aren't dripping before I get under my umbrella. I only feel marginally better when my hair is no longer soaking wet.

We spend some time air-drying while Nate catches me up on all that I missed while I was stressed with wedding planning. Eventually, both of us tug our clothes on and get ready to leave the beach.

"This wasn't so bad," I say. "I can't believe I'm saying that about a beach, of all things."

"So, do you like the water now?"

"That's a stretch. But the vibe *is* nice."

The sun is setting behind us, and I know we need to head back to the boat, but I'm happy to stay alone with him just a little longer.

We gather our things and get ready to leave after a few minutes of silence.

"We could walk along the beach for a little bit," I offer.

"Who are you?"

"A changed woman. I just had to fall off the dock."

He shakes his head. "Don't remind me about that. I'm gonna have nightmares."

"Well, you saved me. I like to think of it as the reason you got so ripped. I mean, *damn*, what are you eating to get this?" I jab a knuckle into his abs and he yelps.

"Hey! Don't fondle."

I raise an eyebrow. "That was a bit of an overreaction there. Don't tell me you're still—"

"Shut up, berry. Shut up right now."

"Ticklish."

He knows what I'm about to do and he tears himself away from me. I get one swipe in and he lets out a guffaw so loud that people turn to look.

"You *are* ticklish."

He puts his hands up as he backs away from me. "Now, hang on. I know you have some information that you could use against me—"

"Come here," I urge. "I just want a very nice and normal hug."

Nate is still backing up. "But I think you're the bigger person and can file this away."

I get close enough that I can reach for him again. He yelps and runs.

"Wait!" I yell after him. "Come back! Don't abandon me like my father did!"

"Your father is a very nice man who would never leave you! You can't guilt me like this!" he yells back.

"But I wanna test a theory!"

"I'm not your guinea pig!"

"What are friends for?"

"Friends don't enjoy the other's weaknesses!"

"Best friends do!"

chapter twenty-three

I, of course, don't catch Nate. His long legs make him ridiculously fast.

So, I do what anyone else would do: I tell him while out of breath that I'll forget about it and hit him when he least expects it.

Nate nearly jumps out of the elevator when I go for the same spot. I erupt in a cackle when he tries to get away from me.

"I fucking knew you wouldn't let it go." His bottom lip pokes out as he glares at me.

"Of course I wouldn't. I know a weakness now." I go for it again, but he stops me in my tracks by grabbing my arm.

"You lose reaching privileges."

I use my other arm. I get one swipe in before he's holding both of my arms, and I'm pressed against the elevator wall.

"Don't make me regret letting you touch me."

My jaw drops. He doesn't mean it like it sounds, but my mind goes the wrong way and all I can think is that I *wish* he meant it that way. I wanted him to use that low voice on me and ask for more.

But then he's gone.

"Sorry." The tips of his ears are red. "Let's forget that happened."

I resist the urge to fan myself. "Yeah, definitely. I don't wanna remember that you actually got the jump on me."

Nate laughs. "That I will remember."

The elevator stops at our floor and he gestures for me to go first. I consider it before shaking my head.

"Enjoy your shower. I'm gonna keep going up and hang out on the deck."

"By the pool?"

I roll my eyes. "I won't even go near it. I just wanna sit and not have to see your ass while you shower. Enjoy the privacy." I all but push him out of the elevator.

"I'll come find you when I'm done," he says.

With a nod and a goodbye, I'm alone and heading farther up. Things feel so much better than yesterday, but I can't deny that there's a change in the air between us. Or at least how I'm seeing things. I'm glad to know he doesn't hate being near me, but I can feel myself wanting to take it even further.

The time away is good for me. I pull out my phone, not fully wanting to be alone.

MAISIE

You free for a drink? It's on me.

SCARLETT

I have the all-inclusive package, but it's the thought that counts. Where are you?

I tell her which deck I'm on and lounge until she arrives. It doesn't take long before I see her making her way toward me.

"Hey," I say.

"Are you alive after your great chase on the beach?" She winks at me.

"You saw that?"

"Anyone on the beach did."

"Oh." My cheeks heat. "Uh, yeah. I'm good."

"I'm happy for you two. You make a cute couple."

"Couple?" My voice goes up an octave, and I look around to make sure Nate isn't done with his shower early. This is *not* what I want him to overhear. "No. We're still not dating."

Scarlett frowns. "What? But I saw you two last night. And you were flirting all day when I saw you at the beach."

"I don't think it's meant to be flirting. And I still don't know—"

"If you're about to tell me he's not into you, then you're wrong. And willfully ignorant."

I think about the way we woke up and the way he reacted to seeing me in my swimsuit. "Okay, so there are some signs."

"Thank you."

"But how does one go from being friends for almost two decades to more?"

"Pretty easily, depending on the connection."

"Without ruining things," I clarify. "What we have is . . . amazing, and I don't want to sound like a cliché, but romance doesn't always end well."

Scarlett gets her drink and considers it. I wonder if I finally have a good enough point where she doesn't have an answer.

But then she turns to me.

"You sound like you spend a lot of time wondering what could go wrong. Have you considered what could happen if it went *right*?"

I blink. I know I haven't. Things going right would mean Nate and I would be together. And what would that look like?

The second I consider it, I can see it. Moments like the couch, where we're cuddled up and there's no question about if I should pull away. His hand could always be in mine, right where it belongs.

I already share so much with him.

More seems . . . right.

And now that I see it, I want it.

A lot.

"There you go," Scarlett says with a smile.

I shake off the thoughts. "But, *still*, what if it all blows up in my face, if he says he doesn't have any feelings for me?"

"First of all, I have a feeling he would be lying, but that's beside the point. You two are very dedicated to your friendship. Would you let it fall apart if *he* had feelings you wouldn't reciprocate?"

"Of course not."

"Do you think he would?"

"No." I answer immediately.

"So, the friendship isn't at risk."

"But it might be awkward."

"And then it'll fade. The worst of things don't stay as intense forever."

I immediately think back to when both Nate and I lost people. Those had been the worst times of our lives, but life *did* go on. Eventually, the gut-wrenching, terrible pain turned into something more manageable. And now, we're living.

"You're a genius. An emotionally secure genius."

She laughs. "My work here is done."

"Wait."

"Need more eye-openers from me?"

I shake off the thoughts of Nate. "I'll be honest, I can't handle that. But we've spent all of our time together talking about me. You've barely said anything about you."

She shrugs. "I love helping others. Don't worry about it."

"Is that by design?" I ask.

Scarlett goes stiff. "Wow."

I can't help but laugh. "I might seem emotionally constipated to a therapist, but I'm capable of picking up on things."

"Us therapists aren't immune from being dumb about emotions." She sighs. "We're just good at hiding it."

"You don't have to tell me anything, but I don't even know where you live. That's just not enough information about you."

"Dallas," she says. "I live in Dallas."

"Are you from there?"

She shakes her head. "I move around a lot. Always have. My mom was broke and followed the money. I think I'm used to not settling down. Or I just get bored. I don't mean to hide anything, but it changes day-to-day. Just last year, I lived in Chicago."

"Moving around sounds . . . stressful."

"You sound like someone who has a home. It's not a bad thing to have."

"Nashville's not so bad. You could move there."

She laughs. "Oh no. I've heard about the dating scene there, and let me tell you, it is *not* my thing."

"I thought you wanted to stay single."

"On the cruise," she clarifies. "After this, I'll inevitably find a younger man with mommy issues and get my heart broken again. It's a classic move of mine."

"Are mommy issues a common problem?" I ask slowly.

"Oh, yes. Many guys want a mommy to fuck."

I choke on my drink. "That's an . . . image."

"Think about how many men want a partner who does it all for them, emotionally and physically. They never learn how to be mature before they fly from the nest, and then they find a wife to replace them. And I'm a fool because I'm attracted to people who have problems. I think I can fix them." She laughs. "I can't, by the way."

"Wait, you're attracted to people who have problems?" I frown. "Is that why you befriended me?"

She pauses with her drink at her mouth. "Called me right out. *Again.*"

"I don't know whether to be offended or glad you did it. Maybe a bit of both."

"To be fair, it only started that way. I've really enjoyed having someone to talk to on this cruise. I thought I'd have fun being alone, but it hasn't been all that great." She smiles and then looks at me. "I do hope things work out between you and Nate."

"Really?" I ask.

"Watching you two reminds me that there's real love out there. I think I've been dating man-babies for so long that I forgot about that."

"I still don't know if what we have is *love*."

She rolls her eyes. "Oh, it's love. Even if it doesn't turn into a relationship, he loves you. And I think you know that."

"I do. He's done . . . a lot for me. And we won the Newlyweds game against a ton of married couples."

Scarlett's eyes go wide. "Oh my God, really?" She leans in. "Tell me everything."

chapter twenty-four

NATE JOINS us right when I'm telling Scarlett about Aaron's expression when we explained that we're not together. He slips into the conversation with ease, sitting right next to me, and gets a drink before continuing to talk about his adventures with Aaron.

"Wait," Scarlett says when Nate is regaling her with what happened to Aaron while snorkeling. "You were involved with the jellyfish sting too? Are you a magnet for disaster?"

"Normally, *I'm* the disaster." He shrugs. "Gotta mix it up, I guess."

"And here I was, avoiding all of it." She shakes her head. "At least someone adventured."

"You bought five dresses," I remind her. "That's an adventure."

"And a good one too." She finishes off her drink before standing. "And as much as I'd like to stay all night, I need to go pack. We get off the boat tomorrow, and I don't think I have enough room in my suitcase. Hopefully, I'll see you tomorrow before we get on our flights."

"I'll try my best," I say. "Have fun."

She leaves Nate and me alone with one last wave.

"Yeah, it's really a shame she doesn't live nearby. She seems cool."

"And really smart. Did I tell you she's a therapist? She caught . . . a lot with me."

"Is that why you're so well-adjusted on this trip?"

"It's why I'm *mostly* well-adjusted. It's nice to be around some emotional maturity."

"You say that like I'm not emotionally mature."

"You make it your life's mission to be emotionally immature."

"No, just immature. I've had a lot of practice handling my emotions." He takes a sip of his drink, leaving me to think about what Scarlett had said about talking to him about my own issues.

"Do you wanna walk around the boat?" I ask. "I think I need to move around."

"Uh, yeah. I think I can handle that. As long as you can deal with being near the water in the dark."

"I'll do my best."

We meander, talking about small things that don't really matter. I'm doing my best to work up the courage to say anything when we get to the bow of the ship. Wind whips at my hair and the sky is dark and empty.

"Never got the courage to come out here," I say.

"You'd be looking at the endless ocean," he reminds me. "That's not historically your favorite thing."

"Yeah, well." I bite my lip before turning to him. "I'm working on trying new things."

"And you're doing it well. Never did I think you'd be learning to swim."

"Me either. But I am."

"You'll be wanting to do it soon enough."

I shake my head. "Definitely not. But I've made progress. And I really owe you for . . . all of it."

"I just taught you how to swim."

"Not just that," I say. "You got me to come here in the first place, and you've made sure I had a good time, even when I was being difficult."

"Berry." His voice is soft. "It's nothing. I'd do all of this over again, and more."

More? That's exactly what I want.

I pull him into a tight hug, feeling the way he wraps his arms around me easily. My heart pounds in my ears. Am I really about to do this? Am I really about to ruin the friendship?

As my arms tighten around him, all I can think about is how terrified I am.

But this isn't the first time I've been scared. I was when I got on the ship. When I fell into the water. When I willingly went back into it.

I survived all of those things.

I can survive this too.

Moving away only slightly, I catch his eyes with mine. I don't know if I'll ever have the words to express what he means to me. Maybe I don't have to figure out the right thing to say.

I can show him instead.

And I lean in just the extra inch to kiss him.

Nate tenses, and I don't blame him. Never in my *life* did I think I would be kissing Nate of all people, but I also didn't think I'd ever learn to swim either.

It's nothing more than a press of lips, but it means more to me than anything else I've done. This is the moment everything could change, or it could stay the same. I don't know which will happen, but I'll find out soon.

I give him a moment, and when he doesn't move, I end it. I tell myself I'll be okay if he doesn't reciprocate and we'll move on. Maybe one day we'll laugh about this.

"What was that?" he asks.

"Me trying something."

His gaze flickers between my eyes and my lips, like he's not sure where to look. "Why?"

"I wanted to," I say.

"I don't think . . . this is a good idea."

Slowly, my heart sinks.

"Does it have to be a good idea? The cruise wasn't, and look at where we are."

I wait patiently. If he pushes me away, I'll accept it. I won't be mad, and I'll put in the work to accept just being friends. Both of us will.

"Maisie, I . . ."

Tilting my head, I let him have as much time as he needs. My heart pounds in my chest, but I try to be still.

He watches it all as he tries to work out what to say. I can imagine him trying to figure out how to let me down gently.

His next words are *not* that.

"Fuck it."

His arms tighten before he kisses me again. His lips move against mine, almost making up for lost time.

All sounds fall away around me, and relief hits me like a truck. All the worry vanishes and I wrap my arms around his neck, releasing a breath through my nose.

I've not kissed that many men, but I usually get tired of it. I'd do the usual hello and goodbye kiss, and nothing more, if I could avoid it.

This isn't like that. I have Nate closer than he's ever been and I don't want to let go. I *need* to learn how he moves, what makes him tick. I'm torn between rushing things and taking it slow so I can savor every moment.

I land somewhere in the middle. The kiss stays chaste for a moment before I swipe my tongue across his bottom lip. Nate groans, but opens up immediately, and suddenly we're making out like two teenagers hiding in a movie theater.

God, we should've been doing this then. We should have been doing this for *years*.

I pull away, out of breath, but desperate for more.

"So . . ." I laugh awkwardly. "Wanna go back to the room?"

"A-and what are we doing back in the room?"

Images flash through my mind, ones that feel like a dream come true. There's not much I *wouldn't* do with the man in front of me.

"Whatever we want to." My voice is breathless as I wait for him to agree.

When he swallows and nods, I feel like I've won the lottery.

chapter twenty-five

I JUMP him the second we're through the door.

Walking back to the room like nothing had happened was sheer torture, and I've discovered I am done wasting time when it comes to him.

"Whoa, hey—" he says right as I press my lips to his. "Berry, let me shut the door."

Both of us reach for it, but he gets tired of me trying to help, so he pins me against the wall. "Hang on," he says. "God, you're impatient."

"It took forever to get up here."

The door finally latches. "I'm sorry, I didn't expect you to turn into a monster."

I pull him back to me by the nape of his neck. "Expect the unexpected."

And then he's kissing me again, right against the wall of the room. He doesn't have to keep me pinned in place anymore. His body is doing the work for him.

I'm already a mess, and I tug his shirt off without a second thought. I can feel the skin of his chest as I kiss him, and his hands roam my lower back. Gooseflesh erupts from every inch he touches.

"Wait," he says as he pulls away. I already want him back. "Are you sure about this?"

"Why wouldn't I be sure?"

"We're friends. What if this ruins things?"

I shake my head. "Nothing can ruin us. Absolutely nothing."

And I mean it. This is the next step, the one both of us have waited too long for.

Nate takes a moment to think about what I've said and I wait on the balls of my feet, silently begging him to say yes.

"And what if it does?" he asks.

"It won't."

I refuse to lose him. If he asks me to step back now, I will. No matter how much I want this.

"Okay."

I blink. "Okay? What does that mean?"

"We're doing this. Whatever . . . this is."

"Really?" I can't help the excited smile that crosses my face.

"You know I'll never say no to you. This is no different." He steps closer, ending up right in front of me.

"This is a lot more than me asking for help. You have to want this."

"I do. I have for way too fucking long."

My eyes widen, and I want to ask how long. When did he know? And why didn't he say anything? But his lips cover mine again and I forget all of my thoughts.

Nate kisses me like his life depends on it. His body curls around mine, his hands cupping each of my cheeks, and I want to melt into him.

I didn't know it could feel like this, and now that I'm with Nate, I feel like an idiot for ever thinking Rob's empty promises meant anything. *This* is what matters.

I'm so engrossed in the kiss that I don't notice Nate is slowly moving me toward the bed. Tumbling back takes me by surprise, and I let out a squeak before he's on top of me, right where he's meant to be.

We're a mess of limbs. I want to feel every inch of him, and the feeling is obviously mutual. He moves from my face to my neck, down to my sides. They're gentle, barely there movements, but they light me on fire.

I don't know how much time passes with our lips locked together. All I know is that I never want this feeling to end.

But I also want more.

Finally, Nate takes my shirt off and then goes to the strings of my bikini top. With a firm tug, it comes loose, and he pulls away just in time to see it fall.

"Fuck," he mutters, a shaky breath escaping his lips. "These are incredible. I never thought . . ." He trails off, and I'm about to tell him to finish his sentence when his mouth covers my nipples, and I'm unable to think again.

I can't believe I'm here. I can't believe this is *real*. But as his tongue lavishes me, I know it is. It feels too good to be a dream.

I'm already growing wet, wetter than I ever got with Rob. From what I felt this morning, this is going to be a different experience, and my hand drifts south to make sure I'm as ready as I can be.

But Nate stops me.

"What are you doing?" he asks.

My cheeks burn. "Um, making sure I enjoy things?" It comes out as a question. I doubt he would be the kind of man to tell me *not* to have an orgasm, but I also know that it takes time for me to get there unless it's by my own hand.

Rob and I had an agreement. He could never get me to come, so he gave me time to take care of it myself.

And as I blink up at Nate, I wonder if that's normal.

"That's my job," he says.

I wince. "Um, it takes a while. Like . . . way too long."

"And you think I won't wait that long? What kind of idiot wouldn't?"

"Uh, well." My cheeks grow impossibly hotter as he rolls his eyes.

"Just let me try."

For a second, I wonder if he'll get frustrated, but this is Nate. *My* Nate. He's never given up on me before.

At my nod, he pulls my bottoms off before he kisses me again. His hand drifts downward.

"Tell me if I need to do anything different," he murmurs against my lips. "I can take a little direction."

I can't imagine correcting him at all, but if there is anyone I'd try to, it would be him. So when he presses the pad of his finger to my clit for the first time, I speak. "Go around it. I can be a little sensitive."

"Got it." And he follows my instructions.

I move differently, and my body knows it at first. It's a mix of this being our first time and Nate being at a different angle. It feels good, and I can't deny that I enjoy it, but I don't feel things building like I should be.

"It's . . . you can—"

"Maisie." His voice is soft. "There's no rush here. What do you need from me?"

"I don't know," I admit. I expect him to sigh and tell me to handle it myself.

"That's okay. I could try something, though. If you trust me, that is."

"Of course I trust you." I say it immediately. "I just don't know if it'll work."

"Then tell me if it feels good. Don't worry about the end goal."

"But the end is what matters, isn't it?"

"No, berry. Not with me." He presses a kiss to my warm cheek.

He then changes his angle, using two fingers to go around the most sensitive part of me. I'd never thought of trying anything like that, but it does feel better. So much so I move my hips to it.

"Yes," I say. "That's good."

My fingers curl into his shoulders as he continues. I want my orgasm to come quickly, but I remember his words. It *does* feel good and I enjoy it. I just wish it was easier.

"Do you remember that time that you didn't want to wait for the pizza to finish and you ate it half-cooked?" I say breathlessly. "If it begins to feel like that, then stop."

"Are you calling me impatient, berry?"

"If the shoe fits . . ."

He huffs a laugh into my cheek. "Normally you wouldn't be wrong, but I save up all my patience each day. And *this* seems like a good place to use it."

"But—"

"Stop worrying your pretty little head for five minutes. It's just me."

I take a shaky breath as he continues. I make a conscious effort to not think. To enjoy the moment. I'm in bed with *Nate*. And he just said he wasn't in a rush.

Instead of thinking of all the things I could be doing wrong to make this happen, I focus on each of his movements. Nate's moving up and down rhythmically, going right next to my clit, giving it just enough attention.

I enjoy it each time.

There's no deadline for this, and every time I want there to be one, I remember Nate's words. He's right here, with me, and I can *see* that there's no rush. It's plain as day on his face.

Finally, I feel it build. I try not to put too much pressure on myself, but I know each time feels better and better.

And when the dam bursts, I erupt with a cry. I don't know how, but it feels better coming from Nate rather than my own hand. I'm used to rushed heat flowing through me. My pleasure always had to fit around Rob's.

But this is only my own. Nate's taken the time to make sure I feel good on my own terms, and every nerve ending feels the eruption stronger than I thought possible. I'm a mess of moans as it takes over, and my vision goes black as I feel every millisecond of pleasure I can.

When it's over, I have to catch my breath as if I've been running. Then I finally catch sight of Nate. He's leaning on his hand, smirking at me.

"So, what have we learned?" he asks.

"You don't get to gloat," I say. "I do."

"You're right. You do. You got out of your own head."

"I can do what I'm told sometimes. And sometimes, I do whatever I want."

I roll us over, getting him on his back before I work with his shorts. Never have I been more glad we were in such casual clothes.

When his cock springs free, though, I freeze. I knew I'd be working with more than I was used to by feel alone, but this is . . .

"Uh, berry?" he says, bringing me out of my thoughts. "It's feeling a little like I'm on display here."

"Jesus. How did I not notice this thing before?"

"This thing? Rude."

"This *thing* is massive. It's a compliment."

He laughs, his smirk only growing. "To answer your question, I've mastered *not* letting you know I'm hard."

"You mastered it the last few times we shared a bed?"

"I did it as a teen."

My eyes widen. "You must have been a horny teen, then."

"Obviously. I had you to look at."

It's his turn to bring me down by the nape of the neck to kiss him. My mind stumbles over the words before I melt into him.

Eventually, I can feel him against my leg and I wrap my hand around the base of his cock before moving up and down gently. He sucks in a sharp breath of air. My core contracts around nothing, and I know I need him inside of me.

Pulling away, I hunt down the condoms we'd stashed when we first got here.

"Wha—Maisie? Where are you going?"

"Safety first," I say as I pull them out. "We're gonna need these. Maybe even all of them."

Nate looks between me and the condoms before a laugh jolts out of him. "You're ridiculous, berry."

"I very much am." I go through the condoms. "None of these are mammoth sized, so we'll have to hope they work."

"You're gonna give me a big head."

"At least both of them will match." I tear off one with my teeth before slowly covering his cock. I take my time with it, enjoying the way his body goes rigid as I touch him. Once the condom is on, I straddle him.

As I sink down onto him, there's a pleasant burn that I've not felt before. I didn't have this to work with when I was with Rob, and my orgasm only did so much. The feeling grows as I take more of him in, and I realize that he's hitting parts of me that I didn't know a man could hit.

Nate feels it too. His hands are tight on my hips and I can see muscles flexing under his skin as he's fully inside of me.

"Fuck," he mutters. "This is . . . I don't feel like I'm awake."

"I know I am," I say. And I also know I'll be feeling this tomorrow, but in the best way.

"Are you okay?"

I blink in shock. "Aren't you feeling a little too good to be asking me that?"

Nate levels me with a flat look. "I can still *think*, and I want you to enjoy this."

My cheeks heat, and it hits me once again just how little Rob cared about me. When it was his turn, the only thing on his mind was him.

Nate isn't like that.

"I'm definitely enjoying this," I say softly. "More than you know."

I lean down to press my lips to his. It's a delicate intimacy I'm not used to with sex, but when I pull back, I grind my hips down and Nate groans low and deep.

My movement spurs on his and he jerks upward. I gasp as I move, eyes slipping shut.

This feels incredible. Just like when he was circling my clit with two fingers. I have no idea how long he'll last, but I hope it's forever. I don't think I can come like this, but I enjoy it more than I can say.

And maybe one day I will.

"I-I'm not—" he grunts. "Honey, I don't think I can last long."

My mind trips over what he's called me, but I can't think of anything other than how perfect this feels.

"I don't care," I say back. "Just fucking come inside of me."

"*Fuck*," he mutters as his hips jolt upward again. My core clenches around him, and I wonder if I'm closer to coming again than I realize, but then Nate drags me down for a rough kiss as his cock twitches inside of me.

I'm not disappointed I didn't come again. I'm surprised I did it the first time.

And I already want to try again.

"You're so fucking incredible," he mutters into my lips.

"So, in theory, how fast does it take for you to recover?"

He laughs. "I honestly have no idea. I've never wanted to go again so fast."

"But you do this time, right?"

"You're insatiable," he mutters. "I fucking love it."

chapter twenty-six

I CAN'T SIT STILL as we get our late dinner. All I want to do is go back to our room and have my way with Nate, but nothing on the room service menu sounded good to either of us.

Nate's hand lands on my bouncing leg. "Calm down. Aren't you supposed to be relaxed after what happened earlier?"

"I just wanna be in a place where you can wear less clothes."

"What have I done?" he asks with a laugh. "You'll never leave me alone. We're getting tacos, berry. Your favorite."

They *are* my favorite, which is the only reason I keep my mouth shut.

I might want to be lost in pleasure, but I enjoy this too. We're more open than we ever have been. If I thought that Nate was free with touches before, it's nothing compared to now.

We're sitting on the same side of the booth, our arms pressed together like we're planning a prank we want no one to hear. Every now and again, he'll kiss me and my heart skips a beat.

There can't be anything better than this.

But then I see someone running toward our table, and both of us tense.

"No *freaking* way!" It's Trixie, and she looks like a child who's found a candy store. "You're together! I knew it!"

"Shit," I mutter. If there's anyone I want to run into, it's Scarlett. I haven't spent a lot of time with Trixie and Aaron, and I still feel defensive about the way they insisted we should be together.

They were *right*, but still.

Nate inches away from me. "Hey. How is Aaron feeling?"

"Not as good as you two, I'd guess." She winks.

"Babe," Aaron calls. "Can we go to our table?"

"But I'm catching up with our friends! They're together now!"

I tense and Nate does too. Neither of us have talked about what we are. We agreed we wouldn't let any of this come between us, but I'm not sure what he wants. Sure, he's dated before, but is he ready for commitment?

Fuck, commitment is all I'm used to. I'd love to have it with him.

We'll need to figure it out without Trixie announcing it.

"Um, we're not." I say it to her gently. "We're just . . . close."

She turns back to us with a frown. "Really? But I saw you kiss."

"Like I said, we're close."

Her bottom lip pokes out as she considers us, but Aaron walks over. "If they're insisting on being blind to their feelings, let them. I'm hungry, babe."

Aaron drags Trixie away and I cross my arms. "I'm not being blind," I mumble.

Nate is watching me, lips pressed together. "Right. So . . . 'close' is the word?"

"It's what worked." I shrug.

He slowly nods. "Right. Close it is, then."

"We can—"

"So, steak or chicken tacos tonight?"

Nate obviously isn't worried about defining anything, and I'm not sure how fast he wants to go. I look at the menu and tell him I want steak tacos before pushing it out of my mind.

A few inches have appeared between us, and we never quite get as close as we were before.

That fact bothers me more than I want to admit.

WE'VE JUST RETURNED from dinner when my phone rings. I'm determined to get the mood back, but when I see who it is, I know I'll be taking this call.

"Is it your parents?" Nate asks.

"No, it's Quinn. I'll go on the balcony and take this."

Once I'm out in the fresh air, I hit accept.

"Hey," I say.

"Maisie! Hey, how's the cruise?" She sounds out of breath, and I can imagine her surrounded by party decorations, slowly losing herself to the madness that is planning a party with Andrea.

I'm thrilled it's not me.

"It's . . . good," I say. "I think I *just* got used to being on vacation. Too bad we're back in Florida tomorrow."

"That sounds about right. The best part is the end." She laughs. "Has anything fun happened?"

It's tempting to tell her about Nate, but she's one of the people that never questioned that he and I were just friends. Probably because I was dating her brother.

It's going to be a massive shock to everyone.

I don't want people involved in this until I know what we are.

I should've said it better at dinner. *Close* isn't good enough of a word for the two of us.

"I fell off a dock." That feels like it was a year ago, even though it was only a few days.

Quinn gasps. "What? How?"

"Someone was in a rush and knocked me right off. Nate had to jump in after me."

"Only you would fall off a dock on a trip. You're okay, right?"

"You know Nate would never let anything happen to me."

"That's Nate for you," she says. "I'm glad he went. He's the only person other than Rob who could manage it. Or maybe he's the only person . . . uh, considering how things ended." Her voice goes quiet. "I shouldn't have brought him up."

"No, it's okay. I can't ignore Rob's existence or anything even though we're over." I've known I'll see him again, but the thought of it makes a shudder run down my spine. I know I can't avoid it, and my fear means nothing.

But it's definitely there.

"Yeah, definitely over." She lets out an awkward laugh.

"So, you heard about what I did?"

"I heard that you went on vacation with Nate, which I knew. But nothing else."

"I poked the bear a little bit, and he hasn't reached out since. So, it's definitely over now."

"Um, maybe don't get *too* used to the idea."

I shake my head. "He's pissed at me."

"From what I've heard, he still wants a chance."

I sigh and rub my forehead. "Not happening."

"Just stick to your guns," she says. "I'm definitely on your side here. That video was wildly inappropriate. But I also have to let you know he's being stubborn about this. And sometimes he can be . . . good at apologies with you."

I wince. After what Nate said, I know I let Rob get away with way too much.

"There's not an apology in the world that can make up for what he did. And even if there was, I'm not so sure that we were right for each other. I don't think I would've enjoyed this honeymoon if it were with him."

"Really? Has it been better with Nate?"

"Yes, definitely."

"Then you have your answer. Just remember that when you see Rob again."

I think about all of the ways Nate has taken care of me, and I know I won't forget it.

"I will," I reply. "But I'll also try my best not to add any stress to your party."

She groans. "Right, that. I swear, Mom won't leave me alone about it. She wants it to be *perfect*."

"I'll do my part. Trust me, I know how Andrea can be."

"You're still coming, right? Nate too?"

I dread it, but not because of her. And while I'm terrified of how angry they must be with me, I also won't avoid my fears anymore.

"Of course I'll be there. Nate too."

I'm determined not to let anything happen on her birthday. It's her day, after all.

"Good. I can't wait to see you in person. I've been so worried about you."

"I'm doing the best I can."

"You sound good for someone who dumped an idiot. And before you defend Rob, he's my brother, and I can say it."

"I wasn't even planning on defending him."

"Wow, you really are doing well." She laughs. "I'm happy for you. Still can't wait to see you, though."

I tell her I feel the same before she says she has to get back to party planning. I promise to send her some pictures before I hang up and go inside.

"How's Quinn?" Nate asks.

"Planning the party of the century," I say with a shake of my head. "At least it's not me."

Nate laughs before the smile falls off of his face. "Did she mention Rob?"

"In passing." I wave it off. "It doesn't matter."

"What did she say?"

"That he thinks he has a chance, but he doesn't." I expect Nate to laugh and agree, but instead, his gaze meets mine. His shoulders are tense. "You do know he doesn't have a chance, right?"

"Yeah, sure."

"Nate, I'm not getting back with him."

"I would hope not, but that little weasel doesn't give up."

I blink. "Did you just call my ex a weasel?"

He shrugs. "The shoe fits. Sorry not sorry. And don't defend him."

"I wasn't," I say with a roll of my eyes. "You're the one who saw how he was acting at the bachelor party. You get to call him what you want."

"Actually, I don't want to call him anything. I don't want to think about him at all."

"And what do you wanna think about?"

"You." He says it in the same way he had when he was at my door picking me up for this cruise.

Relief hits me. We'd gained distance at dinner, but he seems willing to let go of it now.

That's exactly what I need.

"I think I can work with that," I say. "Up for sharing the bed again? Or do I need to prepare for a night on the couch?"

"I swear, if you go for that couch, I will drag you across this room again."

A laugh escapes me. "As much as I would love to fight you, I was kidding. There's nowhere else I'm sleeping."

"Good," he says. "Now get over here, berry."

I don't even think twice as I lie next to him on the bed. He doesn't hesitate to pull me in closer.

My worries evaporate as his lips brush my neck. I know that this is where I'm meant to be.

"I believe you wanted a round two." I can feel his breath against my sensitive skin and it's all I can think about.

"Can you deliver now?"

"Oh, I definitely can. Roll over. There's something I've been dying to do."

I have no idea what he could be referring to, but I do what he asks anyway. I'm on my back when he kisses me once, and then he goes downward.

All at once, I tense.

He sees it immediately.

Nate is at my lower belly when he looks up with a silent question. My cheeks burn.

"Uh, remember what I said about things taking a while?" I ask. "That definitely goes for what you're offering."

He raises an eyebrow. "And?"

"*And* I'm sure you don't want to be down there that long."

"Let's just get one thing out of the way. Would you enjoy me going down on you?"

My face gets even hotter. "Nate," I hiss.

"What? Communication is key here. So, answer the question."

I don't even think I talked about sex this much with Rob, and I was with him for a decade. I mostly went along with what he wanted.

But Nate asked me something, and even if it's awkward, I know I need to answer.

"Honestly, I'm not sure. I've tried it before and it didn't result in anything."

"Let me guess, Rob got tired."

"Yeah, pretty much."

"I'm not him." The words are laced with a firm tone.

"I know that, Nate. Seriously, I do. But I've had a not-so-fun experience, and I don't want that to happen again."

"Then I'll hold off. Or we can try it. All you need to do is enjoy it. If you won't, then we'll find something you do enjoy."

"And what about you? What do you enjoy?"

"Fucking anything when it comes to you. Seriously, berry, you could step on me and I'd be down for it."

I can't help the shocked laugh that escapes me. "Step on you? Is that a kink I've not heard about?"

"Maybe. I don't kink shame." He presses a kiss to my hip. "But I'm serious. Anything to do with you and I'm happy."

If it were anyone else, I would think he was feeding me a line. But he's more than proven himself every day on this vacation.

And I can't be restricted by what happened with Rob.

"O-okay then. Let's try it."

"Are you sure?"

I nod. "Nervous, but sure."

"You know you can tell me if you wanna switch it up, right?"

"I do. And I will."

"That's my girl. Now get the hell out of your head and let me eat you out."

Jesus. I didn't know he could talk like this. But I like seeing this side of him.

With a tug, my shorts and underwear come off in one movement. I have to resist the urge to hide like I would with anyone else. It's *Nate.* He would never judge me.

Slowly, my thighs part, and he's in between them.

Nate remembers what I said earlier. I don't like direct stimulation, so he goes around. His tongue feels different than his fingers did, different from the one time I tried this before and it didn't end well.

It doesn't feel bad, but it's new. Historically, new things take me a while to get used to.

"Th—" He gets a really good movement in and it stops me, but then I continue. "N-Nate, this'll take a while. Just a warning."

Nate lifts up just enough to say, "Good. I'm having a great time down here."

When he goes back in, he's bolder. His tongue catches the edge of my clit, and I have to stop myself from flinching as the sensation rushes through me.

"Too sensitive?" he asks.

I shake my head immediately. I've always been so sure of what I want, but *that* is perfect. That is what I need.

Nate does it again. And again. Not one after another, or else I'd be jumping out of my skin, but just enough to make me feel like I'm at the edge right before he drags me off it.

I forget about time. About the end goal. It's just me and him on this bed, and he's making me feel like I'm floating in the sky. Finally, I have no thoughts other than what he's doing to me.

My hands comb through his hair as it builds. My legs tighten and my eyes screw shut. It starts with warmth. And fire.

"*F-fuck*, Nate. Just like that."

This time is better than the last. I thought the first was earth-shattering, but it was just a candle in the night compared to the fire in my veins now.

It's incredible, and I'm a mess when all the sensation finally fades. My chest heaves as I catch my breath.

Nate is watching me, and I wonder how long I have before he tells me how right he was about going down on me.

But when I finally look at him, there's no pride on his face. Instead, there's a small smile and eyes so warm it makes me flush.

"Wh-what?" I ask.

That snaps him out of it. "Nothing."

I raise an eyebrow, a silent challenge.

"You're just better than anything I could have imagined."

Feeling slams into me. He could easily keep things sexual, but this is soft and loving in a way I'm shockingly used to.

"You are too," I reply, and I mean it. Never in my life did I think I would be here.

And there's nowhere else I'd rather be.

I reach down to cup his chin before bringing him up to me.

When our lips meet, I taste myself, but also him. It's a flavor I never want to forget.

Nate's hand moves to hold my face, his body pinning me down as if I could float away, but there's nowhere I would want to go.

He seems content to stay here and make out on the bed, but I can feel how hard he is. And I feel empty.

I arch against him to get us back on track, giving the tiniest bit of friction against his cock. His breath stutters at it.

"So impatient," he says, his usual smile on his face.

"I can't wait forever," I say against his lips. "There's a condom right next to us."

"You're always prepared." He lifts off of me to get rid of all his clothes and grab protection, then he's right back where he belongs.

When he kisses me again, I bite down on his bottom lip and he groans. "Do that again and this won't be lasting nearly as long as you want this to."

I immediately want to do it again, but this time, I move to his neck. I get a shocked gasp before he's gone. I don't even have time to complain before I'm tugged to the edge of the bed and bent over it.

"Holy *shit*," I say breathlessly.

"Can't bite me if I'm taking you from behind."

"But I *want* to."

"And I'm telling you that will send me over the edge. Warn a guy next time."

"No."

He huffs out a laugh. "I expect nothing less from you, but I'm making this last as long as I possibly can. So sit still and let me fuck you."

"You better—*ah!*" I don't get to finish my sentence as he slides inside. This angle makes his cock rub against new parts of me, parts that I thought were exhausted after I'd already come.

But my body is alive, and it loves this.

"Fuck," he mutters into my skin. "You feel so fucking good." His voice is basically a growl.

"God, you do too. I could—I want this to last forever." I'm not sure if I mean him fucking me or us in general.

But both are true. I know it more than anything.

"You have no idea how long I've wanted you to say that," he says as he pulls out and goes right back in. I gasp as I'm shoved into the sheets.

I didn't know sex could feel like this, but now that I know, there's no way I can ever accept anything but him. He's too perfect.

My body clamps down on his cock, and a new kind of heat builds as he moves. I don't know if I'll come or not, but this feels so good that I don't care. I let myself feel, not worrying about anything but the moment.

And it grows. My hands twist in the sheets as I try to push back into him. I'm a mess, and I'm sure he is too.

Nate's pace picks up and I know he's close.

"I'm gonna—*fuck*."

I want to tell him to come, but I can't even form words. I'm too lost in us. Finally, he slams into me and holds me close. Once again, we're both out of breath, and my body still sings as I feel him empty inside of the condom.

The more time we have, the more I want to explore this.

I hope he meant the same thing I did when I mentioned forever.

"I think . . . you're about to be the reason I have a normal sleep schedule," he says into my shoulder.

"Tired already?" I ask.

"How are you not?"

"I am, but tomorrow is the end of the cruise. I guess I'm not ready for it to end."

His lips land on my cheek. "Nothing is ending tomorrow, berry. In fact, I think it's just beginning."

I let out a long breath. He has no idea how much I need to hear those words.

Now I just need them to come true.

chapter twenty-seven

I WAKE up with a pleasant ache between my thighs and neither of us are wearing clothes. After we cleaned up, both of us fell into bed and immediately slipped into sleep. It's tempting to take it easy and have a slow morning, but I know that we're supposed to be back in Orlando today. One check of my phone tells me we really need to get up and get packed.

The goal is to get out of bed and pack for both of us, that way Nate can sleep in as long as he can, but the second I try to wriggle out of his grasp, he's pulling me back into his arms.

"Bad pillow," he mutters into my hair. I'm not even sure he's awake.

"Not a pillow. It's Maisie."

"The point still stands."

He nuzzles my head before he goes right back to sleep. I feel like my heart could explode and I let myself enjoy his embrace for longer than I probably should.

"I'm sorry. We have to get off the boat."

"Let's just sign up for the next cruise," he says.

"My job wouldn't like that very much. Plus, I miss my own cooking."

He hums. "I miss your cooking too." Finally, he lets me go. "Let's just get this over with."

"You can stay in bed," I offer.

"And miss the view?"

"We're at the dock, and the curtains are closed," I remind him.

"I don't mean the one out the window." He rolls over, eyes following me as I get dressed. My skin grows hot, but I can't deny that the attention is nice.

I get my belongings together the best I can. Eventually, Nate joins, and I get a similar view to his.

At least this time I can stare at his ass as long as I want.

Soon, we have our two suitcases and we're double-checking that we have everything before getting off the ship for the final time.

I can't deny the relief I feel as we step onto the dock. Finally, I'm home. Or at least close to it.

"I'm both sad and excited to never be on a boat again," I say as I turn to look at the boat one final time. It's massive, and I can't believe how much happened there.

He looks over at me and laughs. "Did I not convert you to be a cruise girl?"

"Listen, I didn't hate it. Which is high praise."

"I'll take it," he replies.

We can leave at any moment, but I still stay and stare at the ship. A feeling of nervousness hits me, something I haven't felt before when *leaving* water.

"We need to find a ride to the airport," Nate mutters as he leads me away. I go willingly, but I can't help but feel like I'm forgetting something.

That's when I see her. Blonde hair and a red shirt.

Scarlett is just across the dock. She's got her suitcase and her hair's in a messy bun. She looks as overwhelmed as the rest of us.

But it hits me that I haven't said goodbye.

"Hang on," I say. "I wanna say bye to Scarlett."

"That's fine. I'm trying to find an option that won't cost an arm and a leg. I'll hold your suitcase."

I thank him before I make my way through the crowd.

"Scarlett!" I call as I get close.

She turns to me with a raised eyebrow. When she realizes who I am, her face lights up. "Maisie!" she says. "There you are. I was worried you'd try to sneak away without a goodbye."

"I didn't mean to," I say as I pull her into a tight hug. "It's been a mad dash this morning."

"Agreed." She sighs before eyeing me. "You seem to be in a good mood."

"I *am* in a good mood. Someone gave me some great advice and things have changed."

"Oh, finally." She laughs. "I didn't know if you would have enough time to."

"I made it work. And I have you to thank for it."

"Some of my best work," she replies. "Did you like the part where I let you come to your own conclusions?"

"I did. Very therapist of you."

She laughs again. "You would've gotten defensive if I brought it up too early. But you know we all saw it, right?"

"I do. And I wonder how the hell I didn't."

"Emotions make us miss things sometimes. And you care about him. A lot."

"That I do."

"Then you've got the main thing you need." She pulls me into another hug. "I'm happy for you. Seriously."

"What about you? I didn't ruin your vacation with all of my drama, right?"

"Nowhere near it," she replies. "I think I needed this. Maybe I'll go through my own life with more hope. Until a man inevitably ruins it."

"They always try."

"Keep in touch, okay? And maybe I'll make it to Nashville soon so I can see more of you and Nate in action."

"I would love that." We say goodbye one last time before I make my way to Nate. He's still on his phone, but lets me lean on him.

"Okay, *finally*. Remind me to make plans for rides way sooner." He looks up. "Wait, where's Scarlett?"

I look back, but she must have made her way through the crowd. "I already said bye."

"I wanted to at least say goodbye. She must think I'm such an ass for how little I've said to her."

"She likes you, don't worry." I roll my eyes. "She mentioned visiting Nashville so we could all hang out."

"I look forward to it."

Leaning my head on his shoulder, I say, "There's a lot I'm looking forward to. Ready to make it happen?"

"Always, berry."

～～～

THE FLIGHT back to Nashville is better than the one to Orlando.

Still, the second I sit, I can tell travel has taken its toll on me. Even though I got a full night of sleep, I find myself leaning my head on Nate's shoulder.

"And this is what we call travel exhaustion," he says.

"Do you feel it too?"

"Oh yeah. I'm gonna crash when we get back. *Hard.*"

"You could crash with me," I offer. "I promise my bed is more comfortable than the one on the ship."

"Is it?"

"It's bigger too. Though, I think we won't need to worry about that."

His hand grabs mine. "I'm sure we won't."

I hide my smile in his shoulder and get comfortable. I'm able to drift off for a little while on the flight, but for the majority of it, I read the book for my book club.

This time, the romance doesn't bug me. I enjoy it, for once.

It's raining in Nashville when we land, and I can't wait to get to Nate's SUV and go home. This feels like the beginning of something incredible.

And I need it to start.

I only let go of Nate in the baggage claim so I can hunt down our suitcases. I'm so focused on getting out of here that I don't notice my surroundings.

And a hand gets my suitcase before I do.

"Oh, hey, I—" Looking up, I expect to see a stranger who's made a mistake.

Instead, I see Rob.

"W-what?" I blink at him as if he's a bad dream.

"Maisie," he whispers. "My God, you look beautiful."

My body revolts at his words, but I tamp down the reaction. I still need to be friendly with him. Quinn's party is *tomorrow*.

"Rob." I take him in, seeing that he's in his finest suit with a bright blue bear tucked under one arm.

Behind him, there's a sign that says, "I'm *bear-y* sorry. Will you forgive me?"

No. *No.* Why is he here?

I look to Nate, who's still in the spot I left him. His entire body is rigid, his mouth pressed into a thin line. When my eyes meet his, he shakes himself out of his thoughts and strides over to us.

"What are you doing here?" Nate asks. His voice is flat, but it contains a barely there anger that I've never heard from him before.

"I wanted to apologize in person," Rob says to me. Then he

looks at Nate. "And thank you for taking care of her while I was an idiot. I owe you one, man."

My teeth grit. When he was drunk, Rob was saying how much he didn't want us around each other.

"I—" Nate shakes his head. "Maisie, I need to talk to you." He pulls me away before I can say anything else. "Fuck your luggage," he blows out. "You have your purse, which is good enough. We need to *go*."

I can see his logic, and I *want* to say yes.

But I shake my head anyway.

"No, I can't do that."

"What, why not? Quinn could get your bag. Hell, we could just replace the shit in there. Let's just go before he comes and tries to apologize again."

"Nate, stop." I rub my forehead. "I need to talk to him."

"What?" he asks, his voice suddenly deeper.

"I knew it was possible he would try something else. I didn't think it would be this, but still . . ."

"You knew this could happen and you didn't tell me? When did this happen?"

"Quinn warned me it wasn't over."

"Dammit, Maisie."

Nate huffs out a breath, and dimly, I realize this might be the first time I've ever seen him this angry. His jaw is tight, and he glares at Rob with a ferocity I didn't know he had.

"Nate," I say. "Don't—"

"Don't *what*? Be pissed that you're saying you're willing to talk to him after what he said? Maisie, be smart."

"I am," I say. "I can't just turn my back on what he is."

Nate jerks back like I've hit him, but I'm not sure why. "What he *is*? Seriously?"

His defensiveness is so unlike him that I take a step back.

And I feel my own flare.

"Nate, I can't avoid him. I might not want to, but I need to talk to him. I can't hide from it."

"You should."

"What? You, of all people, are telling me to hide? After all that support with swimming?"

"Don't compare him to that. He's different."

I shake my head. "It's not. I don't run from what I'm scared of anymore. I'm gonna talk to him, explain things. And you can't stop me."

He grabs my hand. "Maisie, *please*. Don't do this."

"No. This isn't a big deal. He's just being Rob. I'm gonna walk over there and we'll just talk. Okay?"

He stares at me and then Rob. "Why?"

"I need to give him a chance to . . ." I trail off. Be my friend? No, I don't think I want that. See if he means his apology and if we can be civil? That's close enough.

I regret not giving this more thought. If I had, I would have seen this surprise coming. Now I have to deal with trying to figure out my words.

"Of course." Nate says it slowly. "I knew this would happen."

"The surprise? Maybe we both should have, but—"

He steps away, fully putting the distance we used to have back between us. "Just go talk to him."

"Wait, are you—" I try to reach out, but he moves away even farther.

"Maisie!" Rob calls, and he's running over to us. I guess our time is up.

Nate still looks angry, and I know I need to clear this up. I need to talk to him more about what he's thinking, because I'm not sure we're on the same page.

"Rob," I say. "Can you give us just a minute? I was—"

"We're done here," Nate cuts me off. "I'll see you later, b—" He stops, and his face goes tight. "Maisie."

My eyes widen. He didn't say my nickname. He used my actual one, and it cuts me like a knife.

"You're my ride here," I say, a last-ditch attempt to get him to stay while I tell Rob to never do this again. "We should—"

"I'll get you to where you need to go," Rob says. "Don't worry about it."

I shake my head, not taking my eyes off Nate. "No, just give me one second. Nate—"

He holds his hand up, lips still pursed. "You're really going to talk it out with him?"

"Well, yes, but it can just be—"

"Stop. This is a terrible decision, but it's yours to make, I guess. I just thought . . ." He shakes his head. "Whatever."

"Nate, hang on."

"No," he snaps. "I'm not watching you do this. Not *again*. So, go talk to Rob. I'm going home."

And then he walks away, not looking back *once*.

"Wow." Rob laughs. "That was kind of rude."

"Don't," I hiss. "Just don't."

"Okay, I can see you're tense. And you can act out when you're mad." My temper flares once again. "Let's just go so you can calm down."

I hate the way he talks to me when I'm angry. It's why I stopped letting him see me mad. But I just had a fight with *Nate*, of all people. I'm not in my right mind.

It's not like Nate and me to not be on the same page. And I don't understand why he was so upset by me simply talking to Rob.

Rob shoves the bear in my arms, pulling me out of my thoughts. "Here you go, babe."

"Please don't call me that," I say. "And I can't hold this and my—"

"I've got your bag. Let's go."

My jaw tightens as I follow him. I'm all kinds of unnerved, and I throw the bear into the back seat the second we get to his car.

"Whoa, don't be so rough with your new buddy."

I glare. "I didn't ask for a new buddy."

"You're playing hard to get still?" He sighs. "Fine. I can be stubborn."

"I don't want you to be stubborn," I say as I get into the passenger's seat.

"You say that, but I know you."

"I don't think you do."

Rob's smile falls for all of one second before he starts the car. "I'm working on it."

"You don't have to. Seriously, Rob. Just let it go."

"No." He's serious and I want to bang my head against a wall. "What we have is good, Maisie."

"We barely *talk*." I shake my head. "What kind of relationship is that?"

"We talk." He laughs. "Of course we talk."

"Then how do I take my coffee in the morning? What time do I usually get up?"

He blinks. "What is this? A quiz?"

"My point still stands."

"Listen, I'm here. I got you a very expensive stuffed animal that I can't return, and I'm not even saying anything about who you took on that cruise. I'm doing all I can here, Maisie."

"Doing all you can?" I repeat. "This is your best?"

"No one is going to compare to your *perfect* best friend, Maisie. Although, maybe he isn't so perfect now. He's mad at you, isn't he?"

His words hit me right where he means for them to. Just thinking about how Nate and I left things makes my chest hurt. "He didn't want me to talk to you."

"Of course he didn't. He knows I'm going to win you back."

"I'm not a *prize*. You can't just win me."

"Is that not what I've done the last decade?"

My jaw drops and I go to argue, but I remember the video Nate showed me. When he talked about marrying me, he mentioned he thought he was winning then too.

Just who was he winning *against*?

"Why did you want me, Rob?" I turn to him the best I can. "Because it wasn't my personality."

"I mean, look at you."

"Yeah, yeah. I'm hot. Whatever. It takes more than that to spend a decade on *winning* someone."

"What do you want me to say?" He laughs uncomfortably. "I mean, you're a good person. You, uh, clean up really well. Speaking of which, those shorts you're wearing . . . Are they new? They're a little short."

I'm about to argue with him when I realize he's changing the subject, which is what he always tries to do when I'm getting close to a conclusion he doesn't want me to have. The cracks in our relationship are obvious. They always have been, but I was too afraid to look into them. I still am, but I survived the water.

I'll make sure to survive this too.

"Did you see Nate as your competition?" I ask.

Rob jerks back, jaw opening. He thinks about it for a moment and then laughs. "What? Why would you ask me that?"

"Answer the question."

"Is that an idea *he* put into your head?"

"No. I can have my own thoughts, you know. I may have forgotten it over the last few years, but it's still possible."

Rob glances at me. Instead of the guy he's been playing, I see a glimpse of the man he really is. His jaw is tight and his eyes narrow into a glare. He doesn't like me fighting back. He doesn't like this side of me at all.

That's why he got rid of it.

"One little vacation and you're very different. I should have known. *He* makes you this way."

"*I* make myself this way. This is who I am, and I guess it's someone you hate."

He shakes his head. He doesn't say anything in response and I scoff, realizing now he's avoiding the conversation entirely. For the first time during the drive, I look out the window and focus on the road. Once I'm home, I'm going after Nate.

But the only things I see are tall buildings. We're pulling through a gate, one that leads to a high-rise I know all too well.

"Rob, why the hell did you bring me here?" I ask. "You said you would take me home."

"I said I would get you to where you need to go. This is it. You need space from Nate. And I have a delicious dinner waiting on us. After, you can use my tub and—"

I go for the handle of the door. The car is too stuffy and I need to *breathe*.

"This isn't what I want!" I yell as I turn to him. "God, do you not understand the word no?"

"Maisie, calm down. You're acting—"

"Take me to my fucking house, Rob!"

"No!" he snaps as he climbs out. "I'm not letting you have another second with that man. Not after he turned you against me!"

"You did that yourself! You won't listen to me, you don't even *know* me, and the only reason you want me is because you think you can take me away from the man who actually cares about me!"

"I *can* take you away from him. I've done it before and I'll do it again."

"Not this time," I say. "I'm not going into your apartment. I'm not getting back with you."

"Yes, you are! You said it yourself, you're giving me a chance!"

"A chance to *talk*, not get back together."

"What else are we going to talk about, Maisie? A friendship? I don't want that from you."

"Wow, thanks for letting me know after all this time." I shake my head in disbelief. "And besides, I just want to be civil for tomorrow."

"Too fucking bad. I want you, and you're at my place. So come inside and let me undo . . . this." He gestures to me and I shake my head.

"You're unreasonable. Empty purchases and dinners aren't gonna make up for what you did."

"What? Hating you? Or finally putting my foot down about you and Nate?"

I take a step back. I know which one it is.

"I should've known." He starts to pace. "I should have seen that you'd always choose him. Even after everything . . ."

"After everything? Like leaving me alone for weeks at a time? Like trying to override who I am so I suit you?"

"I tried to make it work!"

"This isn't how it works!" I snap.

"And you would know, huh? Because of Nate?"

"I would."

"Fine then. Go find him. I bet he'll love to hear you out after he walked away from you."

I flinch at the words. I'm still struggling to understand why he walked away at all. "Nate and I are none of your business."

"Oh, I made it my business. I've watched that lovesick puppy follow you around for years. And that? Him walking away? That's a first."

It is. I *know* it is. "Whatever." I pull out my phone to call a ride, but it's almost dead. I'd forgotten to charge it the night before because I was busy with Nate.

God, will I get that again? Last night alone feels like a different world.

In a rush, I put in my location and Nate's address. I need to talk to him. *Now.*

"You know what I think?"

"I-I don't care what you think."

"I have a feeling he thought you two were finally heading toward being something more. I have a feeling he got his hopes up. I mean, why wouldn't he? You look like *this*, and you're single. And then you get back to the airport and you give me a chance." He laughs. "And you broke his heart."

"The chance was to talk, which you ruined, by the way."

"Yeah, and I bet you made that *very* clear, judging by the way he reacted."

"I—*no*, he would know . . ." I trail off, thinking about what I've said and done over the last few days. Us being physical was new. Did we ever talk about the future?

All I'd said was I'd take what he would give me.

Fuck, I never said the words.

"That's right," Rob said cruelly. "You messed it up."

"Fuck off," I snap.

"You know, I thought it was fun when I was dating you, but this is actually better. You burned your bridge with him. I should've let you vacation with him a long time ago."

"You're an asshole."

"But I'm *your* asshole. When Nate continues to ignore you and you're alone, come find me. I'll tell you I was right, but maybe I'll take a little pity on you."

With one last laugh, he steps away and goes into his apartment complex. I'm left heaving, wondering if he's right. I check my phone to see if my ride is close, and then go to call Nate.

It dies before I can.

"No," I hiss. "Fuck."

Running my hands through my hair, I pace. I need to get to Nate. I need to *explain*.

I'm considering hot-wiring Rob's car when my ride finally arrives. The drive to Nate's apartment is spent with me either begging the driver to ignore all the laws or trying to figure out what to tell him.

I barely even say goodbye to the guy the second we pull in. My heart pounds as I race up the stairs to his apartment door. When I'm in front of it, I take a shaky breath before knocking.

"Nate?" I ask. "Hey, it's me." There's only silence as I wait. I can imagine him on the other side, wondering whether to open it up or not. "Please open the door. We really need to talk."

There's still no answer. It feels like my heart is cracking in my chest and I shut my eyes, wishing I could go back in time and do it all differently.

But Rob can't be right. Surely, Nate isn't done with me.

"I know you're mad at me, and you have every right to be. I'm *not* with Rob, and I said it all wrong. You can absolutely have space from me, but *please*, can I explain myself? I'll leave you alone after. I promise."

I stare at the door, hoping my pleading will reach him, but nothing changes. The door doesn't open and there's no sound on the other side.

My breathing speeds up. No, *no*.

I wait, hoping he's in the bathroom or he's just getting dressed. I silently beg for the door to open. I don't care if he's mad or if he yells at me. I just need to talk to him.

Sinking to the floor, I wonder if this is really where it ends. I didn't realize how much I couldn't live without him. I didn't realize how easily I could mess things up.

There's no telling how much time passes while I sit there. I want to wait it out, but the longer the silence continues, the more I regret *everything*.

We had a chance to get this right, to be something.

And I fucked it up.

The sun has long since set as I sit on the dirty floor of his apartment breezeway. I'm curled into a ball when I finally hear the click of a door opening.

I sit up, hoping this is my chance.

But it's not Nate's door. It's his neighbor, an old woman with two dogs.

"Oh," she says when she sees me. "What are you doing down there?"

Disappointment makes me slump against the wall again. "Just . . . waiting."

She eyes me, and then the door behind me. "You're that guy's girlfriend, aren't you?"

I flinch at the words. "I . . . I don't know, actually."

She puts her hands on her hips. "Well, how could you not know? You young people make everything so complicated these days. Just be together or don't be. There's no reason to sit outside begging for a chance."

"I'm guessing you heard me."

"Oh, yeah. The walls are *very* thin. You're wasting your time anyway."

"I'm not giving up," I say as my fists tighten into balls. "I just need him to open the door and talk to him."

"Well, he won't be opening that door."

My shoulders fall. "Please, can you just—"

"He's not here, kid."

I pause. "What?"

"He's not been here for a week. I would know because I always listen for him. He's very fun to talk to."

"B-but he said he would be here."

"He must've lied. I would know if he came back, and he hasn't."

"Fuck," I say to myself.

"Language," she mutters. "Jeez, have some respect for old ears. You'll offend Mr. Fluff here."

One of her dogs, a tiny ball of fur that doesn't look like it's capable of thought, runs right into a wall.

"Anyway, have fun hunting down your boyfriend. If I stay here any longer, Mr. Fluff might think you're a fire hydrant."

She walks away without saying anything else, but I'm too busy replaying her words. She said Nate didn't come home, but where the hell would he be?

Out of habit, I take my phone out to check his location. But my phone is still dead, refusing to turn on for even a second.

"Fuck," I mutter. I need to get to a charger, but I left my luggage with Rob. And I don't have my extra key to Nate's place.

Not that I should go in anyway.

My only option is to go home and let my phone charge, then continue tracking him down.

Technically, Nate lives close enough to walk. It's not the safest thing, but it's my only option. Heaving a sigh, I get up and pocket my phone, setting out to my house.

The second I step out from the staircase, it starts raining again.

"Are you serious!" I yell at the sky. "I get it, I fucked up! You don't have to keep punishing me!"

The rain keeps falling.

With one more curse at the sky, I break out into a jog. The sooner I get home, the sooner I can plug in my phone and then find Nate.

I round the corner to my neighborhood and I push myself even harder. The second my house is in sight, I try to go even faster.

I'm pulling out my keys as I start to head up my driveway, but I'm stopped when arms wrap around me. My heart lurches and I let out a scream as I try to get away.

It would be my fucking luck that I would get robbed right on my own property.

"Wait, berry!" a voice breaks through my panic. "It's me. It's Nate."

I blink against the water in my eyes. Pushing my soaked hair off my forehead, I finally see him. He's not as wet as I am, but it's definitely Nate.

He's staring at me like I've lost my mind.

"Wh-what?"

"Why are you running at night in the rain? Where the hell is Rob?"

My jaw is still open as I try to catch my breath. I'm not sure if this is a dream or if I fell and hit my head on mile two. Nate checks me over before shaking his head.

"All right, I'll murder him for this later. Let's just get inside and get you dry." He goes to grab at me, but I step away as I shake my head.

"What are you doing here?" I ask.

He pauses. "I—we can talk about that later."

"You said you were going home. You're mad at me. So, *why are you here*?" I nearly yell it. Not because I'm angry, but because I don't understand. I hurt him. I pissed him off.

I fucked up.

He sighs and runs a hand through his hair. It's nearly soaked by now. "I . . . I regretted leaving you at the airport. I should've stayed. But by the time I went back, you were gone. So, I waited here."

"Y-you said you weren't watching me do this again, that you were going *home*."

"I shouldn't have said any of that. I'm sorry, Maisie."

I shake my head. Nate shouldn't be the one apologizing. I should be. I need to tell him that wasn't what it was at all, that I only wanted to be civil with Rob, and that I'm so fucking sorry for not being clear.

But the words get clogged in my throat. I'm so relieved he's here, so angry at myself for letting us even get to this point, and hurt by all the things Rob said.

Before I can stop it, tears are running down my cheeks and mixing with the rain. I'm a complete mess, and Nate is seeing it all.

"Come on," he says. "Let's get dried off."

Tears turn into sobs as he leads me to the house. He grabs my keys from me and unlocks the door before finding me a towel. I don't understand why he's willing to be here with me.

Didn't I mess this up?

Warmth wraps around me as he dries me off. I step away and take the towel myself, trying to get it together so I can say *something*.

"Don't be with Rob." Nate says it softly, and the words are so shocking that I finally look at him. "That's what I came here to say. Don't give him another chance. Not this time."

"I—"

"I want the chance instead. Just one. Let me prove that I can be better. If you say no, that's fine. I'll let it go and we'll be friends. But *please*, let me be better than he is. It might be too late. Maybe he already got through to you, or maybe not, considering you were in the rain, but still. Just . . . one chance. Please."

"You came here . . . while angry at me for going with Rob to ask for me to be with you?"

"Yes. And it might be stupid, but—"

"It is," I say. "Because you . . . you walked away."

He winces. "I did."

"You're angry."

"*Was*. And I stupidly hoped for more when I knew I was just a rebound to you."

All the breath rushes out of my lungs. "You . . . *what*?"

"I know you've never felt like that about me. But maybe there's an inkling there. If there is, then let's try it. *Please*."

"What . . . are you *doing*?" I manage to ask.

"I'm telling you how I feel?"

I shake my head, still stuck on what he believes has happened. "You thought I was using you as a rebound and got back with my ex. You should be pissed at me."

"I'm not, I—"

"Don't make excuses for that." I push his shoulder and his eyes go wide. "If that's what I did, then you should absolutely never talk to me again."

"I would never do that, Maisie. You have me for life. Whether as a friend or . . . whatever else."

The words are what I need to hear, but I still can't believe I'm hearing them. I've not apologized yet. I've not told him what I meant.

And yet he's here. He's asked for a chance.

He would forgive me if I asked.

Nate's love isn't conditional. It's just here. Always here.

And I refuse to be blind about it.

"Nate, I wasn't giving Rob a chance to get back together with me tonight. I was giving him a chance to be civil with me. For Quinn's party tomorrow."

He jerks back. "You did?" I nod. "Did he know that?"

"Obviously not at first. I tried to make it clear, but he . . . wasn't thrilled. I don't think I did myself any good, which is probably why I let him call all the shots like a fucking idiot." I rub my forehead. "But he did make me realize how it sounded. And I would *never* use you like that. You hear me? *Never.*"

Nate takes a shaky breath. I give him a moment to answer, but he looks lost, like these were the last words he ever expected to hear.

So I continue. "You don't need to ask me for a chance. You never did. I chose you. And I'd do it again."

He blinks. "You chose me tonight?" His voice is quiet and raw.

I shake my head. "Not just tonight. I never told you about why I actually dumped Rob last week. Honestly, I was afraid of what it meant until recently." I hold the towel tighter around my body and suck in air before continuing. "Rob wanted me to move in with him. It was about to be a huge fight."

"Wait, why? You own the house. It makes more sense for him to move."

"That's what I thought. But while he was drunk, I heard his friends saying to make me choose. And he told me that he wanted me to move in with him so he could make sure you never came over. It was forcing me to choose between you or him. And I dumped him."

Nate only stares and I look away. I need to fill the silence with *something*.

"I should've done it a while ago. The only reason I was fine with how Rob acted was because I had you. And that wasn't fair to you. I should have seen it for what it was, but I was . . . afraid, I guess. I'm trying to be better about that. If anything, I should be begging *you* for a chance. And I would. I *want* this. So bad that I—"

Lips cut me off, and I let out a squeak of surprise as Nate invades my space. He holds me tighter than when I fell in the water, tighter than when we had our fight. A whine escapes me as I run my fingers through his hair.

He's *here*. He's *kissing* me.

I can't believe it's real.

"Maisie, I love you," he says against my lips. I pull away only to stare at him with wide eyes. "I know it's too early to say it. But I do. I have since the day we met. Since before I fucking knew what love *was*. And I always will. *That's* why I'm here."

"All this time?"

"All this time," he replies as he puts his forehead against mine. "And I didn't care that you didn't feel the same way. I was serious when I said I'd take anything you would give me."

"And what if I want to give you everything?"

His breath hitches before he smiles. "Then I might just be the happiest man on the planet."

"I love you too. Probably for way too long. Probably when I was with someone else. And I'm sor—"

He kisses me again. "Don't apologize. Admittedly, I didn't have the words for it until it was too late. And then we both lost people and . . ."

"Then I met Rob."

"The timing wasn't right."

"I still wish we had more of it."

"Well, honey, we have it all now. What do you want to do with it?"

The world shifts, turning into something that once felt impossible to me. I'd only just realized I wanted Nate, and now I have him. Instead of the dread I felt only a week ago, there's hope.

So much of it that tears gather in my eyes.

"I don't know." I tighten my hold on him. "But let's figure it out together."

chapter twenty-eight

UNFORTUNATELY, the first thing I do is pretty boring.

I'm exhausted from running all the way home. Nate is too. And the second everything is cleared up, we both long for a comfortable bed.

Both of us are out the second our heads hit the pillows.

Travel and subsequently spilling our feelings must have been exhausting, because even when light filters through the windows the next day, I still feel like I've been hit by a train.

The sun is at an angle that tells me it's late. Way later than usual.

I blindly reach for my phone and check the screen.

It's noon.

"Fuck," I say. I'm tempted to go back to sleep, but Quinn's party is in five hours, and I need to remember how to exist.

"Berry, I love you, but this is not the time to be a morning person." Nate is blindly reaching around and presses a hand to my face as if he can silence me as an alarm clock. I'm tired and grumpy, but the action makes me laugh.

"It's not morning. It's noon."

He groans. "Dammit. Why are vacations so exhausting?"

"You can't forget the emotional crash outs my ex started," I say as I slowly sit up and take stock of my body. "God, I need a shower. And coffee."

"I can help with both of those. Once I remember how to function." He rubs a hand over his face, then slowly gets up. "I'll get the water started for your shower. And then coffee."

"You're so hot right now," I mutter. "Love you."

The words are so new that he jumps when I say them, but then he grins at me. "Love you too."

I'm an odd mix of uncomfortable yet grateful to have him when I finally drag myself out of bed. The second I step into the hot steam of my own shower, I feel like I can breathe. My body is sore and needs relaxation.

When I'm done, I feel more human. I throw on comfortable clothes before going to meet Nate in the kitchen. He's putting together some kind of meal from my meager food stores, and I wind my arms around his middle.

"Hi," I said.

"Hey," he says back, leaning into me. "Feel better?"

"Now I do."

"As much as I hate to pull away, I'm making you food and I can't do that with you being my backpack."

I roll my eyes. "I'm not a backpack."

"You're about the size of one."

I poke him right in the ribs, feeling ridiculously proud of myself when he yelps and tries to get away from me. I'm tempted to torture him for longer, but I give him space.

"So, you never told me why you were in the rain," he says as he starts to boil water. "And I should probably know before I'm in the same room as Rob."

"Oh, *that*." I rub the back of my neck. "Yeah, that was partially me."

"You were at his place before that."

"You checked my location, didn't you?"

"I did. You were there for a while."

"Only because my phone died. And he wasn't even supposed to take me there anyway. I wanted to come here. He thought a nice dinner would convince me to give him another chance. I didn't even go inside."

"Thank God," Nate says. His shoulders are tense, but he takes a breath and releases them. "Sorry, I still don't like the guy."

"Neither do I. But I promise I wasn't there long. I actually used the last bit of my battery life to go after you. At your place."

He pauses. "You did?"

"Yep. I, uh, may have thought you were ignoring me up until your neighbor told me you hadn't come home yet. Nice lady, actually." I let out a laugh. "But it all worked out."

Nate doesn't find it funny. "You thought I ignored you."

"Yeah. Part of it was Rob. He said he'd never seen you so mad, and with how it sounded, I'd have it coming."

"Maisie, *no*." He puts the container of oats down and turns to me. "I would never ignore you, even if I was pissed."

"But—"

"No. You need to hear this." He only continues when my mouth shuts. "Maisie, I'm with you always. Even when I'm angry. Even if you mess up. I'm never going to ignore you."

My eyes water, but I slowly nod. "I hear you."

"Good. Now let me cook for you."

I'm not used to this level of care. I had a part of it before, but this is next-level.

I love it. So much so that I have to go get my phone and distract myself or else I'll start crying again. I should probably let the people who care about me know I'm home safe.

My parents are the first on the list. After I message them, a text from Quinn comes through.

QUINN

I heard that Rob surprised you at the airport yesterday. Are you coming with him or is Nate still your plus-one?

MAISIE

Nate's joining me.

QUINN

Good.

"If it's Rob, I'm insisting you block him." Nate's voice pulls me out of my thoughts and I shake my head.

"That was Quinn. She was making sure you're still coming. I don't think Rob'll be reaching out any time soon."

"I wouldn't put it past him. He's like a roach. He never gives up." He sets a bowl of hot oatmeal in front of me.

"He can do whatever he wants. I'm not changing my mind."

Nate smiles. "It's nice to see you like this. I was worried I was losing you when you were with Rob."

"You're not. Never."

"Good."

Both of us settle into silence only to eat. After getting back into town and subsequently skipping dinner, both of us are starving. It's only when I've finished my food and my coffee that I feel like I can talk again.

"Quinn's party. You *are* going, right?"

"Of course I am. It'll be . . . *fun*."

"It'll be something," I admit. "I want it to go well, and considering how things went with Rob, I'm worried."

"Did you mention anything about him just now?"

"In passing. She was asking if we were back together after his little surprise. I said we weren't."

"I bet it'll be a big deal when we tell her about us." He laughs as he finishes off his coffee.

I pause at the thought. He's right. This will definitely be big news.

"Berry?" he asks. "Please don't tell me you're having second thoughts."

"No!" I say immediately. "Not about us. Just about the party."

"We could skip it."

"I want to see her," I reply with a shake of my head. "But it's her birthday. And it's already drama filled because I dumped her brother. I just don't want anything else to happen. Either with us or her family."

"So, what do you want to do?"

"What if we kept the news about us quiet until after the party? Not because I'm ashamed or anything," I rush to say, "but because of how her family might act, and the fact that it's her day."

"I can see the reasoning, but I'm not very excited about even pretending to only be your friend."

"Me either," I say. "But she's put a lot of work into this. And I've already done enough to her by dumping Rob."

"Technically, Rob did enough to *you*."

"Fair, but I don't wanna add anything."

He considers it before sighing. "Fine. But you have to get me more coffee."

"Gladly."

"And we tell her right after?"

"Right after," I agree. "Be right back with coffee."

I get him his drink and refill my own before I sit back down. He accepts it gratefully and gets through half of it before he speaks again.

"We also have to tell your parents." He says it quietly, and I tilt my head at him.

"Why do you sound worried? You get along with them just fine."

"Yeah, when I'm your friend. Judy'll be shocked, but I'm not worried about her. Jeff, on the other hand . . ." He trails off and shudders.

"My dad isn't going to do anything."

"You weren't there when he *grilled* Rob."

"What? Seriously?"

"I didn't even like Rob, and I thought it was too far."

I frown and try to imagine my dad intensely asking Rob questions. I *can* see it, but he's always taken a hands-off approach to me.

"How much do I not know?"

"He asked me not to tell you. He wants you to be your own person, but he's also fiercely protective of you. I'm just not excited for that to be turned around on me."

"Nate, if my dad tries anything with you, then he's dealing with *me*." I shake my head. "The last thing I'm letting him do is make you uncomfortable because he's trying to protect me."

A slow smile spreads on his face. "Protective of me, berry?"

"Yes." I say it immediately. "I love my dad, but he doesn't get to flip a switch because I date someone. I'll be watching him."

"I like it when you get all defensive."

"Get used to it. Because you're my boyfriend now."

He laughs and looks down at his cup. "Hearing that still feels like a dream."

"It does to me too," I reply as I grab his hand. "And no matter how people react, we've got this. Together."

THREE HOURS LATER, I'm staring at a pile of wedding decor that I'm determined to get out of my house.

As much as I'd love to completely change who I am, my house is a mess, and I need to get it somewhat in order. After the caffeine hits my system, the urge to get my life together is strong.

I can tell Nate doesn't have the same urge, but he helps me anyway.

"My wedding dress can be donated. Or do you think I should give it back to Andrea?"

"What could she possibly do with it?"

I shrug. "Maybe she can get her money back. I don't really care what she does with it, though, I just need it out of here."

Looking at it now, I'm glad I didn't wear it. It's a full turtle-neck and covered in beads. It's not my style at all. There's so much about that relationship that wasn't me.

"I'll ask her at the party tonight," Nate says. "And if she says no, can we burn it?"

"As tempting as that is, no. And I'll ask. It's my mess to clean up."

"Fine, but I'll be there for backup."

"I might need it against Andrea," I mutter. "If she doesn't want it, I'll donate it."

"Who could use this thing?" he grimaces.

"What if I really liked the dress? I did have *some* of a say in choosing it."

He winces. "I know I said I would support you through anything, but this is pushing it. When you showed it to me, I almost told you to dump him right then."

I roll my eyes. "Then what should I get next time?"

"There'll be a next time, huh?" He leans in. "Are you putting me through you marrying someone else *again*?"

"Not someone else." I tilt my head at him. "Are you gonna tell me your opinion, or do I need to guess?"

"Here's my opinion. Wear something you *like*. I can tell the difference."

I hum. "Noted."

We work through more of the wedding stuff, throwing about half of it away before we have to get ready to go to Quinn's party. My nerves get to me as I'm picking out an outfit, which leads to me being more indecisive than I've ever been before.

"Okay, but what about jeans? Are jeans too casual?" I've been at this for thirty minutes and have gotten nowhere. Nate is on my bed, waiting patiently.

"Hey, Maisie, you don't happen to be worried about this party, right?" He asks it in a soft voice, like he knows that's exactly what I am.

"I'm obvious, aren't I?" Throwing the jeans back into the closet, I flop onto the bed next to him. "I was doing so good with facing things on the cruise. But now that we're in real life, it's harder."

"You also faced your ex, who's an absolute idiot."

"That too."

Nate's hand lands on my back. "It's a good thing that you're not hiding out. I'm glad you feel safe enough to face the hard stuff now, but it's not gonna go well every time. Just like last night."

"So, should I hide?"

"Not necessarily. This isn't talking to the man who love bombed you. Sure, he'll be there, but so will other people."

"Yeah, his family."

"And your best friend," he reminds me. "Say the word and we'll stay, but I know you wanna be there. Don't let what happened with Rob affect this."

I let his words sink in. I know I'm disappointed that I couldn't be civil with Rob. All of last night was a mess.

But Nate's right. Things don't always go to plan.

Slowly, I sit up. "Okay. Not letting Rob affect today. I think I can do that. Once I pick an outfit."

"Can your new boyfriend offer his humble opinion?"

"Since when do you have an opinion on fashion?"

He gasps and puts his hand to his chest. "Excuse you. I picked out those shorts for you *and* bought them. They're *obscene*, berry."

My cheeks heat. "Is that why you got all weird?"

"Guilty." He shrugs and gets up. "And I'll get even weirder if you wear this."

He pulls out a purple dress, one that I've had for years but had forgotten about. "Really? Can I pull that off?" Nate's answering glare tells me I should *not* be putting myself down. "All right, all right. I'll wear it."

"Thank you." He tosses it to me before going back in my closet. "Now it's my turn to find something. I have a feeling I can wear one of the shirts you stole from me."

"Hey, you left them here."

"Potato, potahto."

I shake my head at him and head to the bathroom to get dressed and work on my hair. I've gotten more comfortable with wearing it down, even when it's inconvenient. I'd let it air dry when getting out of the shower this morning, which has left it wavy and slightly frizzy.

I debate on whether to leave it down or put it up and settle for a half updo that gives me the best of both worlds.

"All right, Nate," I call as I step out of the bathroom. "Moment of truth."

Nate comes around the corner and does a double take when he sees me. "You look . . ."

"Different?" I ask. "Yeah, I'm trying—"

"Incredible," he finishes.

I step close and he pulls me into his arms.

"Are you trying to make sure I can't stay away from you tonight?"

"Not really. That's just a bonus."

His words remind me that we're supposed to be just friends, at least for tonight.

"Can I rip this off of you tonight?" he asks. "Please say yes."

"If we're good and don't get caught, yes."

"Now you're challenging me. And I don't know if I can do this one."

"Just for tonight," I remind him. "Then everyone'll know."

"Fine," he says. "You're driving, though."

"What? Scared of the traffic?"

"Not at all. I just wanna be able to stare at you."

A surprised laugh escapes me as I grab my purse and pull him out the door.

The Nortons always went overboard on parties, but this was even more so. I knew Quinn would have a lot of people at their house, but this was *busy*.

"Are you sure Rob isn't turning this into a surprise wedding? I swear this is how many people were attending yours."

I glare. "Don't even put that energy out there. It might come true."

Thankfully, when we walk into their ostentatious home, it's clear that this is a birthday party. On the right is a massive photo booth with a sign congratulating Quinn on turning thirty.

"You know, when I hit the big three-oh, I don't wanna call a lot of attention to it." Nate's eyes roam slowly. "And I'm also pretty sure they reused decorations."

I gasp. "Andrea Norton reusing things? Say it isn't so."

He shrugs. "I've seen a lot of this before."

I go to elbow him, but he catches me and tugs me closer. I'm about to lean into him when I realize where we're at, and I spring away.

He frowns and the realization dawns on him. "Shit," he says. "I didn't even think."

"Me either." I rub the back of my neck. "This might be harder than I thought."

Nate doesn't get to say anything because Quinn is running to me. She's wearing bright pink and a literal tiara. I wonder if Andrea bought it from an actual princess.

"Maisie!" she yells. "God, it's so good to see you!"

I get a tight hug from her before she pulls back to look at me. "You're so tan! And your hair!"

I fiddle with it. "Yeah. I'm trying something new."

"You should do this more often."

She looks at Nate and me. "So, everything went well?"

He and I share a glance.

Play it cool, I silently beg.

"It was fine." He shrugs. Once he cuts eye contact, he doesn't look at me again. Normally, I'd be annoyed, but this was perfect. Eye contact turned into me wanting to touch him.

"Yep. Fine."

"Oh," Quinn says. "You'll have to tell me all about it."

"Another time," I reply. "This is your birthday, and I bet you have a ton of people to talk to."

She sighs, and I know I'm right. "At least we can all get some photos, right?"

"You two go. I'll hang out here," Nate says.

"Yeah, okay." Quinn looks between us one more time before dragging me away. As I go, I give him a thumbs-up.

He laughs and shakes his head, letting just a bit of that man I know through before he gets it under control.

I pose for at least ten photos in the booth before the curtain opens and Andrea appears. My heart jumps into my throat when seeing her, but I keep my gaze steady. She gives me a cold stare.

"Mom, we talked about this," Quinn hisses.

"Yes, yes." She finally looks at me. "Hello, Maisie. Vacation looks like it suits you."

"It was something," I reply. "Happy to be back to see everyone, though."

"Someone tried to see you last night," she mutters. "I hear you turned him down."

"Maisie can make her own choices," Quinn says.

"Sure." Andrea finally looks at her daughter. "Your grandfather wants to see you, dear."

She sighs and turns to me. "Sorry."

"Don't worry about it. Go see your grandfather. I can entertain myself."

She gives me one last frown before Andrea pulls her away. I find Nate still by the entrance.

"So she hates me," I say. When I get close, he eyes the space between us. "What are you doing?"

"Trying to stay one foot away to keep up the pretense. It's how far I used to make sure I was."

"You measured it?"

"Any closer and who knows what I'd do."

I want to pull him to me and remind him that he's the only one I want to keep close, but I shake off the thought and give us even more space.

"We should mingle. Apart."

"Too tempted?"

"I wouldn't last as long as you did, that's for sure. I'll see you around?"

"Stay away from Rob."

"Don't need to tell me twice." I wink before walking away.

Most of Rob's family isn't interested in talking to me, so they're easy to avoid. As I sift through the sea of people, I come across two familiar faces.

Lia and Ellis are newlyweds, and I was a plus-one to their wedding. They're Quinn's friends from her work, and she often hangs out with them. Their wedding was gorgeous, and at the time, I wondered if mine would ever measure up.

I know it definitely wouldn't.

"Hi!" Lia pulls me into a tight hug, her curly hair in a gorgeous bun. "Gosh, it's been way too long."

Ellis is behind her, two glasses in hand. They're always together, and I wondered how they managed it.

Now I know.

"It has been. Sorry I was so busy with wedding planning. Doomed wedding planning, I mean."

Ellis and Lia glance at each other, and it's almost like they're communicating without words. "We heard about that," Ellis says gently. "How are you doing?"

"I'm okay. It was the right decision in the end. Nate helped me see the light." When I say it, I immediately regret it. If either of them sniffs out anything about Nate and me, it'll get back to Quinn.

"Oh, Nate. Is he here?" Lia's eyes light up. Before I knew she and Ellis were destined to be together, I wondered if there was a chance she would go after Nate. They always vibed whenever he tagged along with me.

"He is. He's just doing his own thing. We better not bother him." Lia's smile fades as she studies me. "Anyway." My voice is a little too high. "It was great seeing you. I need some more punch!"

I run before they can think too hard about how I acted, and then find someone else I know to talk to. That hadn't gone well, but at least no one knows that Nate and I are together.

I run into some of Quinn's other friends that have also become mine by proxy, so I catch up with them and make a mental note to reach out to Amy and Riley to go to the next book club. I'd gotten bad about going when planning for the wedding.

Now, I have time. Now, I feel like *me*.

Once everyone knows about Nate and me, all bets are off. I'm finally living life.

It's an hour before Quinn finds me again. I'm by the dessert table, watching as one of her uncles talks to Nate about sports. "Whew," she says. "This is exhausting."

"I can't imagine," I say. "You're doing great, though."

"And how are you doing?" She peers over at me.

I pause. "Why are you asking?"

"Just checking in, you know? Like if anything is . . . different, you can tell me."

I immediately shake my head. Have Nate and I been too flirty?

We've not even talked. "Everything's fine," I insist. "You have a birthday to enjoy."

"Right, but—"

I put my hands on her shoulders. "Seriously. This is a massive, beautiful party. You have people to chat with, or corners to hide in if you're overwhelmed. I'm good."

"Are you and Nate good?" she asks.

Shit. "Um, we're—"

"Speech time!" Andrea is on the stairs, a champagne glass in hand. "My beautiful daughter is celebrating her thirtieth today, and we all need to shower her in praise."

"Speeches?" I ask.

Quinn's jaw is on the floor. If she wasn't wearing makeup, her face would be beet red. "I thought she was kidding about that."

"Who wants to go first?" Andrea asks. "I suppose I can, if no one else does."

"Oh no. She's gonna bring up the bathwater incident again. Maisie, you have to volunteer."

There are many things in that sentence for me to process, but Quinn's urging me forward, mortification in her gaze.

"What, but—"

"Please!" she begs. "I'll buy you whatever you want. Do whatever you want. Just stop my mother."

I groan before collecting myself. I'm *so* going to regret this.

"Um, I will!" I say it loudly, and everyone's eyes turn to me. *Oh God.* This is terrible.

"Oh." Andrea says. "Fine, I suppose so."

"I owe you my life," Quinn says in my ear.

"You really do," I reply through gritted teeth. Slowly, I walk to the stairs and try to think of what to say. Nate's in the back of the crowd, watching me with widened eyes. He knows more than anyone that I hate this.

At least I'll laugh about this later.

"Wow, what do I say about Quinn?" I begin. I'm asking myself more than anyone else. It's not that I can't talk about her, but a speech? Unprepared? This is the worst. "She's just so incredible. She's helped me through a lot, even this past week." I let out an awkward laugh. Nate shakes his head in the audience. *No talking about last week.* Fair. "I never thought I would say this, but I'm so glad both of us had the worst teacher for algebra in college. Bonding over trying to figure out what she was saying is one of my best memories. I owe my degree to her. I owe a lot to her. She's the best friend anyone could ask for. So, here's to her. I hope you have the best birthday, Quinn."

I raise a toast, proud that I didn't completely mess it up.

I rejoin Quinn in the crowd. "Maisie . . ." She trails off.

"Please tell me that wasn't terrible. God, everyone was looking at me." I shudder.

"You called me your best friend."

I blink. "Kind of. Mostly. It's true, though." Especially since Nate is more to me now.

"Really?"

Oh, boy. "Uh, yeah. But don't worry about—"

"My turn, if that's okay," a man says. It's the very voice I *don't* want to hear.

Fuck, Rob's speaking. I haven't seen him the entire time, and I'm not sure if that's by design or if I've just gotten lucky.

"No," Quinn says. "Anyone but him."

Rob can't hear her, nor would he care if he could. He walks in front of the crowd like he's meant to be there. He's wearing the same smile as he had in the video, and it sends chills down my spine.

"I can't believe my sister made it to thirty. In all honesty, I thought she would stay eighteen forever. In some ways, she has." He laughs and others join him. I can't resist the urge to roll my eyes.

"But, you know, she's my sister. So I'm here for her, even

though I've had a"—his eyes find me in the crowd—"rough time lately, as you all know."

"What the fuck?" Quinn asks.

I tense, wishing I could melt into the floor.

Or that Nate was with me.

"But, you know, I'm glad I came. I get to be here for my sister and see something I needed to see. My relationship is over, but I'm happy to say that's not the only thing that went downhill. To Maisie and Nate, may your friendship get the same ending I did."

Something shatters on the ground, and I realize that I've dropped my champagne glass. I don't even remember my grip going slack. All I know is that he's just wished Nate and me the *worst*, on Quinn's fucking birthday.

At first, I'm rattled. But I've had my fill of embarrassment for the evening. It quickly erupts into something else.

Something fiery.

"Oh, shit." Quinn grabs me and pulls me away. "Can someone clean this up? Maisie, we should find somewhere to—"

I don't even hear the end of the sentence. I'm tearing after Rob. Maybe I'll skin him alive. Maybe I'll rip his dick off. I'm not sure which will be more satisfying.

"What the fuck, Rob!" We're in Andrea's kitchen, thankfully out of sight from the rest of the partygoers.

"What?" Rob asks. "I had to honor my sister."

"You made that about you. Like a complete *dick*."

"Well, it's exactly what you deserve."

"Watch it," a third voice says, and I immediately know it's Nate. "Now that I know how you've talked to her, it's not happening again."

I turn to him, eyebrows raised at his dark tone. With me, he's always so gentle. But this side of him, the part of him that would protect me from anything, sends a thrill down my spine.

He's staring Rob down like he's preparing to take him out. For *me*.

I shouldn't love that as much as I do.

"Oh, come on." Rob spits it out. "You two are supposed to be fighting."

"Unlike you," Nate starts, "we're capable of being subtle."

"Yeah, right. Everyone knows something is going on."

"Is that why you did that?" I ask. "You just *had* to call attention to it?"

"Maybe if you'd acted right yesterday—"

"Don't even try to blame this on her. You ambushed her in the airport, took her where she didn't want to go, and—"

"She gave me a chance anyway." He smirks. "That pissed you off, didn't it?"

"A chance to be a decent person," I snap. "Which it's obvious you can't be."

Rob laughs humorlessly. "I'm perfectly decent."

"When you get what you want, and that's not happening this time."

"Is it not? You two are barely talking. I seem to have won."

"Fuck *off*," Nate snaps, about to stalk over to Rob, but I hold up my hand to stop him.

Rob is a petty man. He played the long game to separate Nate and me, and now that he doesn't have me, he's acting out. I'm tired of it.

It's time to play dirty.

"You know . . ." I say it as softly as I can. "I actually owe you a thank you, Rob."

Nate's gaze cuts to me, but I keep staring at Rob, who only blinks. "You do?"

"I definitely do." Tilting my head, I smile, and he starts to return it. "It's because of you that Nate and I are in love."

The smile immediately falls off of Rob's face. Behind me, Nate laughs as he realizes what I'm doing.

"You're together?"

"Yes. And you helped *so much*. So, thank you. I owe the fact that I'll probably marry this man to you." I lean on Nate, who presses a kiss to my forehead.

"You're being mean," he murmurs. "I love it."

"No. No way." Rob shakes his head. "You were just fighting."

"Nate knows how to resolve a fight really well. It's nice."

"Oh, fuck you. Fuck you *both*."

"No thank you. I'm a taken woman now." I pat Nate's chest and Rob goes red in the face before he storms out of the kitchen, pushing past us both.

The second we're alone, Nate and I burst into laughter.

"Did you see his face?" I ask as I wipe tears out of my eyes. "It was perfect."

"Like I said, *mean*. Please do that more often."

We're both still getting ourselves together when Quinn bursts into the room.

"I'm so sorry. It took me *forever* to get here. People kept stopping me. Are you o—" She pauses when she sees Nate and me. "Oh. Am I interrupting something?"

I take a step away from him and shake my head. "No. Definitely not."

"If I am, I—"

"Quinn, I'm *so* sorry for that." My focus is entirely on her now. I hate Rob for what he did, but she's the one who's had her birthday messed up. Guilt crashes into me.

"Yeah, it's not ideal." She blows a piece of hair that fell out of her updo out of her eyes. "Mom shouldn't have let him talk at all, but she always defends him."

"I don't want my drama to follow you here. It's your birthday and my focus should be on you." I glance out the door where Rob stormed through. I have no doubt he'll bitch to Andrea immediately. "But other things happened. I completely understand if you want me to leave."

Out of the corner of my eye, I see Nate reach out to comfort me, but he stops.

Quinn is the one who grabs my hands instead. "What? *No.* I want you here. We still have to talk about the cruise . . ." Her eyes cut to Nate. "And anything else that could've happened."

I tense. "You know, don't you?"

She nods. "It's hard *not* to know. But it's okay. I wanna help."

"Help?" I ask and glance at Nate. He seems as lost as I am.

"Of course. If you and Nate are fighting, I wanna help."

That gives me pause. "Fighting?"

"Yeah, obviously. You two are avoiding each other and acting stiff. Everyone's talking about it."

Slowly, my gaze slides to Nate, who's staring right back at me. Oh. Oh *no.*

We've played our part *too* well.

"We're not fighting," I say as I turn back to Quinn. "I promise. You should just focus on your birthday."

"Don't lie. I know something happened between you two. Was it Rob? He said Nate was mad at you, and while I had a hard time believing it at first, with how you two are acting, something's gone wrong."

"N-noo, Rob didn't. Well, he mostly didn't." I shake my head. There's no way to explain this in a simple way. "Quinn, it's your party. Something you put a lot of time and effort into. Focus on that."

"But—"

"Seriously, go back out there—"

"Oh my God, Maisie, fuck the party."

I blink. "I—what?"

She lets out a sigh before she rubs her forehead. Her shoulders sink in the same way they did when she was planning it. "I don't care about this party. Or the speeches, or *fuck*, this stupid tiara." She rips it off of her head. "I'm done with it. It's taken over my life to the point that I really don't even care about it. I'd honestly rather be home eating cake, but Mom has to show off."

"Quinn, are *you* okay?"

"Obviously not. Mom's been on a warpath, which is *not* your fault, but she's a lot. Rob is a lot. And I wish they would just take five steps back and be normal. Or at least let me have a normal fucking birthday."

"I didn't know this wasn't what you wanted. We should get together in a few days and do something more casual. Oh! What about a movie night? One where we actually finish the movie. I can bring cake."

She gives me a half smile. "That would be nice. But I'd also like Nate to be there, and for you two not to be fighting." She points between the two of us. "So. Tell me what the fuck is going on."

"But—"

"*Please* distract me from that out there," she hisses. "Consider it my birthday request."

Slowly, I look at Nate.

He shrugs. "It's her birthday. You kinda have to do what she wants."

"All right," I say and take a deep breath. "Nate and I aren't fighting."

She rolls her eyes. "Do I also need to request that you don't lie to me? I know something's up. You called *me* your best friend. While I love you and consider *you* my best friend, with you, that title's always been for Nate."

"Yeah, you really slipped up there," Nate adds, and I don't need to look at him to know he's smirking.

"I was on the spot. In front of people. I was in a sensitive place."

"You're always in a sensitive place," he replies.

"Keep that up and you're sleeping on the couch."

"All right. Shutting up now."

I shake my head and focus on Quinn, who's looking between us as if we're a puzzle and one piece is missing.

"So, Nate and I are together." It's the first time I've said it out loud to someone whose opinion I care about, and it speeds up my heart rate. This is so new and so important to me. Saying it out loud to someone who could easily judge us isn't easy.

"Together," she repeats slowly. "Like working on a project together?"

Oh boy. Our years of insisting we were only friends hasn't helped us out.

"N-no."

"Roommates?" Her eyes go wide. "No way, are you moving in together? That makes so much sense. You'll save so much money on bills!"

"We're dating!" I rush to say. "Like actually dating." She stares at us. "Quinn," I say gently. "We've kissed. We've slept together. I've seen his pe—"

"I'm gonna stop you right there, berry. I think she gets the message."

"Oh. My. God." Quinn starts it quietly. Then she grabs my shoulders. "You're *dating*? You and Nate?"

"Yes."

She screams. "No way! Why didn't you say that? Why didn't you tattoo it on your forehead? This is great news!"

"I . . . thought it would be more of a shock. And I have a feeling some wouldn't take it very well."

She sobers slightly. "Okay, fair. Mom does *not* need to know about this one yet. But I do. And why did you two act like you were fighting?"

"We were trying to be casual!"

She laughs. "You're terrible at it. Absolutely terrible. Now we need to sneak into my room. I need to hear everything."

"Not *everything*." Nate laughs uncomfortably. "Right?"

Quinn cackles. "I'm gonna know how big your penis is, and there's nothing you can do to stop me!"

Nate goes green in the face, but I put a hand on Quinn's shoulder.

"Um, are you sure you wanna talk about that? I thought we avoided the topic."

"We did when it was a man I'm related to." She says it like it's obvious. "But now it's free game. Tell me, is it big?"

"I'm right here!" Nate says. "Berry, don't you dare—"

I nod.

"Hell yes! Congratulations to you *both*."

Nate sighs and rubs his face. "I have a feeling I'm gonna regret this."

"You're the one who said you'd take anything I give you. And this time, I give you embarrassment."

"And there better be more." Quinn bounces on the balls of her feet. "Start the story from the top. I want it all!"

chapter twenty-nine

IT's late in the night when we finally pull up to my house. Nate drove back, mostly because I couldn't keep my eyes open. Even sleeping in until noon wasn't enough for either of us. Socializing only added to the exhaustion.

Rob *did* wind up telling everyone about us. Most people congratulated us. Andrea looked at us like we'd shit in her stew.

Quinn told us not to worry about it. And I didn't. My friendship was with her and her only.

I didn't owe the rest of them anything.

"We're home," Nate says. I can't resist the smile that crosses my face when he says the word *home*. "Or at least you are."

"Shh. You're staying the night, right?"

"If you'll have me. Eventually I'll annoy you to the point you kick me out."

"If you haven't done it yet, you never will."

He laughs, but it has a soft edge to it. I crack one eye open to see him with the lovesick expression he'd had the night before when I told him I loved him.

"Should I carry you in?" he asks.

"I can walk. Just not for long."

Nate begins unbuttoning his dress shirt when we get inside. "Well, that's over. We survived."

"It went well. After we told Quinn, that is. I really thought she would be more shocked."

"She's your best friend for a reason. Though, I could've done without you telling her how big my dick is in my presence."

"You got a glowing review from me," I reply. "Isn't that what you want?"

"I suppose I can't complain."

"Will you help me get the hell out of this dress? I'm done with clothes."

His head snaps up. "Now I *really* can't complain."

Nate wastes no time. I gather my hair and his hands find the zipper. I feel like I can breathe when it's off of my body.

"You looked gorgeous in it, but I prefer the view when that thing is off."

Nate presses a kiss to my neck. I may be tired, but I have an instant reaction to that. It's a shame that we didn't have the energy to do anything the night before.

I want to find a way tonight.

Leaning into him, I tilt my head to the side to give him better access. "Bed or couch?" he asks.

My eyes pop open. "Forward, aren't we?"

"I had to watch you in that dress all night and barely touched you. Trust me, I was a *saint*."

The bed would be more comfortable, but we don't wind up making it there. Once I spin around to kiss him, he's backing me up until we're plopping on the couch. I wind up in his lap, straddling his hips.

When we did this last time, our future felt like it was in flux. Neither of us were on the same page, and this felt so delicate that I was afraid of breaking it.

This time, we know exactly where we stand. It doesn't have to be delicate. It's just us.

I work to get his clothes off, needing to even things up, and he removes my underwear, leaving the two of us completely naked. The only time we stop is to grab a condom from my purse.

When all of this started, I was worried we would ruin things. What I didn't know is that it could be *better*. Instead of worrying about what could go wrong, I should have seen what would go right.

I can feel him against my pussy, and I'm tempted to take him inside of me. But as I shift, his cock brushes against my clit, and I can't help but let out a moan at the contact.

"Does that feel good, honey?" he whispers into my mouth.

"Ah, yes. But—"

"Then do it again and again. However long you want to."

I should know not to argue with him about this. Nate knows me far too well, and he's only been patient about how long it takes me to come.

I don't know why I keep forgetting.

It's nice to drive this time, and I move my hips up and down along his hardness, chasing a feeling that's new to me. My fingers dig into his shoulders, but the pressure is exactly what I need.

Nate stops kissing me long enough to bury his face in my neck. His teeth gently nip my skin and my entire body erupts in goose-flesh. He immediately notices and does it again.

My hands move from his shoulders up to his hair to keep his mouth against my neck. This time, his mouth attaches to my skin, and I know that I'll have a hickey tomorrow.

It's *so* worth it.

As seconds turn to minutes, this is usually when I start to get insecure about how long it takes for my body to respond. I'm arching into him, so focused on the moment that I don't care what time is passing. I know Nate is here with me, and there's no race to the finish line with him.

It hits me as I continue rubbing up and down that I have so

much more to experience with him. I want to find everything that makes him tick, and I want him to do the same to me.

I don't think something purely for my own benefit will do anything for Nate, but as I move, his jaw tightens and he throws his head back against the couch.

"Fuck, berry. You feel so good."

I don't realize how out of breath I am until I try to speak. "R-really?"

"Yes." His hips jolt upward, adding to the pressure. I gasp and try to keep it together, but it feels way too good.

His hands curl through my hair, keeping me pressed into him. Normally, something like that would be a distraction, but every one of my cells is on fire, and the things he does send me careening even closer to the edge.

My hands tighten as my body lights up. Nate must know what's coming, and he moves from my neck to a spot right on my collarbone, a place where I'm even more sensitive.

I shudder against him, my orgasm washing over me like a wave I don't want to stop. My eyes close and I let out a moan that sounds like his name as I'm taken captive by pure pleasure.

"That was fast," Nate says sometime later.

I take a second to catch my breath. "I didn't keep track."

"Good. You shouldn't." He arches his hips up one more time and I nearly jump into the air. I'm so sensitive, I feel like a live wire. "Sorry. Too much?"

"For now. But that just means we can do other things."

"I'm at your mercy," he says. "Do whatever you want."

I feel him at my core and I press down slightly. I'm tempted to make this slow, to take him in one inch at a time so I'm not sore in the morning.

But I *like* remembering what we've done. And I want to remember this.

"I don't want you to be at my mercy," I say.

Nate pauses and raises his eyebrow. "And what do you want?"

"Flip me over and fuck me. *Hard.*"

"You sure?"

I nod. "Yes. Very sure. Don't take it easy on me."

He presses a kiss to my lips. "Then I feel the need to apologize in advance and say I love you."

"I love you too, but there's no need for apologies."

"Save that thought for after."

It feels like I'm airborne when Nate flips me over. I'm pressed into the couch as he takes me from behind. I have no time to adjust to the new position before he lines himself up and slams inside of me.

"Oh, *fuck.*" That's all I can manage as he fucks me exactly how I want him to. My pussy burns as I'm stretched to the max.

It's too much. It's perfect.

I never want it to end.

Everything around me disappears and all I can focus on is him. Nate has stamina that lasts, and he only seems to speed up. I'm a mess of broken moans as he thrusts into me with a ruthlessness I didn't think possible.

Something builds underneath the movement. Something with no expectation, just feeling.

"Fuck, honey. I'm gonna come."

All I can do is moan in response. His hand curls through my hair, tugging it back.

And then I'm thrown over the edge into an orgasm that I don't expect. I'm not used to coming twice, and the fire that washes over me takes me away, shooting me into the stars as I lose myself.

I need to do this again. I need to do this a million times, actually.

When Nate finally stops, he's just as out of breath as I am, and leans over my body.

"Holy shit," he says with a ragged breath. Then he kisses my shoulder. "Are you okay? Was that too much?"

All I can do is laugh. "I'm definitely *not* okay, but in the best way."

"Good," he says. "We need to try that again."

As usual, it's like he's reading my mind.

"Give me until the morning, and then we'll *definitely* try that again. And many times after that."

chapter thirty

Two days later, we pull up to my parents' house. Mom invited us over to catch up after the trip, telling us that Dad was barbecuing. Other than woodworking, one of my father's greatest passions is cooking meat.

Dinner is guaranteed to be incredible.

But despite the promise of good food, Nate is tense the entire drive. He's said over and over that he's ready to tell them, but he still seems to dread it.

I'm trying to decide if I should fight my dad or not.

"I'm sure they'll be happy for us."

"It's different with dating," Nate reminds me.

I hate seeing him serious. He's so rarely worried that it feels like he floats through life with ease.

Panicking is *my* job.

"Seriously, I'll go off on him."

"No, I need to face this. He'll get over it . . . eventually. After he grills me over my intent with you and how I plan to take care of you."

"Ew," I say with a shake of my head. "If I hear that, I'll remind him I can easily take care of myself."

"Still, I'll have to survive it."

I'm tempted to tell him to turn around and go home, but before I can, he gets out of the car. I have a moment to take a deep breath before he opens my door for me.

"Let's do it." A smile crosses his face, but it's not the easygoing one I know.

I *will* be fighting my dad today. If only because whatever he did with Rob has Nate this stressed.

Mom is waiting for us at the front door, and when she sees us, she practically bounces on her feet. She pulls me into a hug so tight it almost strangles me. Then she goes for Nate, but pauses before she gets close.

"Oh, pardon me. I should ask permission before a hug. Maisie tells me you might not like people touching you."

"She did, huh?" He laughs and then hugs Mom anyway. "I'm happy to tell you she was very wrong about that, Judy."

"Yay!" Mom says before trying to crush Nate like a soda can. He lets her, but he winces when she lets go.

"You both look like you had fun!" She eyes me. "Maisie, is that a tan?"

"A little bit of one."

"And your *hair*." She gasps. "I just knew a vacation would do you some good."

"You were right."

"Come on. Let's go say hi to your father."

She grabs both of us and leads us to the back patio, where Dad is staring at his smoker intently. When he turns to see us, he has the same stern expression he always does.

"Take it easy on him," she murmurs to us. "He's had a rough day. Something about a newbie using the wrong kind of wood at work."

"A rough day, huh?" Nate asks weakly. "Awesome."

"Nate, Maisie," Dad says. "Come smell dinner. It's the only decent part of this god-awful day."

Nate stares at him like he's a snake ready to attack, but I join him to see what he's made. "It smells good," I reply. "It always does."

"Thanks. You look good. Healthy." He turns to Nate. "You both do."

"That's what I was thinking, Jeff." Mom walks over and throws an arm around Dad. "I told you she would be fine on a cruise."

"Yeah, but not with that idiot fiancé." He eyes me. "Take a little more time with dating next time. Really think about it."

My laugh is stilted and I glance at Nate.

We are *so* fucked.

Mom loops her arm through mine and tugs me into the backyard. "Oh, Maisie, I've missed you. Have I shown you how the tomatoes are doing? I'll have to send some home with the both of you."

"You haven't. I'm sure Nate would—"

"Nate hasn't seen my barbecue yet," Dad says. "Why are you hanging out in the corner, kid? Get over here."

Nate slowly walks over to Dad as I'm dragged away. My parents don't have a massive yard, so I'm able to hear everything Dad says. Luckily, my father seems none the wiser to us as he tells Nate every detail about how to cook meat.

"And you have to take it really slow. Patience is key. You get me, right?"

"Uh, yeah. Of course I do."

"Good kid. You always were smart."

"So," Mom says. "You seem a little . . . tense."

"Tense? Me?" I laugh. "Not at all. I'm fine. Good, even."

She raises an eyebrow. "I'm guessing there will be some news at the dinner table, yes?"

"M-maybe."

"I'll prepare myself." She pats my arm. "And your father."

I have no idea if Mom has any inkling of what I'm about to say, but she doesn't give me a chance to probe because she launches into talking about all of the tomatoes she has. I help her water the garden before Dad announces the food is ready.

Nate and I always set the table, so we go inside to do just that.

"How are we playing this?" he whispers as we put forks down.

"Mom knows something is coming."

"She figures things out way too quickly," he says with a sigh.

"Like the time we snuck into a rated-R movie when we were fifteen?"

He shudders. "I've never seen her so mad."

"I seriously doubt she'll be angry. And Dad might disagree about the timing, but we'll be okay."

"I know we will be." He takes a breath. "I just . . . like how things are right now. It feels like I still have a family, even after my mom died."

My eyes water immediately. "You do. I won't let this change anything."

"I know. But it'll be different from here on out. I'm just preparing."

I want to say more, but Dad is bringing in the food and I try to get myself together. Mom follows, and we finish getting everything ready before sitting at the table.

"So, start from the beginning," Mom says. "I wanna see every photo from the trip."

"I sent most of them."

"But not all. And I want details. Such as how you fared near water."

"Oh, it was something." Nate laughs. "It was mostly panic at first."

"I thought you got over your fear of it," Mom says.

"Not exactly." I say it slowly. "Rob was the one who wanted a cruise."

Dad huffs. "Of course he did."

Mom elbows him. "Jeff. Let's be respectful."

Dad doesn't seem happy about the order.

"It's fine," I say. "But having Nate there helped a lot. I actually got over some of my fear."

"After you fell off a dock."

Mom chokes on her food. "What? When did that happen?"

"They could've done without that detail," I hiss.

"Second excursion. Some asshole knocked her in. I pulled her out."

"It was heroic, apparently." I elbow him. "And it taught me that I need to face some things. I finally had Nate give me swimming lessons."

"Really?" Mom leans in. "Did you like them?"

"I don't think I'm ever gonna *love* water, but I can be convinced to go near it now at least."

"It's a win in my book," Nate adds.

"Did anything else happen on the trip? Or when you got back?" Mom is hedging the news, and I see Dad's grip on his fork tighten.

Nate and I glance at each other.

"Yes. There's another thing that happened. It's big."

"I have an idea what it is," Mom says.

"You do?" I ask.

"Yes." She nods. "You're back with Rob, aren't you?"

"No!" Nate and I say at the same time. It comes out with such a ferocity that both of my parents startle.

"That's some mighty defensiveness there," Dad says. "From both of you."

"Let's just say Rob caused some problems," I reply. "And that will never be happening again."

"Good," Dad mutters.

"What's the news then?" Mom asks, her eyes wide. "Now I have no idea what it could be!" She scoots to the edge of the chair, watching us intently.

My heart kicks up speed as I say it. "Nate and I are dating."

I'm careful not to use the word "together" when Quinn had taken it entirely the wrong way.

Throughout the drive, I had been going through ways that they could react. I considered anger. I considered shock.

And judging by the way Mom's eyes turn into saucers, I'm definitely getting the second one from her.

I look at Dad, wondering if I'll see anger on his face. But he's gone still.

Nate has too.

I hate this.

"So, yeah." My hand rests on Nate's leg, which is as tense as stone. "We got together on the trip, and made it official when we got back. That's the big news, guys."

I laugh, but both of my parents are silent.

"We meant to tell you as soon as possible," Nate adds. "But Maisie had Quinn's party and we both were exhausted."

"It's a huge change from what we said we were," I say. "So, take as much time as you need."

I wait for a barrage of questions from Mom and the expected quiet contempt from Dad. But they're still staring at us.

Then Dad breaks the silence with the most shocking sound I've ever heard in my life.

He doesn't laugh often, but when he does, it's a high-pitched giggle that sounds wrong coming from a man like him. I've heard it just a few times in my life, mostly when his favorite team pulls off a move that no one else should have, or when he sinks his teeth into ribs that came out of the smoker perfectly.

It starts quietly as if he's trying to contain himself, and then it gets louder and louder until his giggle echoes off the walls.

He's smiling. He's laughing.

"You . . . aren't mad, Jeff?" Nate asks slowly.

"What?" he finally says. "Mad? Ha! I *knew* this would happen. Ever since you two were kids, I was hoping you'd end up together. I almost lost hope. You had me with that loser, Rob, but this? Oh, finally! Didn't I tell you, Judy? They were never just friends."

Mom sighs. "You did tell me. And now you'll never let me live it down."

Nate looks between them, shaking his head. "You asked Rob so many questions that I thought you were planning his funeral. You're really not upset?"

"God, no! This is what I needed to hear! Finally you two saw what we all did years ago!"

"To be fair," I say, "I was the one who didn't see it."

"You had a man-child clogging up your vision. I knew what Rob was and I tried to scare him away. But he stuck around." Dad's nose scrunches. "Like a little cockroach."

"That's what I think about him," Nate says with a childlike smile. "He never gives up. One day, I feel like he's gonna grow extra legs and turn brown."

"Oh, he gave up after I was done with him," I say.

"True. She thanked him for getting us together."

Dad laughs again. "That's my girl! If only I could have been there. I'd love to see that little idiot realize he never stood a chance."

Nate finally laughs, all tension melting from his body. I turn to him with a smile. "And to think, you were nervous this would change things."

"Oh, Nate." Mom reaches across and pats his hand. "We care about you no matter what. Nothing is changing."

"Except your marital status." Dad is *still* smiling. "Which better be soon. I have thoughts on this one."

My jaw drops. "Dad!"

He pays me no mind. "Judy, it's time to get out the scrapbook. I have a *real* wedding to plan now."

I sink lower into my chair as Nate laughs. Mom gives me a sympathetic smile before she joins in too.

And it's the best dinner I've ever had.

ONE YEAR LATER

THE HALLWAY IS dark as I tiptoe down it. No one should be awake at this hour, and my empty bed is making it impossible to sleep.

That's when, of course, I trip over someone lying on the floor. I nearly go tumbling, but manage to catch myself before crushing whoever was stupid enough to sleep in my hallway.

"I knew it," Quinn mutters as she sits up. "You're trying to sneak out again."

My face erupts into heat as I realize why she is where she is. "You told me you were sleeping on the couch."

"That's what I wanted you to think. I gave the couch to Scarlett. She needed it anyway."

Quinn knew about Scarlett from my stories, but I finally got my cruise friend to come to Nashville for one major occasion. It should make me happy that they were getting along.

But I am *not* in a good mood.

"Please let me pass," I beg. "I need sleep."

"You told me you didn't want the bad luck." She rubs her eyes. "It's not even been twelve hours yet."

"That's way too long," I say. "Just forget what I asked you. Who needs luck?"

"And have your dad kill you? He's not taking chances here, Maisie. I don't want that smoke."

I sigh. Dad definitely isn't playing around.

And I hate whoever told him that it was bad luck for a bride to see her groom before the wedding day.

I don't like to think about the last time I almost got married, but Dad wasn't as involved that time. But he's taken center stage with Nate and me.

He threw a *party* when Nate proposed. A literal party with balloons. And now that we're only one night away from the wedding, he's been involved in every step.

I'm not sure who's more excited about this.

Still, I want to sleep with my man. In both ways, preferably.

"Quinn," I beg again.

"You'll survive."

It's not like Nate and I are never apart. We get plenty of time on our own, but we both prefer being together. It's been like that since the day we met, even when I didn't realize it.

Being together opened more doors. To some, Nate and I moved way too quickly. But to us, it feels like we're catching up on lost time.

I attempted to strong-arm my way past Quinn and go sleep in the same bed as my fiancé. But I'm the one who put her up to this, and I know Dad is going to check in.

"Fine. Just know I'll be miserable." I poke my bottom lip out and hope for some sympathy from my friend. She only laughs.

When I get back to my room, I flop on the bed and wonder if I'm going to get any sort of sleep. There are a lot of things that my wedding makeup can cover, but I'm not sure it can conceal the dark circles I'll have tomorrow.

I'm still mulling on sleep when there's a tap at my window. At first, I think it's a tree branch, but it's persistent. Sitting up, I go to check, only for my jaw to drop when I open the curtains.

"Nate?" I ask as I shove the window open. "What are you doing here?"

"Sneaking in. Doesn't it remind you of old times?" He hops through the window right into my room. He's not wrong. This is exactly like when Mom and Dad tried to separate us when we were teenagers.

"You do know we're not supposed to see each other before the wedding, right?" I ask.

"You do know I was never gonna listen to that, right?" he parrots back. "And besides, I heard you trip over Quinn."

I have to hide my smile. "Yeah, yeah. Whatever."

Nate leans in, a shit-eating grin on his face. "Just say it, berry."

"Say what?"

"You have a crush on me."

I almost laugh, but I elbow him instead. "You're such a nerd."

"But I'm about to be *your* nerd."

"You've always been mine. It's just in marriage now."

"You're very right about that." He kisses me once before pulling out his phone. "Now, I have an alarm set so I can sneak back in before anyone else is up. Shall we try to get as much sleep as we can?"

"I wish we had time for other things," I say with a sigh. "But I should sleep."

"It's almost like we have a wedding tomorrow."

"Huh, how strange." I grab his hands. "Now, get in bed. We have cuddles to catch up on."

I can't sit still the next day.

"It's like you've had four cups of coffee," Scarlett says as she curls my hair. "I've never seen anyone this excited about getting married . . . ever."

"They're ridiculously in love," Quinn replies with a roll of her eyes. "This is all your fault, I hear."

"My best work yet. I tell all of my clients in denial about their love."

"Hey," I say. "One of them is right here. And are you almost done?"

"Almost," she says. "You'll have to wait, though."

I groan and both of my friends laugh.

Neither Nate nor I were worried about having a big wedding. We have our families and our friends and need nothing more. I'm at my house while Nate will be arriving at our wedding venue any moment now. After our vows are exchanged, we'll come back here and have a party.

It's perfect.

"Who's going to cry more?" Scarlett asks. "My money's on Nate."

"On Nate?" I ask. "You've barely spent time with him."

"That man is down *bad* for you," she says. "I don't need to spend time with him to know that he's gonna be emotional today."

"My bet is on both of them crying an equal amount. It'll be a sob fest. I can't wait to get pictures."

"I hate you all," I say.

"We're putting you in waterproof mascara for a reason," Quinn says.

My leg bounces as Scarlett finishes my hair and they talk about things they want to get up to while I'm on my honeymoon. Apparently, Scarlett is staying for a bit, and I'm bummed I don't get to see her the entire time she's in town. The two of us have kept in contact, but it's not the same as it was when we were on the cruise.

One of these days, I'll convince her to move here.

Amy and Riley will no doubt be joining. At our rehearsal dinner, they all talked like old friends, and it's nice to see such a big day come and go without any drama.

Today's wedding is going to go the same way.

Once upon a time, I had a different idea of how all of this worked. But as I think about Nate being my husband, I'm so glad I got my head out of my ass.

I'm counting the seconds until both of my parents walk me down the aisle to him. I have a feeling they'll be in as big of a rush as I am.

I don't feel anything but that excitement until we pull up to the venue. Then I see Nate in the distance with his wavy hair styled, wearing a perfect suit, and it finally hits me.

We're going to be *married*.

My heart rate kicks up. Not out of fear, but out of pure happiness. *This* is where I'm meant to end up. This is where I want to be.

That happiness grows until it causes me to tear up.

Quinn, who's sitting beside me, hands me a tissue. "There it is."

"Thanks," I say as I blot the wetness from my eyes. "Now let's do this."

I'm pretty sure Mom and Dad congratulate me before they walk me down the aisle, but I can barely focus on anything other than Nate. The second our eyes lock, it's all I can do not to run to him.

The same goes for him. He's shuffling his feet as if he's also fighting the urge.

I go through the motions of what we practiced, but I'm on autopilot, even as the officiant starts speaking.

The only time I'm truly listening to a thing anyone says is when Nate recites his vows.

At first, he clears his throat, looking uncharacteristically shy as he starts reading. My heart rate is probably dangerous for me, and tears are already welling up in my eyes again before he's even spoken.

I'm so not making it through this unscathed.

"It was always a dream to marry you, berry. And for a long time, I never thought it would come true." He squeezes my hands and takes a breath before he keeps going. "Now that it has, I struggle to put vows into words, but I'll do my best. The first thing I'll do is always share the last strawberry with you, even if I'm starving. I'll always make you smile, even when I'm being annoying. I want to be there for you, both as your protector and the one who pushes you to do something difficult. But most importantly, I vow to love you every day, throughout every trial life may throw at us. It's all I know how to do." He sniffles and wipes a tear.

I'm openly weeping as he finishes.

I want to kiss him right then and there, but I still have my own damn vows to do. "Wow, you really went for good ones, huh?" My voice is rough. I'm surprised I can talk at all.

"Well, you only get one wedding." He shrugs.

I laugh and take a breath to get myself together. Then, I say mine.

"It's taken me a long time to understand what love can be. Sometimes it's putting your feelings second when you want the other to be happy." Nate's eyes widen when he realizes I'm not talking about what I've done. It's all the things he's done for me. "Other times, it's telling the truth even when it hurts to hear. It's holding hands when the other is scared, but also pushing them when they need it. These are all things you've done for me since the day we met, and I have no idea how to repay all of those little things."

"Y-you don't have to." More tears run down his face now. I wonder if Quinn is cheering at the messes both of us are.

"But I'll try. I vow to see you, to hear you. To accept the love that you've shown me for nearly our whole lives, and to give you just as much in return."

There's still more that the officiant has to say, but Nate's done waiting. Right when they start talking, he pulls me for a kiss and slips the ring on my finger, a detail we both had forgotten during our vows.

And we don't separate until it's over.

<center>~~~</center>

"I CANNOT BELIEVE I'm doing this again," I say as we walk hand in hand along the dock.

"This was your idea," Nate replies as cool air brushes over us both. "I would've been fine to stay in Nashville and never leave the bed."

"We can never leave the bed here too," I offer. "But we have to pay homage to how we got together."

Both of us are in front of a massive boat. Instead of being on the tip of Florida, we're in Alaska in the middle of summer. The sun will barely set, and it'll be an adventure for us both.

I wasn't sure I could handle another beach vacation, but this? This seems fun.

He squeezes my hand. "Are you ready?"

"Of course I am." I lean my head on his shoulder. "I have you with me."

"And you always will."

I press my lips to his one more time before we get on the boat. The last time this happened, I was a nervous wreck and heartbroken.

This time, I have everything I could ever want.

want more?

Tap the QR code or click here to get access to bonus content from Nate's perspective.

thank you

I'm going to start this a little differently than I usually do, and the first people I want to thank are Nate and Maisie. I know they're only characters, but I genuinely feel grateful that I was allowed to be the one to tell this story.

After my last book, I was determined to write whatever my inspiration told me to. With all the health issues I'd been facing over the last few months, I was scared nothing would come to me, but this novel came to me in a way nothing else did. Don't get me wrong, I love my other books, but this one is the first where I genuinely wish I *was* there. I want more time with Nate and Maisie. I wish I knew them in real life.

I mean it from the bottom of my heart that this is my soul story. It's what I'm most proud of. It's so close to me. And I'm thrilled that I was able to fit it into an already-busy release schedule and tell it in the way it deserved to be told.

To Mae, who championed this book from the moment she read it, I can't thank you enough. This book was pretty much written on video call together, and one of the best parts of writing it was you getting to see me laugh maniacally as I put it all together. Next, I need to thank Kasey, who always copyedits my work. You're incredible, and I'm so lucky that we work together. And last but certainly not least, Rachel, my cover designer. You were an absolute dream to work with, and I cannot believe how gorgeous this cover is. I can't wait to see what else we create together!

looking for another read?

Read Levi and Amy's story now! Ill Will is available in ebook, paperback, and audio formats here.

also by elle rivers

The Failure to Thrive Series

Failure to Thrive

Under Any Conditions

The Aisle and Error Series

Contractual Obligations

Ill Will

Summers in Christmas

Snow Stuck

The Family Business Series

Forces of Nature

Man of Action

Movers and Shakers

Strawberry Springs Series

As It Was

As They Are

As I Grow

Standalones

To Make Matters Worse

Fakecation

Ruin the Friendship

about the author

Elle Rivers writes fun romance books filled with real-world problems wrapped in beautiful, heartwarming happy endings. When not writing, she can be found speed-reading other authors' amazing romance novels, curling up next to any warm object she can find, or singing obnoxiously loud to Taylor Swift.

Elle was born and raised in Nashville, Tennessee, and she considers herself one of the few native Nashvillians who does not like country music. She has eight cats who fight for the spot on her lap and eight chickens who couldn't care less about her unless she is bringing them food. She lives with her romance hero of a husband who endlessly supports her writing endeavors, and her son, who is the biggest, but most adorable, distraction.